About Apollo Africa

The original Heinemann African Writers Series was launched in 1962 with the publication of Chinua Achebe's *Things Fall Apart*, Cyprian Ekwensi's *Burning Grass* and Kenneth Kaunda's *Zambia Shall Be Free*, with Achebe himself acting as an editorial advisor. Over the next 40 years, the series continued to publish the best writing from across the African continent.

One of the founding aims of the Heinemann series was to make books by African writers available to as wide a readership as possible. Apollo Africa – a collaboration between Black Star Books and Head of Zeus – is proud to continue this work, ensuring novels, essays, poetry and plays from the original series are once again made available to readers all over the world.

Eyes of the Sky

Eyes of the Sky

Rayda Jacobs

Black Star Books and Head of Zeus would like to thank the following organisations: The Miles Morland Foundation, The Ford Foundation, and Africa No Filter. This publication was made possible through their support.

First published in South Africa in 1996 by Kwela Books

First published in the Heinemann African Writers Series in 1997 by Heinemann Educational Publishers

This edition published in 2024 by Black Star Books and Head of Zeus, part of Bloomsbury Publishing Plc.

Copyright © Rayda Jacobs, 1996

The moral right of Rayda Jacobs to be identified as the author of this work has been asserted in accordance with the Copyright, Designs and Patents Act of 1988.

All rights reserved. No part of this publication may be reproduced, stored in a retrieval system, or transmitted in any form or by any means, electronic, mechanical, photocopying, recording, or otherwise, without the prior permission of both the copyright owner and the above publisher of this book.

This reprint is published by arrangement with Pearson Education Limited.

This is a work of fiction. All characters, organizations, and events portrayed in this novel are either products of the author's imagination or are used fictitiously.

9 7 5 3 1 2 4 6 8

A catalogue record for this book is available from the British Library.

ISBN (PB): 9781035900831
ISBN (E): 9781803288291

Typeset by Siliconchips Services Ltd UK

Printed and bound in Great Britain by
CPI Group (UK) Ltd, Croydon CR0 4YY

Head of Zeus Ltd
First Floor East
5–8 Hardwick Street
London EC1R 4RG

WWW.HEADOFZEUS.COM

Dedicated to the memory of OUPA REGOPSTAAN

Acknowledgements

When I started this novel four years ago, I had this notion to tell a nice little story set in the Karoo in the 18th century. I had no idea what I was in for. My thanks go first to two great brothers: Ghalick and Hymie, for all those special favours, and never saying no. Dan Sleigh, for giving me the names of Twa and Smoke in the Eyes. The people of Calvinia, especially Alta Coetzee who arranged for me to stay in the Karoo Boekehuis, and Danie Poggenpoel and his wife who told me many stories. The Richvale Writers' Club in Toronto for being the first to encourage me to 'tackle' historical fiction and listening to the opening scenes. My daughter, Zaida, who was there the whole time behind me on the bed doing homework. And a special thanks to my South African publisher, Annari van der Merwe, who after a first reading, said, 'this book is too eurocentric' and forced me to look at it differently. This book could also not have been written without the wonderful stories and information contained in numerous books on animal behaviour and the history of the early Cape. I am especially indebted to the following works: *Cape of Good Hope, 1652–1702, The First Fifty Years of Dutch Colonisation as seen by Callers*, translated with notes by R. Raven-Hart, Vols I, II, A.A. Balkema, Cape Town, 1971; *Journals of Jan van Riebeeck, 1651–1662*,

Vols I, II, III, edited by H.B. Thom, A.A. Balkema, Cape Town, Amsterdam, 1952; *The Kalahari Hunter-Gatherers, Studies of the !Kung San and Their Neighbours*, edited by Lee and DeVore, Harvard University Press, 1974.

I have decided to tell the story the way it is. It is a book of fiction, after all, and sometimes we go too far with all this de-labelling. In the words of the late Oupa Regopstaan who responded to a question of mine in 1994 on whether he liked being called San, 'Wat is San? Ek is 'n man van die bos.'

Rayda Jacobs
September, 1996

Chapter One

It was an intensely still night, the radiance of the moon spilling into the back of the lonely little house on the rise. Inside the house were four beds, and in one of them, a boy stirred in his sleep. Some noise had scratched into his dreams. He opened his eyes and listened. Had the servant entered the house? Sanna was practically his mother the way she fussed over him, part of the family. She was always stumbling into things, especially with the baby strapped to her back. Pa? Oupa Harman? He didn't think so. It had sounded sudden and far away. Outside was mile upon mile of dry and broken land studded with kareebome, skaapbos and vygies, the house on the slope of the rant with its sheep kraal and huts breaking the monotony of the vast, featureless plain.

Then he heard it again, the growling of Ratel and Riempie, and sat up, looking at his brother asleep in the next bed. A sudden scream made him throw off the covers and run to his father's bed. Willem Kloot already had the loaded musket in his hand.

'Sounds like trouble out there.'

Roeloff ran out after his father without bothering to put on his veldskoene.

The soil was warm under his feet as he ran in the direction

of the kraal, arriving to find a dead sheep with arrows in its back and Ratel and Riempie at the neck and arms of two Bushmen boys twisting about in the dust.

'I'll kill you!' Willem pointed the gun down at their heads.

'No, Pa!'

Willem turned at the voice of his son, a sprightly boy of twelve with blue eyes, and hair the colour of Karoo sand when the sun arched directly overhead.

'What are you doing out here?'

'Don't shoot. Twa can talk to them.'

Willem kicked the intruders viciously in the ribs. They balled up like caterpillars, but made no sound of their pain.

Roeloff turned to run to the servants' huts and saw the old Bushman, dressed in skins, come limping up.

'Pa wants you, Twa. Come quickly!'

'Ask where their camp is,' Willem barked.

A proliferation of click sounds knocked at the roof of his mouth as Twa addressed the boy trapped under Willem Kloot's boot.

The boy tucked his head between his knees and refused to speak.

Willem aimed the gun.

Twa kneeled down on his good leg and tried harder, waving his hands angrily in order to make them understand the seriousness of their crime.

'They won't talk,' he said finally.

'Tell them to stand.'

When they were up on their feet, Willem shot one of them point blank in the chest. The boy was lifted from his feet and fell back with a thud, blood snaking from the wound under his heart.

Roeloff looked at his father in horror.

'Ask him if he wants the same.'

Twa addressed the other boy. With the gun pointed at his head, he spoke quickly. He didn't know the gun needed reloading before the white man could shoot again.

'A waterhole near the hanging rock, he says. Behind the Hantam.'

'Tie him up. Tomorrow he goes to Joubert. Joubert will know how to tame him. And bury that bosjesman before he attracts other animals.'

'You killed him, Pa.'

Willem looked at his son.

'He's a thief. That'll teach them to come here and steal. Now go back inside.'

David had heard the shot and was up when Roeloff returned.

'Pa killed a bosjesman.'

'What were they doing on our land?'

'Looking for food.'

'Stealing, you mean. The kommando should get the lot of them. Last month they raided Maatie Muller's kraal and killed six sheep. Just killed them and left them there.'

'Pa's getting dangerous. He's changed since Oom Jan came. Oom Jan should have stayed in Roodezand. If it was so green and wet where he was, why'd he come north? Pa wouldn't have done it if Ma were alive. And I heard Oom Jan talk about the kommando the other day. He wants Pa to join up. Pa's thinking on it.'

'The kommando protects us. The Hottentots come at us from one end, the bosjesman from another. At least a Hottentot respects cattle and sheep. He's not going to kill out of revenge. A Hottentot with two sheep will make six, you get some clever Hottentots. A bosjesman will kill both and shove it all down his gut in a day.'

'That's not true. He only kills what he can eat, he respects animals,' Twa said. 'He says all this land belonged to his people.'

'Belonged?' David laughed in the dark. 'They're thieves and savages, all of them. How could anything have belonged to them? What have they done with the land?'

'There were many animals before we came. We scared them off.'

'Scared them off?'

'Yes. With our guns. Our loud noises. We have disturbed the harmony of the veld. Even the bees, he says, are making their homes far away.'

'You spend too much time listening to that jong. What does he know, an old bosjesman like him? Now, stop all this nonsense and go to bed.'

Roeloff listened to his brother's even breathing, haunted by the face of the dead boy, the cold-hearted calm of his father. What was it about his brother that sometimes made Roeloff dislike him? He liked all the people on the farm, he almost loved Twa. Twa was a friend, a teller of stories, a provider of food. Left for dead by the kommando who'd wiped out his camp decades before, Twa, the 'thin man', was picked up by Roeloff's grandfather, Oupa Harman, behind the Hantamberge, the two almost killing each other in the process. Twa became Oupa Harman's voorloper and tracker in 1765, and later, Willem's. Twa had never done a day's work in his life, David always said, and sometimes the sheep got taken out and the manure transported to where Willem Kloot wanted it, and sometimes Twa just squatted on his heels like an old king at his small fire, fixing the tension on his bow, saying he'd worked the previous day and was tired. When he got like that nothing budged him, and Sanna, the Koi-na servant, refused him food from the three-legged pot. But Twa had a different understanding of work. To him, hunting was work, and hard work at that, not looking after sheep who knew what they had to do anyway. What did he know about sheep? Some Sonqua had sheep, but his tribe had never looked after them. That was white men's work. White men had the magic of their fire sticks if they wanted to hunt large animals. The Sonqua relied on instinct and a big heart and the poison on the tip of his arrow. Roeloff agreed. Twa was a wonder to him, more intriguing than the travelling German teaching the unlettered farmers and children how to read and multiply. Twa's stories were full of animal people, trickster gods, and ancestors advising on everything from the burrowing habits of the porcupine to when to expect rain. So far the rain god had miscalculated and they were barely surviving on the brackish dribble in the well, but Twa waved this off with the explanation that that god had many areas to cover and wasn't always nearby.

Roeloff's grandfather, too, could tell a tale, especially about the trekboer and the original settlers at the Cape, but Oupa Harman's stories, true and courageous as they were, didn't touch Twa's for magic and lifting you out of the sameness of the Karoo. It wasn't only their fantastical nature, it was how Twa told them: laughing, gesticulating, retelling the same story many times, embellishing greatly on the original. A story could have several endings, depending on the point he wanted to convey, but however it turned out, the little yellow-skinned hunter always emerged the victor.

They had learnt each other's language, much to the consternation of his brother who couldn't understand Roeloff's association with the bosjesman, and Twa could now speak Dutch, and he, !Khomani. Twa looked after him. When the two of them were out in the veld with the sheep, Twa would never let him go hungry. 'Hey, Kudu,' he would call to him. 'You hungry?' And he would get out his bow and arrow or set a trap. Before the sun dipped in the sky, they would be sitting at Twa's small fire, watching the meat sizzle on the coals. He didn't always want to know what Twa brought down with his arrow—Twa knew he ate kolganse, kraanvoëls, and ostrich—and had even tried tortoise, which he liked, and porcupine, which he didn't. His father's musket worked much faster than the tiny arrow, and they had blesbok any number of times, but it was more satisfying eating with Twa who could spend days tracking an animal and hunting it down. Roeloff didn't have this closeness with his brother. His brother was his brother and that was it. David had no time for him.

His thoughts returned to the scene at the kraal, the fear of the two boys, one killed in front of the other. Were they brothers? Where had they come from? Was the rest of the camp nearby? What gnawed at him was the tremor of excitement he'd felt in his father when the boy was lifted off his feet.

The night passed with agonising slowness and he lay there disheartened, watching the shadows dance and disappear on the walls, the light sifting slowly into the room.

He got up at cock crow and found Sanna in the circular skerm outside putting the bread pans into the clay oven, her two-year-old son, Kleintje, strapped to her back with a blanket tied in a knot under her huge breasts. He could tell by the way her bottom lip jutted out that morning that the news had spread among the Koi-na. Sanna would have something to say to him later on when they were alone. He seemed to have become the recipient for the grumbles and groans of the Koi-na who funnelled all their grievances through Sanna. The yard was coming to life with people going about their jobs; the day started with the strong smell of coffee already brewing. In the open doorway his grandfather stood looking out at the activity, lighting his pipe.

'You are up early this morning, Oupa.'

'I am always up at this time. Listen, son, your father be with the devil this morning. There'll be war if he finds no milk in the beaker. We can't wait for Twa to bless us with his presence.'

'I'll get some.'

'Be quick about it, Roff. Your father's out there inspecting the kraal. He'll come in any time now to eat.'

Roeloff stopped by Twa's hut to shake him awake, then headed for the kraal where he milked one of the goats. He had lots of questions for Twa, but saved them for later. His father and David were in the kitchen when he returned.

'Where's Twa?' Willem Kloot asked, holding his coffee, shoving a piece of bread into his mouth. It looked like he and David were going somewhere.

'His leg's hurting him this morning,' Roeloff lied. 'He's getting up.'

'That bosjesman's lazy,' David said curtly. 'And always Roeloff's making excuses for him. Twa doesn't have enough to do, that's his problem.'

Roeloff looked at his brother taking the powder horn from the wall, the two guns. David, older by three years, had that week had his first taste of the apricot brandy his grandfather brewed, after the Sunday service his father held in the yard for the Koi-na, and thought he now had as much right as older people to criticise. He was strong-shouldered and thick-necked, with every look and mannerism of his father, down to tightening his jaw and grinding his teeth when he wanted to make a point. When he was nasty like this and spoke badly of Twa, Roeloff couldn't stand him. He knew David did it to stir up his father. And his father needed little incitement in the state he was in. His father had a big voice and Roeloff had heard him yelling at Hennerik and the others all the way from the barn. Yelling at the workers made all the Koi-na shiver, and after the killing of the intruder, knowing the mood of the grootbaas, they would cower all day in their huts.

'He's not lazy,' Roeloff countered, keeping the anger out of his voice.

David smiled.

'See what I mean? You're doing it again. When are you going to learn, Roff, they're just Hottentots?'

'Twa's Sonqua. And it's not Hottentot, it's Koi-na.'

Willem Kloot looked from one son to the other, then wiped his mouth with the back of his hand. His look said that he didn't have time for their nonsense that morning. He picked up his gun and turned to Oupa Harman, who'd sat quietly smoking his pipe.

'We're going to Jan.'

'What for?'

'To take care of things.'

Harman Kloot inspected his fingers as if seeing them for the first time. 'You'll make it worse,' he said.

'It has to be done. The others will come looking for them. When they see what we have, that will be the end of our sheep.'

Roeloff watched his father and David walk out to the stable and mount their horses to go to Jan Joubert on the other side of the Hantamberge. By horse, they would be back by the time the sun was halfway in the sky. What were they going to take care of? His father would never leave Kloot's Nek at such a time if it wasn't to consult Jan Joubert on what had happened, and Jan, with his hatred of the Sonqua, was the last person to ask for advice. Roeloff turned to his grandfather.

'What are they going to Oom Jan for? Are they going to look for the Sonqua?'

'Yes.'

'Oupa should have stopped them. I can't believe Pa shot a bosjesman. He killed him, just like that, without thinking. He was only a boy.'

'They killed one of our sheep.'

'But that's a sheep. Pa killed a child.'

Oupa Harman knocked the pipe against his boot and caught the dead ash in his hand.

'Did I tell you about the night your father was born, Roff?'

Roeloff knew what was next. His grandfather, born in the Cape, had made the arduous trek with the Steenkamps and Retiefs over perilous mountains with his bride in a tent-covered wagon to come to the Hantam. He'd heard the story several times, but there was always a new reason to tell it, and always the grit and spit of it enthralled him. But his mind was on other things now—he wanted to know where Twa had buried the body. Not in the family plot, surely, where his mother and grandmother were; his father would never allow it. He was also anxious to take a look at the boy Twa had been instructed to tie up.

'I didn't know there would be a baby coming when we spanned in our oxen and packed up our world's belongings in 1760,' Oupa Harman continued. 'I didn't know anything about crossing mountains with women and children and sheep. Africa's like an old woman, Roff. Disagreeing. Unpredictable. She has little patience with fledglings and will spit you out at the first sign of weakness. But the call of the interior was very strong, and we'd heard about this river way up north where there were water and plenty of trees. No man with half a brain in his head would choose land where life had been choked out of the earth. So, with nothing more than God and our guns and a whole lot of courage, we attempted the uncivilised womb of Africa.'

Roeloff shifted in his seat. He could hear a commotion

outside. He heard Hennerik's voice, then his wife, Sanna's raised above it. The Koi-na were in a nervous state.

'On a moonlit night, at the foot of a dangerous pass, with thick bush behind us and a steep wall of mountain ahead, your grandmother's water broke. Men can do anything, Roff, but when it comes to birthing babies, they'd outstare a cobra first. The light was just beginning to change, in that grey hour before dawn, and everyone was fast asleep except for Katrijn Steenkamp with your grandmother in the back of the wagon. I was slumped against a tree, in a doze by the dead fire, everything was quiet. Maybe too quiet because I opened my eyes and saw a shadow roll down the pass. It happened so fast, I thought I'd imagined it. But even as I thought this, I knew I must stay still. So I remained with my eyes half closed against the back of the tree and saw two of them head for the flock. At the same time I saw the arrows aimed at us. There was no time to warn anyone. My gun was loaded. I would have only one chance to get it right, as it would take time to reload. I was lucky. The shot caught the second bosjesman, and he tumbled over the one in front of him down the kloof, just as the first arrows thrrrrd into the canvas of the wagon. Then all hell broke loose, with Steenkamp and Retief grabbing their guns and firing, womenfolk and children screaming, the sheep looking for the first opening to bolt. I could have stopped there, because the bosjesman, alarmed by the crack of the gun and his dead friend, fled up the mountain, but someone handed me a loaded gun, and I fired again, and again, until he, too, lay dead on the rocks.'

Roeloff had heard the story of how his father was born

in the middle of a raid and lay unattended between his mother's legs, but he hadn't known that his Oupa Harman had killed a bosjesman.

Harman Kloot looked at him, pursing his lips.

'In a civilised country, a man can stand back and give another the benefit of the doubt, Roff. This is Africa. Here you put your own mark on the land. The warning that comes from your gut is the one that saves your life. Remember that.'

Chapter Two

The day was dizzyingly hot, the Bushmen quiet and listless in the stingy shade of a quiver tree. Two winters had come and gone, and morning after morning they rose to cloudless skies and dust in their throats, to a land as forlorn as their souls.

The lines and folds in Koerikei's face contrasted with the smooth bronzeness of his hunter's physique, making him look older than his thirty years. Sitting slightly away from the group, he looked at the desolate landscape, mottled and red, feeling the needle pricks of the hot wind on his back. The drought had killed more than the land. It had deadened their spirit, the children's laughter, dried up the milk in the women's breasts. And always they accepted. Always it was their destiny to wait.

He studied the despondent faces about him: his wife, Tau, lying sleepily against the tree; his brother, Kabas, exchanging harsh words with Nani, his wife; Kabas's children asleep in the sweltering heat with ants crawling over their legs; Limp Kao carving a pipe out of bone. Only his daughter, Karees, sitting outside their skerm carefully adorning a steenbok hide with ostrich eggshell beads, made him smile. Karees had worked the hide into a fine kid, scraping off fat and other waste, and tanned it using a mixture of plant juices, bone marrow, urine and rotted brains. He had no doubt Karees had someone special in mind to be the recipient of this handsome gift. Who did his daughter have her heart on to mate?

They split up every two seasons to avoid overworking an area for game and plant food, and the rest of the clan was several days away. But dispersing hadn't helped much. The animals had left the region, the land too shrivelled and dry to maintain them. They were themselves tempted between the big river up at the top of the world, and the mountains in the Hantam where the others had gone. They knew of several waterholes in the area. Perhaps there was game, the land there a little more merciful to animals, with thorn bushes and grass, and people with sheep.

The heat vibrated over the plain, and Koerikei rested his chin on his knees and closed his eyes. His expression softened as his mind wandered back to the dust clouds on the horizon, the thunder of hooves. There was no sound like that bleating and snorting as hordes and hordes of pale brown buck rushed the plain, a brown wave stretching across the veld as springbok trampled everything in their path in their frantic rush. But that was long ago, before the white man's arrival and their forced migration to this parched, forsaken, and uninhabited land. Rain was the heartbeat of life, but it was withheld from them like some guarded possession. Kabas's children had never seen it, never tasted its sweetness or witnessed the transformation of the Karoo when the wind stirred and the sky belched and fire forked the land and water rushed down on them. The dryness was pitiless, but its breaking, the smell of moist veld after rain—that forgave everything. The smallest ant, the oldest tree, the driest pan, all waited patiently under baked skies for relief. A few thin showers had brushed them briefly with hope a season before, but evaporated before reaching the ground. Why were the gods being so cruel? What stupid ancestor had angered them?

His people reclined like a pride of lions under the tree waiting for the soft shade of late afternoon. Then the women lit the fires, and Koerikei and Kabas visited the hearth of Limp Kao.

No one knew how many winters Limp Kao had seen. He was crooked and bent, the loose skin on his belly undulating like rippled desert sand. A bad leg had prevented him from hunting as a young man, making it impossible to take a wife. Stained with weather and time, he depended on the system of sharing to stay alive. The system demanded that if you couldn't hunt, you could provide the weapon for the kill and get your due, and if one family brought home game, they had to share it with those who didn't have. Meat was thus divided and redivided until debts and obligations were incurred and the old and crippled were also fed.

Koerikei and Kabas sat just at the edge of the circle of light. Even though they were the ones seeking counsel, they waited for Limp Kao to start.

'These are very bad days,' Limp Kao said, stirring the coals in his fire.

'Very bad. We are starving, old father. No animals, nothing in the ground. We don't know if we should go to the others down at the Hantam, or travel to the river at the top of the world.'

'It will take many days to the river.'

'What is your opinion, old father, on when the rains will come?'

'My bones are starting to hurt.'

Koerikei looked hopeful.

'Your bones have never been wrong.'

'There are no clouds. There must be clouds for rain to come.' He shifted on his heels. 'I will not go with you when you leave.'

The brothers looked at him. They knew what he meant. He was old, holding them up. He would stay and let nature take its grim course. And it wouldn't be long, with the jackals.

'These legs will not carry me any further. I can stay till I'm stronger, then follow.'

'We're not so poor that we have to leave you behind, and so wise that we can do without your counsel, old father. We'll carry you, if we have to.'

Limp Kao stuffed his pipe with a clump of foul-smelling leaves, then passed it around. The matter was settled.

'We'll see if there are clouds in the morning. Then go up to the river.'

'There are sheep in the Hantam,' Kabas said.

Limp Kao nodded. 'And people with smoke in their sticks. We have not been attacked by them yet. I think we will go to the river, if we get rain. The others will know we have gone there.'

The next day, like the days and weeks and months before that, erupted in a wave of torrid air. Limp Kao's aching bones and rain talk forgotten, Tau and Karees set off early with their digging sticks in an easterly direction. The women walked for hours in the heat, closely inspecting the ground, but found nothing. They were thinking of returning to camp when Tau, squatting behind a thorn bush, saw a tiny vine winding around the trunk. She pulled gently at its base to see where it led, then with her digging stick tried to work it loose. The stick was useless in the hard ground and, using both hands, she sat back on her heels and scratched and scooped until a deep hole revealed a huge bi root tightly wedged in the packed earth. She took a stone, scraping around the root, then reached in with both hands and pulled. Her face creased into folds as she strained. The root suddenly came loose, sending her flying back into the bush. She rocked back on her heels, the root still clasped in her hands.

'It's a big one,' she laughed. 'Perhaps there'll be others.'

But a thorough examination revealed nothing more, and after painstakingly scouring the area, they collected twigs for firewood and returned home. The others saw them coming and waited eagerly under the tree.

'Karees!' Kabas's youngest daughter came running up. 'My father's killed a snake.'

Karees wrinkled her nose.

'Snake? We're not snake eaters.'

'We have eaten it before. Come see how my mother's roasted it. Have you found anything?'

'Only this,' she opened her kaross and showed off the bi root her mother had found.

Tau was invited to her brother-in-law's hearth with her family where Kabas and his wife offered everyone generous portions of meat.

'It's not bad,' Koerikei said. 'Tasty.'

'My belly's full,' Tau rested her hand on her abdomen, paying her hosts a compliment.

Nani smiled. She had been greatly honoured.

Later on, at her own hearth, Tau took the root she'd unearthed and scraped it into thin slivers with a stone. Dividing it into three portions, she, Koerikei, and Karees held the scrapings over their mouths, and squeezed until thick drops of juice trickled down on their tongues. It didn't amount to a swallow, but at least changed the taste in their mouths. When the last drop was squeezed out, she mixed the scrapings with grass and sand and built it into a pile. Koerikei urinated over the mixture and scooped out a hollow grave with his hands. Tau and her daughter eased themselves into the pit, and packed their faces and bodies with the spongy waste, leaving only their noses exposed. Closing their eyes to the intensity of the sun, they remained in their moist graves until dusk. The pit offered a brief respite from the heat.

Roeloff was in the yard with Twa trying to get the captive to speak when his father and Jan Joubert rode up with a Bushman girl on the back of the horse. Naked except for a small leather flap dotted with beads over her private parts, antelope strips round the elbows and knees, she had slanted eyes in an almost flat face with high cheekbones, and a full, delicate mouth. Her head was small and round, with tight balls of hair, her dusty skin the colour of ripe apricot.

'That's him, there,' Willem Kloot pointed. 'You can have him.'

Jan Joubert jumped down from his horse and examined

the boy's shoulders and back, peering into his mouth. There was a scar running from the boy's left brow across the forehead, and he felt this to see how old it was.

Roeloff watched. He didn't like Oom Jan even though he was the only farmer whose company his father sought regularly. Oom Jan was a man of three words—*schiet hom vrek*—and murderous actions. Roeloff knew of his raids with the kommando and his brutality towards the Hottentots on his farm. His wife, Elsie, was a religious woman with thin lips that rarely smiled, and his daughters made Roeloff think of frogs whose eyes seemed ready to pop from their heads. Diena wasn't too bad with her constant references to God, but he disliked Soela, the prettier one. He blamed Oom Jan for his father's actions the previous night. His father would never have killed a human being in his mother's time. Oom Jan liked no one, especially not the brown-skinned people. The other day when Twa brought wood into the kitchen, Oom Jan said he stank up the air. Had he smelt himself like others smelt him? Twa's odours were not of the mouth and the body, but of fire and tobacco and the rich scent of the land.

Jan finished his examination of the boy and turned to Willem, satisfied.

'He's insolent—you can tell from his eyes—but strong.'

'Tell Sanna to give her clothes,' Willem said to Twa. 'She's to help in the house.'

The men went inside and Twa helped the girl off the horse.

'What's your name?'

She put one dusty foot on top of the other, and looked up timidly.

'He doesn't bite,' Twa laughed, sensing her apprehension of a white boy. 'What's your name?'

'Zokho.'

'Smoke in the Eyes,' the male captive blurted from the other side.

'Smoke in the Eyes?' Twa's eyes twinkled. 'I can see why. I'm Twa, and this is Kudu,' he pointed to Roeloff. 'We call him this because he blends in with the veld and is fast as an eland.'

'Roeloff,' Roeloff said quietly. He was immensely taken with the girl.

'You know this boy, Smoke in the Eyes?' Twa asked.

'He's Toma.'

'Where did they find you? Where are your people?'

Zokho dropped her head and started to cry.

Roeloff looked at Twa. He had no knowledge of girls, but from her mutterings made out that her mother and father were dead. Moved by her distress, he came forward and touched her arm. She pulled away.

Twa laughed at the hurt look on his face.

'Don't worry, she'll get used to you. Sanna will take care of her. She has no girls of her own.'

'And him?' Roeloff turned to Toma. 'He knows her. Maybe they're family.'

'Are you family?' Twa asked Zokho.

Roeloff caught the look between the girl and the captive. He knew they weren't.

'They have played together,' Twa said.

'Oh. My father's giving him to Oom Jan. You know what Oom Jan does with them. He chains them up, he …'

'Your father *killed* one last night,' Twa said.

The accusation cut into Roeloff's heart and he stopped with his hand on the stallion.

'Why do you think she's here?' Twa continued. 'Her people were killed. Like mine were. Like the one last night. Ask her who did it. Ask her why she's here. You speak !Khomani; ask.'

Roeloff was stung by the words. Twa didn't have it in him to be cruel. Roeloff led the horse into the stable and sat down. He didn't want to believe Twa, but how else would Oom Jan and his father have got the girl? Had they really killed her people? His own father? It was hard enough to understand how he could fire into the heart of a boy; to believe he'd killed a whole family, was to believe him a murderer. His thoughts went to Zokho. Smoke in the Eyes. He liked that name. It suited her soft, slanted eyes. He'd thought all Sonqua were craggy with stained teeth, like Twa, but she was a creature of beauty, with the smoothness and colour of a bronze sun, the most exquisite female he had ever seen.

He got up and studied Toma through a crack in the door. A brave Sonqua, he thought, but the night chained up had subdued him, he seemed shrunken, his earlier spirit gone. It was quiet when Roeloff stepped out of the stable.

'Toma?'

Toma turned at the strange voice behind him.

Roeloff held out the water mug.

The boy looked uncertainly into the blue eyes.

'Take this,' Roeloff said in !Khomani.

The hands reached out and Toma drank greedily.

Roeloff cut quickly into the rope around the ankles and wrists with his hunting knife. He could smell the fear, the disbelief, hear his own heart hammering in his ears.

'Roeloff! What are you doing?!'

He stiffened. It was David coming up behind him, raising the alarm.

'Run!' he whispered. 'Now!'

Their eyes locked for a moment, then Toma catapulted across the yard and was gone.

David ran into the house.

'Pa! Roeloff freed the bosjesman! He's running!'

Willem came out, saw the rope still in Roeloff's hand, and took off his belt.

'Bliksem!' He struck him, catching him on the ear.

'Don't hit him, man,' Oupa Harman stepped between them. 'It was a mistake.'

'Mistake? He knows what's a mistake and what can't be forgiven. Whose idea was it, tell me, who told you to do it?' Willem Kloot raged.

Roeloff touched his ear with his hand and looked at the blood on his hand. He was aware of Joubert and David, the humiliation of a beating in front of strangers. The Koi-na had come out with the commotion, but seeing him on the receiving end of his father's belt, went back into their huts. He was shamed by the indignity in front of them.

'The bosjesman's getting away,' Joubert said. 'Let's go after him, leave the boy.'

'I asked you a question. Whose idea was it?'

Roeloff looked up, his eyes fired with anger.

'Whose?!' Willem Kloot demanded.

Roeloff wouldn't answer.

The belt licked his face and Roeloff flinched. He could tell from the way his father swung the belt that Willem Kloot would chase him around the yard. He wouldn't give him the pleasure of dodging. Not him or anyone else.

'It was my idea, and I'd do it again.'

Willem stopped with his hand in the air.

'What?'

'It was my idea and I'd do it again!'

Willem, shocked by the effrontery of his son, lashed into him with renewed rage. He whipped Roeloff until his hand dropped, exhausted, at his side. Roeloff collapsed to the ground like wet washing.

'Are you mad?' Oupa Harman shouted angrily. 'You nearly killed him!'

'He has his mother's softness. There's no place for it in these parts.'

'This is softness?' Oupa Harman lifted his grandson up in his arms. 'He's brave! And leave his mother out of it, the woman's dead.'

Joubert looked at the welts rising fast and red on the boy's arms. He didn't agree with Willem Kloot's actions, but agreed with the old man that the boy was brave. He liked him, even though he knew Roeloff didn't feel the same way about him.

Three days north, Limp Kao sniffed at the air. There were clouds, but clouds didn't always mean rain. He'd seen them all: thin ones, curly ones, puffy ones, ones that seemed to dodge and dart about the sky like hyenas after a hare. It was the dark ones that held promise.

'The earth is releasing her smells,' he said to the group waiting anxiously for his prediction.

'I think you're right, old father. I think this time it really will come. We'll start out for the river.'

'Someone's coming,' Kabas said suddenly.

Koerikei put his hand over his eyes and squinted into the distance. A puff of dust on the horizon turned slowly into a shimmering dot until finally a figure separated out of the rippling heat and Toma arrived, out of breath, at their sides.

'Where's everyone? Why have you come alone?'

'They are dead.'

A hushed silence fell over the group.

'Dead?'

'Balip and I borrowed the white man's sheep. We were caught. The white man pointed his fire stick at Balip, and he flew up in the sky. Then he landed like a rock on the ground and blood ran from his heart. They tied me up. The next day I got away. When I arrived at the camp there was only the blood and bones in the dust. The vultures had been already.'

'You are telling the truth?' Koerikei asked.

'Yes. Everyone is dead except Smoke in the Eyes. They took her.'

'They've got Zokho?'

'Yes.'

'How did you get away?'

'The white man's son. He cut me loose and let me go.'

They looked at each other.

'The white man's son? You want us to believe that?'

'It's true. He's a strange one, Uncle, with eyes the colour of the sky, and he speaks like us, !Khomani.'

'It can't be.'

'They have one of our people there, too. I don't know him. He's friendly with this boy.'

'Tell us from the beginning.'

Toma related every detail from the time he and Balip had sat in the tree waiting for darkness, to seeing his friend killed and dragged off. When he came to the part where Roeloff offered him water, he was stopped by Limp Kao and asked to repeat it. The story ended and he had to tell it several more times to make sure no one had missed anything.

The men sat back on their heels, faces creased in thought. They'd always managed to evade the white hunters. Toma was telling them strange things.

'We have to go back for Smoke in the Eyes.'

'They will be expecting us, Kabas,' Limp Kao said. 'It would be foolishness. We are this many,' he opened and closed his fists twice. 'I say we wait for three moons to die, then take them in the night.'

'I say we go now,' Kabas insisted.

A roll of thunder clapped over their heads and they looked at each other.

'Rain!'

'The gods have spoken,' Koerikei said. 'It's decided. We will go to the river, wait three moons like Limp Kao said, then come back.'

The sky closed like a tortoise withdrawing into its shell, shutting out the light, and the wind started its wicked dance over the veld, flattening skerms, hearths, erasing all trace of settlement. It came down hard and furious and they ran about filling their ostrich-egg containers with the precious water, laying hides in shallow depressions to catch what they could from the sky. But as suddenly as the rain had started, it stopped, and the sun bragged spitefully through the clouds. Minutes later there was only the soft, springy feeling under their feet to tell them the gods had been kind, the intoxicating smell of wet sand. But the rainy season was started. They had water. Soon the land would swell with plant and animal life.

Chapter Three

Roeloff sat in the shade of a large rock on the hill with Ratel and Riempie, sorting out stones for his sling. Twa had made the sling out of a leather strap and two thongs and had taught Roeloff how to use it, and he went everywhere hitting targets. He had become quite a good marksman and occasionally killed small animals for the Koi-na, who were used to him and his pranks. Kupido told him his sling wasn't as fast as Twa's arrow, but that his eyes, clearer than the old bosjesman's, resulted in a hit every time and that the Koi-na were grateful for the wild birds he brought to their pots.

He fitted a stone into the sling and hurled it across the sand.

'Sa!'

The dogs scooted after it, and brought it back.

He had half an eye on the sheep to his left, the other on Twa, waist-high in an old aardvark hole with a digging stick, looking for beetles whose larvae would be removed and body juices used to provide poison for his arrows. The hunter in him was in the mood for wild meat, he said, and he was on the lookout for game which he would share with his people. Dressing the arrow had to be done with care as even a scratch on a finger could prove fatal. Twa's hands were riddled with cuts and scratches and to avoid contact, he applied the poison directly onto the shaft with a stick. Roeloff hurled a stone in his direction, knocking over the oval shard of ostrich eggshell in which the beetles were being collected.

'Kudu!' Twa shook his fist, imitating Willem Kloot.

'Just making sure you're awake,' Roeloff laughed.

He heard galloping and looked up. In the distance he saw the horseman, an imposing figure in black. He watched his father gallop up the path to the house. Grootbaas. Or was it Jan Joubert who was grootbaas of the Karoo? Big and brooding, he was a force to be reckoned with, but he didn't have Willem Kloot's presence. The very greyness of his father's eyes and the set of his jaw demanded respect. Thinking of his father made Roeloff sad. A terrible strangeness had settled between them since the night of the killing. He could no longer join in when the mood to be congenial struck his father, couldn't look him in the eye. It had separated them, that rush of excitement he'd sensed in his father when the bosjesman boy was lifted from his feet. His father now also beat a regular path to the door of the Jouberts, where Oom Jan's widowed sister had moved in. Drieka was a younger version of her brother, but whereas Oom Jan was blunt and you knew what he thought, Drieka was sly, with a deadly sting. Her true nature had surfaced when, as an overnight guest in their house a year before with her husband before he choked on a meat bone and went straight to heaven, she called Sanna a lazy Hottentot who didn't know her place. The Koi-na didn't like being called Hottentot, and Sanna, especially, coming from the Cape, took particular offence. The Koi-na would never speak back to the grootbaas, but Sanna sometimes defied his father who, surprisingly, took no action to remedy her behaviour. Perhaps it was because she had been his mother's servant, and looked after all of them. If anyone crossed Sanna, she said nothing. She just pushed out that bottom lip and burned the food. When Drieka made the comment and humiliated her in front of everyone in the kitchen, Sanna put out the mugs for coffee, and in Drieka's she put a heaped teaspoon of stomach powder. Drieka spent most of the visit out in the veld.

He was sure the house behind the Hantam was where his father came from now in his Sunday clothes, in the middle of the week.

Please, God—he looked up into the clear, blue sky—don't join us up with the Jouberts. If my father marries Drieka, we shall all have to suffer her mouth and those awful lectures, and David and I will be forced against our will to be nice to Soela and Diena. Correction. I will be forced. David, I think, has feelings for Soela, although I don't think she has for him. Which is just as well. We can't have this family mixed up with theirs and …

'Roff?'

He turned at the sound of Zokho's voice, and saw her poised on a rock, bright as a springbok shimmering in the sun. She had on the tiny leather apron with the ostrich eggshell beads she'd worn that first day, and he noticed immediately how her breasts had swelled. Had she grown this quickly from one summer to the next? They had taken a while to become friends; she didn't trust him at first, then, more and more, as she picked up a few words of Dutch and saw the ease with which Sanna and the Koi-na treated him, they started to talk to each other. When she was finished with her work in the kitchen, she liked to play games with the other children, and sometimes followed him and Twa when they took out the sheep. During these outings, depending on his mood, Twa would tell a story, and they would listen. Sometimes she would start one, then stop. No one pressed her when this happened, but he was curious about her family, how they lived. He liked her more than any girl he'd ever met.

'Your father wants you.'

'Where's your dress, Zokho? Sanna will pull your ears if she sees you walking around like this.'

She'd been with them a year now, and Sanna had taken her under her wing, lavishing the same attention on her as on her own boys, Kleintje and Kupido, scrubbing her down in the tin tub, fighting with her to wear clothes. He'd thought the leather apron had been thrown out long ago.

'It is too hot for the white man's clothes. Roff?'

'Yes?'

'You speak !Khomani like the Sonqua. Was it hard to learn?'

'No. When I was small, Twa spoke to me only in his language. He didn't know mine. When I didn't know what he meant, he acted it out.'

She had a few dry flowers in her hand, and picked at the leaves on the stem.

'One day Toma will come.'

The statement surprised him.

'Why?'

'To take me for his bride.'

'You're a child.'

'My sister married an old man from another tribe. She has run away several times. She's not happy. Her husband forces himself, he's too old for her.'

'Forces himself?'

'He takes her against her will. It hurts very much, she says. Toma's not like that. He's young, like me.'

'How do you know?'

'We have played together. We play and play and that's how we learn.'

Roeloff fitted a stone into his sling and stood up.

'Do you like this game?'

'No. Boys like it very much, but not girls. We do it because it pleases them. One time an old man tried to force me and I told my mother and she told him he was already losing his teeth, he should look elsewhere for a bride.'

'Will you go when Toma comes?'

'He's the son of a great hunter. I'll have food.'

'You will go with him for food?'

'Yes,' she laughed gaily, picking the last leaf from the stem. 'A husband gives you food and things to wear. He protects you.'

He catapulted the stone over the sand.

'Four seasons have gone, Zokho. He hasn't come.'

'He will, you'll see. Toma won't leave me here.'

'Don't you like it here? You have food, you're protected.'

'I'm not protected.'

A shadow fell over them and they looked up. David was standing on the overhanging rock looking down at them.

Zokho's smile froze and she skipped off.

Roeloff watched her run back to the house, his brother following at a leisurely pace. He felt suddenly cold.

'Ratel! Riempie!'

The dogs came bounding up.

He made a signal and they scampered off towards the sheep.

At the house Willem Kloot, still in his coat, his unruly hair made respectable with pomade bought from a smous, waited for Roeloff at the back door.

'You've decided to bless us with your presence, then. Didn't Zokho call you? I hear you've been on Boerhaan.'

For a moment Roeloff thought he was in trouble for trying to ride his father's stallion, but his father was in an exceptional mood.

'He threw me.'

'So I hear. He takes to that bosjesman, though. Twa has a way with him.'

Boerhaan came from champion stock but, volcanic and skittish, he allowed no one except Willem Kloot on his back. He was Willem's favourite horse, greedy for mares, but he'd refused to mount Kobus Steenkamp's brood mare, causing much head-scratching and embarrassment. Twa had watched the performance and come up with a plan. 'We have to dig a hole for the mare to stand in. She's bigger than him, he can't reach.' Everyone had laughed at the ridiculous suggestion. Twa dug the pit himself and led an agitated Boerhaan up to the brood mare, holding onto the rein. It was pump and snort with Twa almost getting hooved to death, but the plan worked, and in due course the mare foaled. The stallion was no further ahead in his manners, but some bond had formed between them, and now Twa, too, could ride on his back. But not Roeloff. He'd tried several times to get on, but Boerhaan had snorted like a high-born prince and flung him off. His father was referring to the incident that morning in front of the Koi-na, who'd all had a good laugh as Roeloff landed backside first on the ground.

'A man cannot live alone in this wilderness,' Willem started. 'God made us in twos.'

Roeloff looked at the other faces around the table. David seemed anxious, as if he'd been wrenched away from something important and wanted to get back, and his grandfather had a strange expression, the same one as he'd had the time the smous had tried to sell him a set of brass candle holders he didn't want.

'Jan's sister's widowed as you know, and she's without children, a young woman like that, and all alone. It's a sin letting healthy people go to waste. God didn't intend it.' He paused for a moment to see if anyone would argue with him. 'This morning she agreed to be my wife.'

'Well,' Oupa Harman knocked the dead ash out of his pipe. 'When does the happy event take place?' The look on his face didn't at all match the tone of his voice, which had to it a quality Roeloff knew he reserved for things he didn't approve of.

'December.'

'Does that mean we're now related, Pa?' Roeloff asked.

Willem combed his fingers through his beard and looked at his younger son.

'You don't like the Jouberts, Roff.'

Roeloff chanced his father's good mood.

'Oom Jan's a …'

Willem laughed.

'Oom Jan's a fine man, and I'll marry his sister in the summer.' Softening a little, he added, 'You'll be related, but only in name.'

'Krisjan must come to the wedding.'

There was an uncomfortable silence. Everyone looked at Oupa Harman.

'The family has not been in touch,' Willem said, the look on his face suddenly changed.

'They can be in touch now. This is an opportunity,' Oupa Harman coughed into his hand. 'What better reason than a wedding to invite him?'

'It will be a small affair. No need to disturb old nests. And there's no one going that way to tell him.'

'Well, that's that, then,' Oupa Harman got to his feet. 'Anything else you want us to know?'

Willem Kloot lost a little of his earlier confidence. Oupa Harman still had the power to unsettle him.

'No.'

'Who's Krisjan?' David asked when his father and grandfather had left the kitchen.

Roeloff looked at his brother. He had never told David, and he wouldn't have known himself if Oupa Harman hadn't surrendered so completely to the apricot brandy at Pietie Retief's grandchild's doopmaal. Retief's fiery brew was known for its tongue-loosening power and Oupa Harman was as affected as anyone by its potency. If Roeloff hadn't happened to be standing near his grandfather when the words popped from his mouth, he wouldn't have known there was a brother, still living, in the Cape. But there was some mystery attached to Krisjan Kloot. Why was his father reluctant to have him visit? Why did no one mention him? One day he would travel to the Cape, look up this lost relative and find out.

Chapter Four

The night was moonless, wet, the rain beating down on the house on the rise.

'Your father and brother won't be coming tonight, Roff,' Oupa Harman said, getting up from his spot at the hearth where the blaze gave the room a warm pleasantness. 'If they're not here by now in this rain, it's tomorrow they'll arrive. You've done enough reading; time for bed, son.'

Sanna was kneading the next day's bread, Zokho folding clothes which had come in damp from outside where they had been spread to dry over bushes and on the grass next to the stream beside the fruit trees.

'Just a little longer, Oupa. I'll come when Sanna and Zokho go to the back.'

Oupa Harman started to wheeze. He had contracted a bad cold at the start of winter and was plagued with phlegm, complaining of tightness in his chest. Bent double by a hacking cough, leaning on the table for support, he spat into his small tin, looking curiously at the deposit.

'What is it, Oupa?'

'Nothing. Don't forget to put out the lamp when you go to bed.'

Sanna folded a cloth over the bread pans.

'The oubaas isn't telling the truth. There's blood in that tin.'

'Blood?'

'I saw it with my own eyes. He thinks it's going to go away, that's why he keeps looking. He knows what it means.'

Roeloff looked down at his book. It had happened to Gerhard Marais. The rotten smell coming up from his lungs, the wasted flesh. The family didn't want to believe it, even when Nico van Wyk, who knew about these things, told them to start thinking of getting the coffin owed to them by the Schmidts for the one they'd borrowed for a visiting uncle. A few weeks later they were eating pumpkin fritters at Gerhard Marais's funeral. And he could tell by Sanna's manner that she had waited to tell him. She had a fondness for Oupa Harman, because his grandfather was always in the same mood and never shouted at the Koi-na. When she was concerned about something, her eyes seemed narrower, her lips more protruding. And she was never wrong about these things. The thought frightened him. What if Oupa Harman never got better? What if he died? Roeloff couldn't imagine life without him. His grandfather was the only Kloot he could talk to and who shielded him from his father's anger. Roeloff loved him dearly.

'What does it mean?'

'There's poison in his chest. It will get worse if he doesn't take something.'

'What? Do you have a remedy? Those potato skins worked when you wrapped up my foot. In four days it was better.'

'Potato skins won't work for this. There's a plant. I haven't seen it around here, but Hennerik can get it.'

Roeloff thought about Sanna's husband Hennerik, a funny little man half Sanna's size who, most afternoons, when Willem Kloot wasn't around, slept under a tree instead of doing his work. Sanna complained about his laziness and Roeloff had once seen her slam a bread pan against Hennerik's head, after which he showed diligence for a few days, then returned to his old ways.

'What plant?'

'I don't know the name, but it has strong powers. It cured the bite of a pofadder once.'

A pofadder? Impossible. You would be dead in minutes. The thought of the snake stirred up ugly memories, and he pushed it aside.

'You must send Hennerik for this plant, Sanna, tomorrow. I know my grandfather's sick.'

'I will. Come, Zokho,' she opened the door. 'We're done. We'll let Roeloff read his book. Aren't your eyes tired, yet?'

'No.'

'Can I stay a little longer?' Zokho asked, holding up a shirt to show she was still folding clothes.

Sanna looked crossly at the girl, but there was softness around the corners of her mouth.

'Not long. He must go to bed.'

Then Roeloff and Zokho were alone and a new silence filled the room. Roeloff tried to return to his book. The yellow light from the lamp was sufficient for him to read, but no words registered themselves on his mind. He was thinking of what Sanna had said, aware of Zokho folding the clothes behind him. He heard the crackle in the fire, the thwoop as the coals dropped onto the tray, the rhythmic patter of the rain, like the feet of little children, on the barrels outside. Zokho had on one of his mother's old pinafores, and even though Sanna had drawn it in at the waist, it hung like a tent on her narrow frame. He was very aware of her presence.

'What are you reading?'

'One of my grandfather's books. He has a few of them in a box under his bed. When I'm finished with one, he gives me another.'

She looked over his shoulder, her arm almost touching his cheek. She was standing uncomfortably close.

'Is it hard to read?'

'Not when you know the letters.'

'Who taught you?'

'My mother. And the German teacher.'

'Sanna says she was beautiful. Her hair was the colour of a lazy sun. You look like her, Sanna says.'

Roeloff looked up. He was aware of his grandfather's sleeping figure behind the straw partition where everyone slept. He kept his voice low.

'And are you beautiful like your mother, Zokho?'

The colour rushed to her face.

'I am beautiful?'

'You are very beautiful. I have not seen anyone like you.'

'Do you want to play a game?'

He tried not to look at the hard little nipples erect under the thin dress. Strange things were happening to him.

'Do you know one?'

'I know many, but we play them outside. It is dark now, and raining. But we can make one up.'

'What?'

'Show me something which you will hide in this room, then fold this rag over my eyes, and I try to find what you've hidden in the dark. If I move away from it, you say cold. If I get close to it, you say warm.'

'All right, you first.'

'Show me what you're going to hide, then cover my eyes.'

Roeloff selected his grandfather's pipe, then blindfolded Zokho.

'Ready?'

He tiptoed to where she had stacked the folded clothes and hid the pipe under the pile.

Zokho stretched out her hands and inched forward.

'Warm.'

She took tiny steps towards the folded clothes, and seconds later had the pipe in her hand.

'How did you find it so quickly? I just put it there.'

'I can smell.' She took off the blindfold, laughing. 'Your turn.'

The blindfold slipped over his eyes and he stood for a moment trying to sniff out the position of the pipe. What he didn't know was that Zokho had rubbed a few grains of the tobacco on her palm and was waving it in front of him.

He stepped forward.

'Warm.'

Another step.

'Very warm.'

He stretched out his arms and bumped into her.

'Very, very warm.'

He came forward some more and was almost on top of her.

'You're in the way, Zokho.'

'No. You are very, very warm.'

He stopped.

'Zokho?'

'Yes?'

'Is it on you?'

'Yes.'

His hand encountered a naked shoulder.

'Where's your dress?'

'You want to lose the game, Roff?'

'What kind of game is this?'

'It's a game boys play with girls. Don't be scared.'

Then they were up against each other and he felt her breast brush his hand.

'Zokho!'

'It's all right to taste them.'

Roeloff felt the blood rush down to his groin. With the blindfold still over his eyes, his hands fumbled with the front of her dress, trying to get it off.

Then the back door opened and Willem Kloot, kicking the mud off his boots, stepped inside with David behind him. A grizzly giant of a man, he shook the rain from his hair, slapping his hat against the side of his leg. With two steps he had Roeloff by the neck and was pulling him off the girl.

'What's going on?'

Zokho folded her arms in front of her, trying not to look

at the grootbaas and his older son staring open-mouthed at her.

Roeloff waited for his father's anger to erupt. He was glad he was still in his clothes.

'You want to stick yourself into a bosjesman?' Willem Kloot shouted. 'Your behind's itching, is it?'

'No, Pa.'

Willem punched him and Roeloff slammed into the trestle table, his head hitting a ledge in the wall, toppling mugs and tin plates and the bread pans of rising dough down on him as he fell to the floor.

'This is what you do when I'm away? Act like an animal? And with a servant! Are you one of them? Tell me!'

Roeloff's head hurt, and he held up his arms to protect it.

'I'm talking to you! Get up!'

Roeloff got to his knees and Willem booted him in the small of his back, pushing him down again.

'You want a bosjesman? Is that it? Go sleep outside and take your food with them, then, and don't come back into this house! And you,' Willem turned to Zokho, 'you will not work in this kitchen again, you'll work with the others outside!' And he took them both by the neck and pushed them out through the door.

Roeloff stood in the rain, watching the door close in his face. Zokho's dress was still on the kitchen floor, and she ran naked into the darkness. He looked about him. What was he to do now? Barefooted, cold, the rain drumming down on his head? Oupa Harman wouldn't have allowed his father to do this but he hadn't even woken up with the commotion. And how would Roeloff face him? The others?

What would he say? Tomorrow everyone would know his sin. A chuckle behind him made him turn.

'Ttt, ttt, ttt,' Twa sniggered from his doorway where he squatted, warming his hands over the fire. 'What did you do now?'

Roeloff looked at the Bushman laughing at him. He walked over.

'Nothing.'

'Nothing? Come, sit with me at my fire.'

'My father just threw me out in the rain. Your fire won't make me forget.'

'You don't know that. I have tabak, that makes you forget anything. And many stories. I haven't told you yet about the day the men came on their horses to our camp. I saved that for when you're big.'

'I don't feel very big.'

Twa looked at him slyly over his foul-smelling pipe. 'What you did in there with Zokho, that is big.'

'I didn't do anything.'

'I can see that,' Twa laughed, his eyes moving down to Roeloff's groin. 'But you were going to.'

'What's the matter with my father?'

'You're reminding him he's getting old.'

Roeloff squatted at the small fire, rubbing his hands in front of him.

'I don't know what happened in there. It just happened.'

'It's like that the first time. I was younger than you when the fever came over me. I remember the girl. She was from the Ein-qua, the people of the river. Your feelings run off with you, you think with your stick. But it's good, hai?' he cackled.

'Tell me the story.'

'Not tonight. Go in there, Kudu, and sleep. You are tired. I'll stay here by the fire.'

Zokho's fate was much worse. Embarrassed by the girl's behaviour although she knew sexual play was not uncommon among the Koi-na children, Sanna took a stick to Zokho when Willem Kloot told her what had happened, and forbade her to speak to Roeloff. Not only had she left behind her dress and caused trouble with the grootbaas, she had fancied herself the kleinbaas' equal, and shamed all of them.

'You're so bad, Zokho,' Sanna's breasts heaved with her guilt at beating the girl, 'I don't know what to do with you. You want to be kicked off the farm? Don't you have food in your belly, you stupid girl? Is the grootbaas not looking after you that you have to go sniffing after his son?'

Sanna didn't have to worry about Roeloff. Torn between feelings he didn't understand and what he'd done, Roeloff felt he'd committed a terrible sin. He'd set himself upon a girl, and one not like himself. He vowed to God that he would never do it again. The next day he went out at dawn with the sheep to avoid running into the family in the yard, and stayed out with Twa until dark. When he returned, he saw Zokho with the Koi-na near the stream. They had made a fire and were dancing around it. Was it full moon already? His father allowed them the big fire for that. He walked the other way to reach Twa's hut, thankful that no one was there.

The following morning he came out of Twa's hut, surprised to see his grandfather waiting outside.

'Oupa …'

'Here,' Harman Kloot handed him a chunk of warm bread just out of the oven. 'You staying with Twa?'

'Yes.'

His grandfather looked around the yard, still empty of people at this early hour, and reached for his pipe in his jacket pocket.

Lighting the pipe was almost a ritual. His grandfather wouldn't talk until he had tamped down the tobacco, lit the pipe, and inhaled. Roeloff felt the need to say something.

'I didn't mean to do anything bad with Zokho.'

Harman Kloot brushed aside the explanation.

'It's done. You can't undo it.'

'I just … touched her.'

Harman Kloot sucked on his pipe, letting out small bursts of smoke. There was a look of amusement in his eyes.

'You just touched her?'

'Yes. I … she … I didn't do anything wrong.'

'Not yet.'

Roeloff felt the heat rise to his face.

'I wouldn't do such a thing, Oupa.'

Harman Kloot smiled.

'You can make a river run backwards? Don't make too much of it. These things happen when you're young. Even when you're older. Don't put yourself in the way of it.'

'You're not angry with me?'

'Angry?' Harman Kloot laughed, coughing at the same time. 'You're not the first one to do it. Won't be the last.'

Roeloff waited for him to stop coughing.

'Your cough's getting worse, Oupa. Maybe it's that pipe. Sanna said she was going to give you something—did she?'

'Sanna's too busy boxing Zokho's ears.' He paused for a moment to catch his breath. 'We miss you. Are you eating?'

'Twa roasted a tortoise last night.'

'A tortoise?' Oupa Harman made a face. 'You must come back, or you'll end up like him scouring for food in the dust.'

'Pa told me not to come into the house.'

'He didn't mean it. You know your father. He thinks with his fists. Afterwards he's sorry.'

'He wasn't sorry about killing the Sonqua.'

'That's different. If you stay out here too long, it'll make it harder to come back. Just come in tonight and say nothing.'

'I can't.'

'You mean you won't. You may look like your mother, but you're stubborn like him.'

'When David makes mistakes, Pa doesn't go on like that. But he hits me. For any little thing.'

'Maybe your father doesn't know the things David does.'

'Some things, Oupa, he does. Sometimes I think Pa's afraid to tell him anything.'

'Your father's not afraid of anyone.'

'He listens to Oom Jan.'

'Well, Oom Jan, that's a different story. Oom Jan's the devil's disciple, there's no salve for him. You don't have to agree with everything Oom Jan does, but it's good to know someone like him when you're out here alone. Oom Jan has his usefulness. Don't think your Pa doesn't know that. And don't think he agrees with all that Oom Jan does.'

Roeloff listened some more, but didn't do as his grandfather asked. After a few claustrophobic nights in Twa's hut, he had grown used to the cold and the smell of smoke clinging to his hair and clothes.

One evening, sharing a plate of food with Twa that Sanna had sent from the kitchen, Willem Kloot's shadow fell over them at the fire.

'So, you'll show me what you're made of, Roeloff Kloot? You'll stay in this hok and show me you don't care to improve yourself? Maybe I've misjudged you. Maybe it's time to test your mettle in the bush.'

'I won't go killing Sonqua, if that's what you mean.' The words came out unbidden, and Roeloff cringed: not only had he spoken out of turn, he'd also remained on his heels while his father spoke.

Willem looked down at his son, squatting beside the fire.

'Yes, I can see I have misjudged you. Another week and I wouldn't be able to tell you from this goat-smelling bosjesman. You've made a mistake; I'll overlook it this time, but I warn you—don't go turning the Kloots in their graves. Now get yourself into the house.'

Spring came with a torrent of rain and a rush of yellow and purple flowers rising from the veld. There was water in the barrels, the well, the house. The tin tub came out for the first time in months. It was a warm October evening, and Roeloff turned his grandfather's chair on the stoep so he could look out directly over the veld. Propped up with a cushion in the mahogany chair with the riempie seat he'd bought from a Roodezand farmer, half dozing, half listening to Roeloff tell of his success with Boerhaan,

Oupa Harman had got thinner over winter. He didn't have to talk or cough or be in a closed room for Roeloff to pick up the gangrenous odour. Roeloff knew, better than his father who didn't want to face the fact that Oupa Harman had poison brewing in his lungs, that it was only a matter of time. His grandfather had no strength in his legs and had to be helped into his chair where he insisted on being instead of in bed. His beloved pipe lay, dried out and dusty, on the window sill.

'That sunset's like a paralysed scorpion bleeding over the rant. Look at that, Oupa. The whole veld's red.'

Oupa Harman shuddered at the description. A scorpion didn't bleed, but what did it matter, he knew what the boy meant. Someone else had talked like that. His difficulty with his estranged brother had always been Krisjan's obsession with words. Visionary verse, he called it. What was a man of vision if he couldn't foresee the result of his actions? But Roeloff was right. It was a rosy sky flecked with gold, and he wasn't yet dead to its beauty. It was his last season. Hewn from the blood dust of Africa, the land would soon claim him back.

'You all right, Oupa?'

'Everything's all right on a day like this, Roff. Beauty is God's cure for despair.'

'You are quiet today.'

Oupa Harman coughed, farting at the same time. His grandfather never broke wind in company; it showed his lack of control.

'I'm thinking of my brother, Krisjan. Your father never wanted him to come here.'

'Is there something wrong with him?'

'No.'

Roeloff waited for his grandfather to continue, but he didn't.

'One day I will travel to the Cape. There are many things I want to see there. I'll look him up.'

Oupa Harman turned sideways to look at him.

'You must leave that part of the family alone.'

'He's blood.'

'Yes, he's blood. And blood's blood, even if it's diluted. But, perhaps your father's right. Listen, Roff, when I'm gone …'

'Don't talk like that, Oupa.'

'There's a wooden box with a green lid … the dockets of the first settlers. My great, great, great-grandmother, Anna Kloot, wrote it. A handful of papers in duiker hide. Also a leather necklace.' He spoke slowly. 'The first Kloots were vrijburghers. Their children grew up with the Hottentots.'

'Koi-na.'

'They came to bush and mountains and murderous winds. They are the ones who made it easy for us.'

'Where will I find these dockets?'

'Your father had them last. When you read them, read what isn't there.'

'What do you mean, Oupa?'

'Anna Kloot was a smart woman. From across the sea. There's a story she tells, and a story she doesn't.'

'Bad?'

'In the eyes of some, not in mine. We all stand still when we pee.'

'A Sonqua can pee while he's running.'

'Who says?'

'Twa.'

'You mustn't believe everything he says. He thinks if you chew on a root, you'll get better.'

'I did, when I had pains in my stomach.'

'Did you get better?'

'No. He said in his hurry to get the root out of the ground, he forgot to put back a piece. You have to pay the land if you take from it. If you don't, it doesn't work.'

'That's what I mean. His head's full of such nonsense. But he's a good tracker. Did I tell you about the day I found him behind the Hantam?'

'Not the whole story.'

The coughing started up again and Roeloff waited for his grandfather to get back his strength.

'I thought it was an animal when I saw the bushes move. It wasn't. It was Twa, crouched on all fours behind a doringboom, stalking an eland. We saw each other, and I fired at the same time as his arrow came flying through the air and into my saddlebag. I wasn't injured, but he was. The shot knocked him over, into the bush. I got off my horse, and as I came forward, he ran off. I followed his spoor on horseback, and soon had him. What puzzled me was why he didn't run when he first saw me. He must have seen me a long way off.'

'Maybe he was afraid of losing the eland.'

'Maybe. Anyway, there was something about him. I couldn't leave him there or finish him off, so I brought him back to the camp. Your father was even younger than you are now, and we were camped a short ride away. I cleaned his wound and put on a poultice, and for three days he lay close to death with a dangerous fever. When he came out of it, he swore my magic was more powerful than his and that he'd been mistaken about us.'

'He doesn't think so any more. We are the robbers, and they the ones robbed.'

'I know.'

'They were here first, he says.'

'True. But they're not the only ones now.'

'We're the ones who don't want to share. We want everything for ourselves.'

Harman Kloot looked at him a long time.

'We live by the same laws of the veld, Roff. Bosjesman takes what he can from the land by his nature, we take by the smoke in our guns. Both of us have to live.'

The farmers in the interior had their own way of communicating. If Gerhardt Brink up on the kopje received tidings of death, he would span in old Maduna and clip-clop over to the dominee's wife at Oorlogsrivier, who in turn would relay the news to the Vissers, Steenkamps, and Jouberts until it reached old Pietie Retief in the valley. When word came at breakfast that Oupa Harman had bowed to the Will of the Lord, the horses were harnessed and by noon the path leading up to Kloot's Nek accommodated five extra wagons belonging to mourners bringing potatoes, pumpkin, biltong and beskuit. Laid out in a black suit stiff with age, attracting a dark knot of flies, Oupa Harman looked irritated at the idea of being on display, the little white flowers at the head of the coffin adding to the sickly sweet smell pressing in on them in the closeness.

Willem Kloot stood dry-eyed among the Jouberts and Retiefs and announced that the dominee was away in Roodezand and that the burial would take place immediately because of the heat. The mourners paid their respects, and the men carried the coffin silently down the hill to the family plot.

Hennerik and Twa lowered it into the grave with rieme, then went to stand with Sanna and the other workers and their children behind the mourners. Willem Kloot read a verse from the Bible, his coat tails lifting slightly in the breeze. He said a few words about the courage and determination and trekgees that had possessed his father and brought him to the Hantamberge forty years before, and how Kloot's Nek would be silent without him. Then he closed the Bible and threw the first handful of sand on the coffin.

Roeloff stood with David and Diena and Soela and watched Twa and Hennerik go to work with their shovels.

'You can move into Oupa's room now,' David whispered.

Roeloff gave him a cold look.

'I mean it, before Pa marries.'

Roeloff took the spade from Twa.

'Let Twa do it,' Willem Kloot said.

'No.' Roeloff didn't want anyone else to do it, and not Twa. He wanted all of them to go away.

The farmers had heard of the Bushman who talked to himself, and Roeloff's fascination with him. They watched to see if there would be confrontation, but Willem Kloot merely nodded at Roeloff to go ahead. Roeloff leaned into the mound of sand with the shovel and started to fill the grave.

Willem turned to the mourners who were watching his son and Twa. They all knew about his fire-loving Bushman and sometimes made reference to his strangeness, but knew nothing of his powers. Willem didn't deem it necessary to inform them. Twice during the long drought Twa had been able to point out where to dig for water. It would strike up at him from the earth through the soles of his feet, he said, and Willem Kloot would kick in his spade in the earth at the exact spot where Twa stood, trembling. The power wasn't always with Twa as it required huge concentration, giving him a pain in his head, and while Willem wasn't selfish towards his fellow farmers—especially when it came to that most precious of commodities—he was afraid that Twa's powers would get used up if everyone knew, and not be available to him when really needed. Willem had his own fondness for the little hunter (Twa had been his protector at one stage) and understood the friendship between Twa and his son.

'Coffee and bread, people?' he asked. 'Let's go back to the house.'

'Come,' David said to Diena and Soela.

'I'm waiting for Roff,' Diena said.

'Me too,' Soela added.

'Stay, then, and get yourselves dirty.'

Roeloff knew the tone in his brother's voice. Tomorrow or the day after David would take his revenge. Roeloff looked up briefly at the sisters in their blue dresses and starched kapjes. He hadn't seen the outfits before and imagined Drieka had had a hand in fashioning them. He returned to scooping and dumping the dirt onto the coffin and Diena and Soela slowly followed the others up to the house. Alone with Hennerik and Twa who paid him no attention, Roeloff threw himself into his task with a vengeance, the tears running freely down his face in hot streaks onto the front of his clothes. He didn't stop shovelling and dumping until Twa pulled at his arm.

'That's enough, Kudu, the hole's filled.'

Roeloff didn't go straight to the house, but sat down with Hennerik and some of the other Koi-na. When the last wagon had left and the lamp in the kitchen had been doused, he came out and joined Twa at his fire.

'Your old father's with his ancestors now.'

'He's in a dark hole, Twa.'

'The shell he came in, not his spirit.'

'My father never cried once. He has no feelings.'

'He has, but he has to show you and your brother that it's not a big thing, death.'

'It's big for the people who're left behind. Who will I have now that he's gone?'

Twa's eyes twinkled in the firelight.

'Me.'

Roeloff looked at him.

'You?'

'And all the trees and dassies and vygies.'

'There aren't any trees in the Karoo.'

'There are, if you look. There are many things in this great silence. You'll understand when you're older.'

For Roeloff the days were punctuated by moments of aching loneliness. The riempie chair looked forlorn, and for weeks he imagined he heard the hacking cough in the house. He went looking for the box his grandfather had mentioned, but there was nothing in the barn, or under any of the beds, and he didn't want to query its whereabouts.

A week before his father's wedding, Roeloff went into the barn to shovel manure. There he found Zokho crumpled in a corner, crying. Her dress was torn, exposing a red smear on her knee.

'Zokho, what happened?'

Zokho clasped her dress hastily about her.

'Who did this to you?'

She wouldn't answer.

'Who, Zokho?'

'You didn't talk to me, so I let him talk to me. And he started to push me for things.'

'What are you talking about? Who pushed you for things?'

'It's not my fault. I tried to be nice to him. I don't want to be thrown off the farm.'

'No one's going to throw you off the farm. Who are you talking about?'

She looked up.

'Who, Zokho?'

'Your brother. I was in here fetching something for Sanna. He came in and forced me to play with him.'

'Play with him?'

'Now my leg's bleeding and Sanna won't believe me. I didn't want to do it, but he forced me. He said he would cut my head off and feed it to the jackals.'

Roeloff looked at her. Despite his father's threats that she would work outside with the other Koi-na, she was back in the house, and he talked to her only in front of others, avoiding situations where they might be alone. But he missed her; their nonsense chatter, her childlike laughter. Everything in him screamed out for her. She was different from Soela and Diena. And very beautiful. Sitting there, with the torn dress pulled about her dust-streaked knees, a delicate flower among the stones, he wanted to touch her, taste her again in his mouth. His father had curbed his behaviour, but not how he felt.

'Go to the house. I'll tell Sanna what happened.' He got up and left to look for David. He found his brother at the water trough washing his face.

'What did you do to Zokho?' He fitted a stone into his sling.

David was tall and thickset. A smile curled his lips at one corner.

'Don't try it, Roff, I'm warning you.'

Roeloff swung the sling in a circular motion over his head. The stone zinged through the air and smacked into David's kneecap.

'Aieee! I'll kill you for this!' David grabbed his knee, hopping around on one foot. 'Pa!'

Willem Kloot heard the commotion and came out.

'What's going on?'

'Roeloff broke my knee with that sling!'

'Tell him what you did, you swine! Tell Pa you forced yourself on Zokho!'

David collapsed to the ground. Willem came over to inspect the kneecap. The stone had shattered the bone.

Three pairs of eyes watched as wagons and horses passed

within inches of the thorn bush behind which they were crouched. They had the patience of a predator awaiting the slow approach of its prey, and had come in the greyness of dawn, sitting all day in the heat, witnessing a parade of visitors to Kloot's Nek.

'You're sure this is the place?' Koerikei asked.

'Yes,' Toma answered.

They sat hidden until darkness, listening to the muted sounds of merriment drifting from the house.

'Get her and bring her to where we arranged,' Koerikei gave the go-ahead. 'Kabas and I will go for the sheep.'

'What about paying them back for Balip?' Toma asked.

'No. If we take a life they'll come with their fire sticks. Limp Kao has agreed, it is best. For now.'

'Limp Kao's too old to make these decisions for us. We should set fire to the house and take the sheep.'

Koerikei looked at his nephew in surprise.

'You're disputing the wisdom of one who has seen.'

'Maybe he's right,' Kabas said. 'Limp Kao doesn't see so well any more with those skins over his eyes. If we burn the house we can take the girl and all the sheep. They'll be too busy to come after us.'

Koerikei looked at his brother.

'We agreed, Kabas. It will take us days to get back. And look how many people there are here, how many horses. They'll find us in no time.'

Up at the house, Roeloff watched old Pietie Retief stab at his fiddle, playing a spirited vastrap. Dancing was in full swing in the front part of the house, Willem Kloot leading Drieka in a twirl of skirts, raising a cloud of dust from the floor. Roeloff had never seen his father engage in any kind of frivolity, and he watched with interest, amazed as always by the power of the peach brandy Willem brewed in a big pot and which everyone seemed to have had too much of. In one corner Manie Steenkamp was trying to hold onto his twin brother, Frederik. In another, Retief's grandson Hennie, who couldn't squeeze ten words out of his mouth on the best of occasions, was actually telling a joke.

Giggling behind him made Roeloff turn. His brother, dressed in brown pants and a white shirt, was standing between Soela and Diena. He'd scrubbed himself all afternoon, using a bucket of water for the event. It was obvious from his smile that things were progressing well in his pursuit of one of the sisters.

'Will you take me for a dance, Roff?'

Diena, who was thirteen and had breasts straining at her bodice, wore a collared dress wholly unsuitable for her round frame.

'I don't dance, Diena,' he said, although he could. No one was watching and he was on his second mug of his father's brew. It wasn't that he didn't want to dance with Diena, he didn't feel like it just then, and the brandy, whatever was in it, was making his shoulders and legs feel awfully strange. He was afraid he would lose control on the floor.

'We'll watch the others, and follow. It's easy.'

'Maybe Roff will dance with me,' Soela broke in, walking away from David.

Soela had thinned out over the hips and had left her long hair down for the occasion.

'David will,' he said, heading for the door. 'He knows how.'

'Where are you going?' David laughed. 'To your bosjesman? Roeloff's not interested in Africaanders,' he added for the benefit of the girls.

Roeloff closed the door behind him. He hated his brother. What David had done to Zokho left no room for Roeloff to consider him any better than an animal; but then an animal wouldn't have done what he had done. And his father had done nothing except tell him to keep his hands off the Koi-na. Nothing! He didn't feel at all sorry that David limped.

It was dark outside and he walked slowly in the direction of the huts. He found Twa at his fire, arguing with something that only he could see in its flames.

'What you doing out here, Sonqua?'

'I'm not Sonqua.'

'You are,' Twa laughed. '*Our* Sonqua.'

'You've been smoking dagga again.'

Twa waved Oupa Harman's pipe under his nose. Roeloff had given it to him after his grandfather's death.

'Try it,' he laughed. 'It'll take you to your ancestors. Do you know your ancestors, Kudu?'

'They came with a ship to this land. They were the first people here.'

'The first?'

'A hundred years ago, yes.'

Twa's eyes closed as he laughed.

'My people came with the locusts and bees. They've seen thousands of droughts. *They're* the first. They, and the Koi-na.'

'Why don't they have their own flocks, then? Why do they take from us?'

'That's the fault of a foolish old man at the beginning of the world when people were still animals,' Twa sighed. 'If I tell you how stupid he was, you will laugh. He came upon some cows in the field and without questioning how they could be useful, he stupidly showed them to the black man. Have you seen a black man, Kudu? He comes from the place where the sun comes up, and is dark as a wildebeest, very strong, the size of two Sonqua. The black man saw the importance of the tame cows and drove them into a kraal. When he'd milked one of them, after tying the hind legs with a thong, he took some of the milk to the old man who, if you can believe it, told the black man to drink first and let him lick the pot. That's what he said! 'You drink first, and let me scrape what's left off the sides of the pot!' So what do you think happened? The black man drank, and the stupid old man licked the pot. Then the black man took the thong and told him to pull the other end. They pulled and pulled and the black man, being the stronger, pulled it out of the old man's hand. He gave the old man a piece of string and told him that he had nothing he needed to tie up with leather thongs, and from that day on, the black man became a herdsman, and we were left snaring guinea fowls.'

'That's a good story.'

'It's not a story. It's how the world came to be. We were the first, before everyone. Now we're the last.'

'That's why you steal?'

'It's not stealing. It wasn't the white man's. He took it from the black man who took it from one who didn't use his head. It was shown to us first, remember? Just like this land was ours first. We're just borrowing.'

'It's taking what isn't yours.'

'See that tree, Kudu? Old and ugly from years and years in the ground. Who does it ask for nourishment? Who asked us for our permission to come and take this land?'

Something crashed behind them.

Roeloff stiffened.

'What was that?'

Twa was instantly alert.

'It came from the back of the huts.'

Roeloff got up and walked towards where he'd heard the sound.

At the first hut, he stumbled over Sanna tied up on the ground, and came face to face with a young Sonqua pulling Zokho by the hand. He recognised him immediately from the scar on the forehead.

'You! What are you doing here?'

'You know what I've come for,' Toma said.

'She won't go with you.'

Then Toma's expression changed. Roeloff turned slowly. Behind him another hunter had his arrow aimed at his back.

'Don't! It's Eyes of the Sky.'

Koerikei lowered his bow.

Roeloff regained his composure.

'Why have you come back?'

'Smoke in the Eyes belongs to our tribe.'

'You will not leave here alive if my father sees you.'

'We've been here all day, and he didn't see us. We'll be gone before he can blink.'

'No, you won't,' Twa came up laughing behind them, pointing Willem Kloot's old gun. It didn't matter that the trigger was broken; the sight of it was enough. 'I know how to use this. Leave the girl and go.'

Koerikei scowled at him.

'You have the heart of a jackal.'

'And the fangs of a lion. This girl is ours now.'

'Wait, Twa,' Roeloff interjected. 'Let's ask Zokho. Zokho? You were right. Toma did come for you.'

Toma and Koerikei looked at each other.

'Do you want to go?'

'She has no choice,' Toma said. 'Why are you asking? We'll take her if she doesn't come.'

'She has a choice. Zokho?' Roeloff asked again.

Zokho looked at Sanna on the ground, wriggling to get free of her knots.

'I have a mother now, Toma. I have food.'

'A mother? What nonsense is this? Your mother's dead. These people killed her.'

'If Zokho wants to stay …' Koerikei intervened.

'Zokho will come with us,' Toma said crossly.

Roeloff came forward. 'You heard her. She wants to stay.'

'Let her go, Kudu,' Twa said behind him. 'It's better for her. This is not her way. Not for long.'

Roeloff looked at the girl.

'Is that what you want, Zokho?' The tone of his voice wasn't lost on the hunters.

Zokho answered in Dutch. 'Do you want me to stay?'

Her meaning caught him unawares.

'I …'

'Let her go,' Twa said again. 'Make peace with these Sonqua.'

Roeloff stepped out of their way.

'What did he tell you?' Toma asked Zokho.

'He said I should go with you.'

Koerikei nodded his head in amazement. 'You're not from here, Eyes of the Sky. Who are you?'

'He's Sonqua!' Twa laughed, his voice trailing eerily after them as they disappeared into the darkness.

Chapter Five

Tau and Nani rose early on the day of the celebration for Zokho and Toma, and selected a spot a few steps from Limp Kao's hearth for the new skerm. While the others slept, they went quickly to work, digging elbow-deep holes a foot apart in a circle, into which they inserted flexible poles that met over their heads, binding branches and twigs around the structure and tying it all together with strips of bark.

'She's learnt bad things while she was gone. "*Don't call me Smoke in the Eyes, my name's Zokho*",' Tau imitated.

'Look how Toma's troubled Koerikei for her. And he's good with his arrow, a good hunter. Before she came, I thought he and Karees would mate.'

'Me, too. What will Toma do when he finds out?'

'What do you mean?'

'She has not been with Toma since she's back, but her body's changed.'

'Of course it's changed. She's started her flow.'

'I haven't seen any blood.'

'You haven't seen any blood because …'

'Exactly.'

They put the finishing touches to the shelter, then fetched wood from their own hearths and built a small fire in front of the entrance.

Zokho went dutifully with the women to the home built for her and Toma. Tau and Nani poured water from a container onto a soft piece of leather and washed her down, winding antelope strips below her knees, adorning her arms with bangles, decorating her short hair with red and white ostrich eggshell beads. When the grooming was complete, they sat her down on the special kaross.

'You are ready now for your husband.'

'Why do I need a husband? I'm still a child.'

The women looked at her in surprise.

'What do you mean?' Tau asked.

'A husband just wants to lay with you.'

'Of course, he wants to lay with you,' Nani laughed. 'What man protects you and feeds you and doesn't want to play with your genitals? You think he does it and wants nothing for it in return? But there's no need to worry about that yet. You will sleep on opposite sides of the fire until the first blood comes.'

'The first blood came long ago. It stopped.'

'How long ago did it stop?'

'I don't know.'

'Did you lay with Toma?'

'No.'

The women looked at each other.

'I think you are growing a child, Zokho.'

Zokho sat with her face in her hands and looked down at her feet.

'What happened?' Nani asked.

'I didn't want to, he forced me.'

'Who forced you?'

Zokho looked away.

'Someone where you were?'

'I didn't want to do it.'

'Toma will not accept a white child,' Tau said gently.

'We can give her the leaves,' Nani said.

'It's too late.'

'Maybe it will still work.'

'I don't want a husband,' Zokho said suddenly.

'What do you mean you don't want a husband? You have no one. Your mother is dead. There are no brothers, no uncles, only Koerikei and me. Toma can look after you. He wants to look after you. He went all that way to fetch you back.'

'I cannot do it for food.'

The women looked at each other.

'What nonsense is this? Of course, you do it for food. And for someone to care for you.'

'I have someone.'

'You have?'

'And I don't care for Toma.'

'You will care, when your belly's full. And who's this someone you're talking about? He's with us? Here?'

'He's not of this tribe.'

'Where's he from?'

'Not from here.'

'You are talking in circles, making us cross. He is the one who did this?'

'No.'

'Then, if he is not here, and he's not there, and we cannot see him, there is no one. Toma will be your husband.'

'I'll run away.'

'You will not. You will have his children and make his fire. You have learnt some bad things, Zokho. You have got answers for everything.'

Zokho's tears fell silently on the kaross.

The women regretted their harshness and leaned forward in comfort.

'It's not so bad,' Nani said. 'A husband can be good.'

'Yes,' Tau agreed. 'I lost two before Koerikei. But Koerikei is a good provider, and kind. In the end it all works out, you'll see. Come, Nani, we will leave Zokho now, to rest before Toma comes.'

Outside the skerm they returned to Tau's hearth where the women discussed Zokho's behaviour.

'Can you believe that, "I cannot do it for food"?'

'She has learnt very bad manners.'

'I feel trouble, Nani. And now, with this child in her belly, she will be difficult. Your husband's brother had trouble like that with his wife in the beginning, remember? She ran away every time she found out she had a baby growing in her belly.'

'She only had two children, Tau.'

'Yes, but she stayed away from one moon to the next. Kwa's brother was thinking of leaving her and taking someone else. We must prepare the leaves to bring the baby down and give it to her right away.'

Inside the new skerm, Zokho sat miserably on the kaross. The sun was still on an upward climb and she was in for an unbearable day in the cloistering heat. Although Toma was just outside, he would only come inside when the fires were lit in the evening. It was customary for her to wait like this by herself. No adults would come with him, only some of his friends who would sit with them at the fire till morning. She looked at the gifts placed in the skerm: a digging stick from Limp Kao, tortoise shell plates from Kabas, the steenbok cloak from Karees and an ostrich egg container from Toma. The creamy eggshell reminded her of Roeloff's smooth skin, and she remembered the night in the kitchen. Never would she forget how she had felt. How he had reacted. The rapidity with which his heart beat. Eyes were the deliverers of the heart, the old people said, and Roeloff spoke with his: grey like the rainy season when he was troubled, bright as the sky when he laughed. She was not of the dust and the wind like his brother said, to be trampled and blown away. She was like a shiny stone he'd found, interested in how she was made. That was his nature. Curious. Always wanting to know things. But why was she thinking of him? How would it help her tonight when Toma entered the skerm and claimed her? Roeloff was far away, in another world. He had let her go. He wasn't Sonqua. Would never be. He spoke the language and played at being one of them, but he was what he was and would always be: the son of a white man. This was where she belonged. At her own hearth, with her own people. The women were right; you couldn't have what was out of your reach. She'd once liked Toma, and she would like him again. Soon she would light his fire and have his children arguing over the milk in her breasts.

'The grass here has been disturbed,' Koerikei said, reaching the area where the women said they'd seen animal tracks. 'There are the gemsbok droppings over there.' He stuck his finger into the crust, examining the spoor. 'Broad and pointed. Female.'

Toma inspected it. Urine in front of the faeces indicated a male. The urine patch here was on top and slightly behind. And the spoor was fresh; she probably wasn't far away. He hoped not. They'd failed in their last two attempts to catch eland and needed desperately to bring food to camp.

'We can't let this one get away, our people are hungry.'

'We'll go in over there. Keep downwind.'

The hunters bent low and crept stealthily through the grass. A short while later they saw twigs moving on a bush up ahead and came upon the fawnish-grey antelope with the black stripe. They had seen lions and hyenas impaled on those long horns, and they weren't taking any chances. Dropping silently to their knees, they got ready to aim. The sudden alarm call of a bird shrieked over their heads, and the gemsbok bolted. Cursing the interfering bird, they released their arrows. Toma's found its mark and the gemsbok fled with the arrowhead lodged in its belly. The hunters gave chase into a clearing, over sand and bush, then back in among the boulders. Poison worked swiftly in the softness of the belly, and the afternoon found them still in pursuit, creeping up on the weakened gemsbok panting under a tree. The animal tried wearily to ward them off with its horns, but it had lost its strength and was no match for the hunters who quickly beat it to death with a stone.

'Your arrow got him, Toma, make the cut.'

Toma knew the honour bestowed on him; knew, that, despite his age, he was next in line after Koerikei. The leader had to be many things, not just accurate with his arrow.

Toma had been told that his ability to decipher spoor over rock and stone was as legendary as his old father's, his eyesight better than anyone's. His people had lived mostly on berries and tubers and plants during the dry months, and the last failed attempts had disheartened them. They would know it was his arrow that had provided the camp with their first real food in almost two seasons. Would it change Zokho's feelings towards him, make him more important in her eyes? She was growing bigger every day with their child. He wasn't sure when it would come although from her appearance it looked like it might any day. The meat from the gemsbok would strengthen her.

He made the cut, then the arrowheads were dug out and examined to establish ownership, the animal quickly skinned and disembowelled.

Toma took out the liver, divided it in three, and handed a piece each to Koerikei and Kwa. They ate it warm, with the blood dripping down their chins and arms, then proceeded to the serious business of cutting up the carcass. The sun was on its downward journey when they left for camp with the meat slung over their shoulders.

The women saw them in the distance and started the fires. The group had swelled to nineteen, and at Koerikei's hearth, the meat was again divided and redivided until everyone had a share. Choice cuts were roasted, the stomach cleaned of grasses and thorns, blobs of faeces squeezed out of intestines turned inside out with a stick, the rest of the meat cut into strips and hung from branches to dry. The feast went on far into the night and they ate until they lay blown up like those swollen snakes they'd seen at the big river after a feed.

Outside her skerm, Zokho moved restlessly on her side. She'd had cramps all day, and a knife-like jab in the lower abdomen made her suddenly gasp with pain.

Tau heard the catch in her breath and turned. Zokho's face was sweaty and strained, and she was propped up on her elbows, her hips cradled in the shallow pit she'd scooped out of the soft sand. The leaves Tau and Nani had ground into powder and put in her food hadn't worked, and Zokho's belly had grown round as a melon. Tau knew her time was at hand. Toma knew, too, she saw, from the way he'd turned. Had he worked it out? Tau tried not to look too obviously at them. She and Nani felt Toma had been greatly deceived. Toma had proved himself an able provider, fulfilling his role, but he was not a contented mate, and most days looked like a hurt fly over Zokho who refused him sexual pleasure and ignored her duties, running off with Karees to play.

She mashed some dried herbs together, and took it over. Zokho, bent double with a contraction, waved it away.

'Give it to him, I don't want it.'

'You'll need your strength. Don't be so stubborn. Take it.'

'No!'

The others tried not to look. Everyone knew of the couple's discord—Toma's patience, Zokho's childishness. And now she was being disrespectful to Tau, who'd treated her like her own daughter. Still, they understood. It was her first child; she was acting out of fear.

'I'll leave it here. Take it. The pains will get worse.'

All this Karees noted from the entrance of her parents' skerm. Her mother had taken responsibility for Zokho, but Zokho could be very disagreeable. Karees knew why; Zokho had told her things. Having lived on a farm, she had experience that no one else had and Karees never tired of hearing about the big woman pretending to be Zokho's mother, giving her food. She particularly liked the stories about the old hunter and Eyes of the Sky. It seemed odd to her, this bond between the mountain man and the white boy, and strange for Zokho to want to be friends with him. Girls played games with boys, they didn't want to just be with them, like Zokho said. And why with someone so different from them? What had Zokho found so exciting that she was willing to ruin everything with Toma—Toma, who wasn't only a good hunter, but was possessed of such humour and tolerance? If she had one like him, she would take care not to lose him.

Karees watched Zokho get up and walk slowly into the bush. Zokho wasn't laughing now. No one could go in her place. No one could take on that pain. Now Zokho had to go and squeeze out that baby by herself in the bush. Karees pulled her kaross tightly about her, eyes fixed on the darkness beyond. She waited, straining her ears, but there were no cries of pain, no sign of mother and child. It was a night for stories and dancing around the communal fire, but it was a still camp as they all waited for Zokho to reappear.

The fires cast their circles of light, the night chilled, and Tau got up from her hearth to go and investigate. She came upon Zokho, frantic with pain, squatting on a patch of grass. Zokho had chosen her birthing spot well, with her back to a thorn bush so she could see oncoming danger.

'This pain is killing my insides.'

Tau kneeled down and put her hand between Zokho's legs.

'The head's there, it's almost over.'

'I can't push any more.' Zokho squeezed her eyes closed against the pain. 'It's not coming out.'

'You have to be strong. Take a deep breath and push!'

Zokho was racked with a contraction.

'Come, Zokho, now!'

With Tau's comforting hand on her shoulder, Zokho dug her heels into the grass and bore down hard into the ground. A trickle of blood collected at her heels, and the night air fractured with her screams.

'He's coming!' Tau eased out the head. 'One more.'

At the first rush of air into its lungs, the infant cried, and Tau went quickly to work, biting off the umbilical cord. As she lifted him into her arms, the moonlight fell on his face.

'Aaiee!'

'What is it, let me see.'

'It's better not to, he's dead.'

'Dead? But I heard him cry. How can he be dead?'

Zokho didn't see the hand clamped over the nose and mouth.

'Give him to me!'

Tau choked the windpipe to make sure, then placed him in Zokho's arms.

Zokho stared horrified at the dead child.

'I've killed him! I'm cursed!'

'Stop it, you foolish girl. It's not your fault. You'll have a child with Toma and everything will be all right.'

'I will not have a child with Toma! I've grown close to this one here, under my heart. How can he come to me dead?'

'You'll have other children, you are young. Now take this and clean yourself. You won't tell Toma about the softness of his hair.'

Zokho cried as the older woman dug a hole with her hands. The others would have understood, perhaps even Toma if she explained. She'd been forced. She hadn't done it willingly. Her feeling for the child was strong; she didn't want to accept that his small soul had departed. She touched the face, warm with her juices, and opened his eyes to see if she could revive him. There was movement in the lashes, but Tau pulled at her arm.

'Give him here.'

'I think he's alive, Tau.'

'Give him to me, Zokho.'

'I will not!'

Tau wrenched the child from her arms.

'Go to Toma. He's waiting for you.'

The night grew dark and deep, and a short while later a lone figure came through the bushes. It was bad manners to stare, but eyes looked on in naked disappointment. There was no baby in Zokho's arms, nothing protruding from her cloak.

'Zokho, you are all right?' Nani asked as she passed.

Zokho walked stone-faced past her to her skerm where she washed the blood from her hands and legs with a handful of water from the ostrich egg container, then lowered herself onto the kaross where Toma sat staring vacantly into the fire. There was a new firmness around her mouth. She didn't look at him when she spoke.

'He was born with no breath.'

Toma sat quietly digesting this news. Then he put his hand on hers, and crawled into the skerm.

In the morning, the men and women came one by one to console the couple, sitting with them at their hearth.

'You will have other children, Zokho. Toma's seed is strong.'

'Yes,' someone else added. 'Before long you will have a son.'

Then Koerikei came up with his wife, his quiver of arrows already on his back.

'You are strong enough, Zokho?' he asked. 'We cannot linger where there's one buried. You don't have to carry anything, Tau and the others will help.'

Chapter Six

Five years passed. Roeloff was on Dorsbek driving the sheep back to Kloot's Nek with Ratel and Riempie when Twa came galloping up on a mare, waving wildly at him.

'Quickly! Vinkie's fallen in the dam!'

Roeloff raced off in a panic. The dam was full with the recent rain, and his four-year-old half-sister had a fondness for playing with Sanna's boy, Kleintje, on the grass near the water's edge. Drieka didn't like Kleintje—so named for his smallness—and complained bitterly about her daughter playing with Hottentots. His father paid no attention. They'd all been raised with the likes of Sanna and played with their children in their youth, he said. Roeloff knew that Drieka was a frustrated wife and sometimes wondered where she thought she'd grown up that she didn't know the realities of living a day away from your nearest neighbour. Finding herself with a rifle stuck in her hand on her first day on Kloot's Nek when the men went out looking for the jackals that had killed the sheep during the night, she discovered in a hurry that the man she'd married wasn't interested in voorkamer discussions about female sensibilities, and that his only concerns were his crops and grazing land for his animals. Willem Kloot was not a drinking man, and the odd times when he did loosen up with a beaker of brandy, the kitchen warmed with his laughter. The next day he was a tight-faced farmer again. Then Vinkie came along, and a softness was born and Drieka had a new way in. 'I don't want that snot-nose infecting my child.' 'Roeloff's too reckless with Vinkie.' 'David has no time for his sister.' Vinkie, with her freckles and dimples and sun-washed hair, had captured Willem Kloot's heart. He started to listen.

Roeloff arrived at the dam to find Vinkie floating face down on the milky brown water, and Kleintje shivering with fright. He had peed himself wet, stammering to his mother—who'd heard the shouts and come with rolling thighs over the veld with Drieka, and Soela and Diena who were visiting—that he wasn't to blame.

Roeloff rushed, hat and all, into the dam.

'She just turned over!'

He reached Vinkie in four strokes and put her over his shoulder. On the bank he laid her down on the grass and pushed his hands down on her chest. Nothing happened.

Drieka gave Kleintje a hard smack to the head.

'I told you to stay away from my child!'

'It wasn't his fault,' Sanna said, pulling Kleintje towards her, where he cowered behind her huge bum.

'Not his fault? You monkey, you're arguing with me?'

'Stop it!' Roeloff raised his voice above all of theirs. He had never taken such a tone with his stepmother, but her arguing wasn't helping and he was frightened himself that he'd come too late to save Vinkie. He knew of one way to resuscitate someone who had breathed in water, but couldn't think of inserting a smoking pipe up his sister's rectum. Taking Vinkie by her ankle, he turned her upside down and gave her a thump on the back. If it worked for babies and animals, it should get the air into her lungs.

'What are you doing?' his stepmother shouted, pulling him back.

He pushed her away roughly.

'I'm trying to get her to breathe!'

Vinkie was hung upside down with her dress falling over her head, exposing her bare behind. Roeloff gave her another thump, and she coughed. A thin trickle of water bubbled out.

'Look, Tante Drieka!' Diena said.

Roeloff put Vinkie face down on the bank with her head lying sideways on her arm. Slowly, signs of life returned.

'You've saved her, Roff. She's waking up!'

Vinkie opened her eyes, bewildered by the commotion.

'It's all right, Vinkie; it's me, Roff. Don't be scared. Cough it out.'

He picked up the exhausted little girl and her head fell back on his arm.

'I'll carry her up to the house.'

Willem Kloot came out of the kitchen as they arrived.

'I came in for coffee and there was no one—what happened?'

Drieka pointed an accusing finger at Kleintje.

'She was playing with this filthy Hottentot at the dam. She almost drowned.'

Sanna stood protectively in front of her son.

'He did nothing, Grootbaas. Tinktinkie's shoe got stuck in the mud and …'

'Vinkie,' Drieka corrected.

Sanna looked at Roeloff. Tinktinkie was Roeloff's nickname for his sister. Everyone called her that.

'Tinktinkie's shoe got stuck in the mud,' Roeloff said, ignoring Drieka. 'She went after it. It's not Kleintje's fault.'

'What were the two of you doing at the dam?'

'Playing, Grootbaas.'

'Playing? What did I say about playing near the dam when it's full?'

Kleintje looked up, wide-eyed and trembling, at the towering white farmer. For once there was no snot in the crease under his nose.

'I don't know, Grootbaas.'

'You don't know? What *do* you know?'

'Nothing, Grootbaas.'

'He doesn't listen,' Sanna said. 'I told him about the dam swelling up. He just runs out like an ostrich with no brain.' She brought Kleintje out from behind her skirts, pulling his ear to show she was angry with him. 'But he didn't make her fall in. Kleintje's lazy, but he's not bad, and he likes Vinkie.'

'How did she get out?'

Drieka opened her mouth to speak, but Sanna beat her to it.

'Twa fetched Roff and Roff jumped in the dam quick, quick. We all thought she was dead. But he turned her over and hit her on the back and the water came out. He saved his sister.'

Willem turned to his son.

'That was quick thinking.'

Roeloff coloured slightly.

'Well, don't stand there like a tree, Sanna,' Drieka said.

'Get her changed and hurry with those potatoes. My brother and his wife will be here soon.'

Roeloff saw Sanna's bottom lip curl. She'd been embarrassed in front of the Joubert girls. Drieka had also called her a monkey. Sanna didn't forget such things. Tomorrow she would leave the loaves extra long in the oven to burn, and Drieka would retaliate by withholding meat from the three-legged pot which fed the servants.

They entered the kitchen and Roeloff gave Vinkie to Sanna.

'I'll change her in front of the hearth, Sanna, give her to me,' Diena said, coming forward. 'You help Tante Drieka.'

Sanna handed Vinkie to her and poured water from the kettle onto a rag. 'You can wipe her with this, it's nice and hot.'

Roeloff studied Diena as she went about tending to his sister. She had a neat brow, with light brown eyes, and the thick plait of hair wound all round her small head. Why was it he didn't find her attractive? The pimples were gone, her waist had narrowed, and he liked her. Much better than Soela. Soela was the handsomer of the two sisters, but her manner belied her looks. Diena spoke straight, and she was kind to the people on her father's farm. A bit too religious, but that was not surprising. The missionaries had made quite an impact when they came all the way from Europe to save the natives' souls, Oupa Harman had said. Many farmers now held services for their workers on Sunday afternoons, and on the farm it was Diena who performed it, instead of her father whose duty it really was. Just as well, Roeloff thought. How could a man with no Christian feeling for his workers impart the word of the Lord when he never gave them a day off, never paid them except in the form of wine to keep them drunk? God wasn't sleeping. And neither were the Koi-na. They were always making off with his sheep; recently six more had been lost to raiders.

Aware of Soela's eyes on his back as he stood with Diena and Vinkie in front of the hearth, he fought the temptation to look up. He wasn't unaware of the snug fit of her dress, the curves underneath, the effect they had on him. It displeased him that she had this power over him.

'I was thinking, Roff,' Willem Kloot said from where he stood at the half door drinking coffee and looking out for Joubert's wagon, 'I'm getting too old for that stallion. I was thinking of giving him to you.'

Roeloff came fully alert.

'Boerhaan?' Champion stock was hard to come by, and a stallion like Boerhaan was priceless, besides being his father's favourite horse. Willem cared for nothing and no one like he cared for Boerhaan. Roeloff couldn't believe it.

'You're seventeen. It's time you took care of some things. I'm putting you in charge of the foaling. You'll run the stable from now on.'

Drieka, cutting potatoes and carrots, stopped with the knife in the air.

'Giving him all this responsibility, the stallion—David's more suited.'

'Roff has his way with horses, David doesn't.'

'David will take a wife. It's a start.'

Roeloff looked at his stepmother from under his lashes. Her hair had greyed prematurely, making her look older than her twenty-eight years, and her size had not decreased much since Vinkie's birth. She'd lost her looks, and her thin lips, mean and unfriendly, bore a strong resemblance to her brother's. Roeloff wasn't surprised that she favoured David. David, wanting to curry favour with the aunt of the girl he had his heart set on, had worked diligently through Drieka to promote himself with Soela, and Drieka, wanting at least one son on her side for future insurance, had responded. Still, Roeloff was hopeful. Drieka had no hold over his father; in the end his father did what he wanted.

'Everyone will take a wife sooner or later. There's enough on this farm for everyone. He's yours, Roff, but I don't want anything happening to him, or any change in his routine. He's still number one around here.'

'Don't worry, Pa.' The thrill of ownership was overpowering. 'He's mine, then, completely? You won't be riding him any more?'

'He's yours. I'll take one of the mares.'

'Thank you, Pa. Thank you.'

'Don't thank me so quickly. I've given you a big responsibility.'

'Yes, Pa.'

Twa appeared at the back door.

'Meisie is ready, Grootbaas.' Meisie was one of the brood mares.

'Come in, Twa.'

Twa came into the kitchen and stood awkwardly in front of them. He was in the same duiker loin cloth he'd arrived in almost a quarter century before, the only additional adornment an old hat hanging from the leather waistband that held up his testicle pouch, a carry-all for his pipe and tobacco. The playfulness he exhibited with Roeloff was seldom seen by the womenfolk.

'When are you going to wear the clothes I gave you?'

'Tomorrow, Grootbaas.'

Everyone knew tomorrow would never come. When it was cold during winter, Twa sometimes wore a kaross over his shoulder, but once back at his fire, he was naked again.

Willem reached into his pocket and took out a piece of rolled tobacco.

'Don't smoke it all in one day.'

Twa took the tobacco, smiling humbly, and said something only Roeloff and Willem Kloot understood. He had come to the farm as a young man, and even though he and Willem Kloot had played and hunted together at one stage, Willem had gone from kleinbaas to grootbaas, and Twa was in awe of him. He and Sanna were the only ones the grootbaas never yelled at, and while he knew he fell into the same category as the Koi-na, their earlier comradeship wasn't forgotten and there was occasional teasing between him and the farmer.

'You two take care of Meisie,' Willem Kloot said to his son. 'I'll come later to see how things are going. I'm waiting for Oom Jan.'

Roeloff took a paraffin lamp and some rags and went with Twa into the barn. The birthing area had been prepared with a thick carpet of straw, and they found an agitated mare, restlessly circling the stall. Her chestnut coat was streaked with sweat, milk squirting in thin streams as she kicked at her large belly with her hind hoof.

'Halt!' Twa trailed after her, holding her still while Roeloff looked under her tail.

'My father gave me Boerhaan. He said he was mine, he won't even be riding him from now on. Can you believe it? That he's given me his stallion?'

'No.'

'He's getting too old for Boerhaan, he says.'

'That horse has the devil in him, his spirit appeals to your father. He won't be satisfied with a mare.'

'Why do you think he did it? My father hasn't been generous to me.'

'Maybe for saving your sister. And he is generous to you. More than to your brother. You don't see it because you are so angry with him for many things. What does David say?'

'He doesn't know. He's away buying wood for that house I told you my father wants to put up at the back. They'll be here soon, him and Oom Jan. Oom Jan wants one, too.'

Twa chuckled. Roeloff had told him about the farmer in Roodezand who shut himself in a wooden contraption to perch on a plank, dropping his waste into a bucket underneath. He thought it queer, this fascination with your own faeces when a kick of sand covered everything, and queerer still that others wanted to copy the farmer.

'Can I watch?'

They turned, surprised to see Soela in the doorway.

'Well, I …' Roeloff stammered, not sure what he should say. A girl in a foaling barn?

'Your father says it's all right.'

'I'll be back soon,' Twa said, taking the tobacco Willem Kloot had given him, and heading for the door.

'Where are you going? I need you.'

'Now, now,' he said and left the barn before Roeloff could stop him.

Meisie whinnied and Roeloff patted her flank.

'My father says they always give birth after dark.'

Roeloff looked at her: the long hair left loose hung down to her waist; the blue eyes innocent, yet with a hint of daring. Why had she come? Alone in her presence, he was forced to be attentive.

'It's the safest time. In the veld there's the danger of predators, so they wait for the quiet of night. It's instinctive.'

'She seems nervous.'

'It's her first foal. She doesn't know what to expect.'

'Have you thought of a name?'

'Neizaap.'

'Sounds Hottentot. My father says your horses all have Hottentot names. Oegaap. Neizaap. Isn't one called Kakaumaap?'

'Your father says too many things. We treat our Hottentot-name animals better than he treats people.'

Soela reddened. She had never heard anyone speak about her father like that.

Meisie kicked over a bucket.

'It's getting close,' he returned his attention to the mare. 'Maybe you should go back to the house.'

'No.'

The mare swung her head wildly from side to side and he concentrated on calming her down, walking her around the stall. A short while later the water broke with a gush, and a small hoof encased in a bluish sac appeared. Roeloff was conscious of Soela in the barn, the silence between them. He watched the hoof slide back into the swollen flesh. As the hoof continued to appear and disappear with every contraction, he became slowly aware of his own body. He was angry with Twa. If Twa had been there, it would have eased the tension. A mare giving birth was ordinary. Alone with Soela, it aroused other feelings. Why was she in the barn? Where was Twa? Smoking with the Koi-na? Sitting at a fire? He didn't dare look down at himself for fear that Soela would see his condition.

Meisie looked for a spot to lie down and collapsed onto the straw with a groan. Moments later the hoof appeared again, followed by a second hoof, the snout, and—slowly—the entire head. Meisie gave a final push, and a shiny chestnut foal slid out onto the straw; sniffing, twitching, blinking its eyes to adjust to the yellow light.

Roeloff clamped the umbilical cord, carefully drying the filly.

Meisie raised herself up from the straw.

'Come, Neizaap, you, too. Up!'

Neizaap began determined efforts to stand, and a few tries later, on wobbly feet, she was exploring her mother's body to find food.

He wiped his hands on the rag and got up.

'Why did you come out to the barn, Soela?'

Soela fidgeted with a button on her dress.

'To watch.'

He advanced towards her.

'No, Soela. You came for me.' His face only inches away from hers, he slipped his hand down the front of her bodice and touched her flesh, feeling her breast in his hand.

Soela gasped.

'Is this what you want?' He stroked the nipple, feeling it harden under his touch. He knew what he was doing was wrong, but he couldn't help it. Through the thin dress, he could feel her heart racing. He ripped off two of the buttons and put his face between her breasts. It was warm there, with a fragrance of soap, and another much stronger smell. Then, as suddenly as he had touched her, he pushed her away.

'Go now. It's better for you.'

Soela looked at him in shock.

Roeloff turned back to his work. 'Go, I said.'

Soela wanted to say something, but she couldn't get the words out.

A noise at the door made them turn.

'Soela! What the …'

Soela rushed past him into the dark.

'What's Soela doing in here? What did you do to her, Roff?'

'Only what she wanted me to.'

'What does that mean?'

'It means what it means. And next time she follows me, I'll show her.'

David's fist caught him under the eye, and he fell.

'You touch her, you're finished!' He kicked Roeloff in the ribs and went after Soela.

Roeloff lay sprawled next to Neizaap, holding his head. He was on the receiving end of too many fists, landing too often on his rear end. A chuckle at the door made him look up.

'Ttt, ttt, ttt,' Twa tittered, standing over him laughing. 'When are you going to learn? I can't turn my back, and you're putting your hands where they don't belong.'

Chapter Seven

Roeloff and Twa stood in the shade of a kareeboom, watching a swell of orange dust roll towards them over the flats. They had followed the tracks to dense undergrowth at the foot of a pass, stopping at the remains of a recently abandoned fire. They had left Kloot's Nek two days before, and were tired and irritable from the heat and burning wind. There was only one calabash of water left, and the horses were thirsty, too, the recent rain having barely moistened the earth, if indeed it had reached this far north. It didn't appear so.

'They look ready to kill, the way they're driving those horses.'

'Your brother will see that path.'

'I hope not.'

The riders galloped up, and dismounted in a flurry of guns and flapping coat tails.

'We thought we'd better come out and see where you were. Any sign of the sheep?' Willem Kloot asked.

'It's not the first time I've come looking for sheep, Pa, you didn't have to come all this way. There are some bones over there.'

Willem kneeled down next to David who was already

inspecting the tracks around a hearth with a few embers of coal still in it.

'A whole lot of them.'

Willem turned to Twa.

'How many?'

'Five, maybe six.'

'How long ago did they leave?'

'Yesterday.'

'Yesterday?'

'I don't think so,' David said. 'These tracks are fresh, and there are more than five or six. It looks like a whole family. Look at all these footprints. The thing is, which way are they headed? I don't think we should waste any time.'

'They've done a good job camouflaging,' Roeloff said. 'They're clearer here, around the hearth, because the area's protected by these rocks. It'll be harder from here on. Besides, it's not necessary for all of us to go. Twa and I can handle them, they're a small party.' Twa's deciphering of the spoor had indicated a group of at least fifteen. The remains of the fire had also told them that the hunters had just that morning departed.

'I disagree,' David said. 'These tracks seem to be going up this pass. Don't listen to him, Pa. I think we should get going. They've eaten one of the sheep already. They've gone north.'

'What do you think, Twa?' Willem Kloot asked. 'North?'

'They came north all this way, but going east from here on,' Twa said, starting to sweat from all the lying.

'Why would they come north, then, suddenly, at this point, go east?' David questioned him.

'And they knew you were coming, they tried to cover their tracks,' Twa continued as if David hadn't spoken. 'They went up here, then walked backwards on the same tracks. If you look where the stones are, you'll see the crossover. This is where they start going east. You can see the scrapings of the branches they used if you look closely where they wiped out the tracks behind them. Sonqua clever, Baas. You're supposed to think they went north.'

'They've gone north, and Roeloff knows it. That's where they're from, bosjesman country! Not even a buffalo can survive in that heat. They live there because they know no one will follow them into that wasteland. They come down to the Hantam to steal. It's easier than hunting game.'

Roeloff knew David was telling the truth. Twa was from the parched land below the yellow river. His family had travelled south because of the prolonged drought, and taken shelter behind the Hantamberge when their camp had been ruthlessly decimated. Where the men on the horses had come from, what they were doing there, Twa couldn't say. He had survived because he'd played dead, lying with his face in the cold ashes. David was right. The Sonqua would retreat to the north until they were hungry again.

'David's right. They've gone north. The truth is, I don't want you with us.'

Willem Kloot was weary from the long ride, his eyes tired. 'So you lied. And you told this bosjesman to lie. Why?'

'I know these parts. I speak !Khomani. You would be in the way. I want to avoid trouble.'

'That's not enough reason. A lot of them together might be dangerous. David can go with you, an extra gun is good.'

'If he comes, he goes by himself. He won't keep his head.'

David bristled under the insult.

'He's too soft for this, Pa. Already he's thinking of a way to bargain with them. These thieves don't know reason. They should be shot on sight.'

Twa walked off and left them talking. Roeloff wasn't unaware of the old hunter's dislike of his brother.

'You want your sheep, or you want revenge? I can promise the sheep. If I find them.'

Willem Kloot blinked at his confidence.

'You're very sure of yourself. They're thieves, Roff, they'll come again.'

'I know, but we kill this lot, and next month another party, hearing of it, will come. And it'll get worse and worse until finally there's no one left. They've only touched our animals, not us. Other farmers have been less fortunate.'

'That's why we have to do it, to show them we mean business. It's not going to stop. We just have to take care of them.'

'I promise the sheep, Pa, that's all.'

Willem considered this.

'All right, Roff, I'm going to trust you. Just don't tell me any stories afterwards. Bring my sheep back.'

David scowled at his father. 'You're going to let them go by themselves? You know what they get up to together.'

Willem Kloot got back on his horse. 'Come on, we've already wasted a day. Roeloff will bring the sheep back. There's work waiting at Kloot's Nek.'

Roeloff and Twa watched them ride off.

'Come Twa, this shouldn't take long. The Sonqua will be

slowed down by the sheep over this pass, we should catch up with them in no time.'

They moved stealthily up the path, leading the horses up the natural stairway of stone and vegetation, past clefts and cliffs until, sweaty and breathless, they reached the top. They found a shelter of overhanging rock scarred with the soot marks of old fires, and fresh evidence of the little hunters. Twa discovered water for the horses in the hollow of a tree, the dark streaks of usage still discernible.

'They've been here.'

'I know. Look at this,' Roeloff pointed to a collection of stones arranged in a circle. 'The sharp edges.'

'Sharp enough to slice the hide off a steenbok without drawing blood. They leave things for other travellers.'

Roeloff looked around the cave. 'Good shelter from the rain. Twa, look over here! What does it look like to you?'

Twa peered at some dull markings on the cave wall.

'Elephants.'

'That's what I thought. It's old, Twa.' He ran his fingers over the rock. 'Very old.'

'I told you. My ancestors were here thousands of years ago. This was one of their homes. Here, stand over here, and close your eyes.'

Roeloff did as he was told.

'Now, let everything inside of you go, and listen. Feel it come into you. Listen with all of your skin, not just your ears.'

Roeloff allowed his muscles to relax and let himself sink into his surroundings. He stood for a long time, smelling the earth, feeling the coolness of the cave on his skin. The silence was overpowering. The buzz of a bee whirred lazily in the background, the razz of birds a distant music. Then he heard it, the light-hearted banter, the soft laughter of children, the sound of stone on stone as men sharpened their hunting tools around the fire and women tended their hearths. Then the voices faded and all was quiet again. Presently he opened his eyes to the dimness.

'You have visited my ancestors.'

'I swear, Twa, I heard them.'

'I know.'

'Twa? Why did you stay on at Kloot's Nek? I mean, you could've run away, couldn't you?'

The question was unexpected. Twa picked up one of the stones and examined it. He didn't answer right away.

'I owed a debt to your grandfather.'

'He was the one who shot you.'

'I flung my arrow at him, too. It missed and hit his bag. I was sick from the sting of his gun. He could've left me for the jackals, or killed me.'

'That's why you stayed?'

'I thought I would stay for a time to look after his sheep—he wanted me to look after them—then I would leave. What Sonqua will tie himself to the white man and a piece of land when the whole world is out there for him? But, the seaons changed, and I was still there, I couldn't leave. It made me sad. A Sonqua doesn't like to be sad. So I would go away, and return, go away, and return. I said to myself, if your grandfather gets angry, he won't see me again. But your grandfather never got angry. Sanna wasn't there in those days, she came afterwards, with your mother, and your grandfather fed me from his own pot. He was good with his gun. There was always eland or springbok.'

'You stayed for the food.'

'Also, your father was young at the time, I was curious about white people.'

'What was he like as a child, Twa, do you remember?'

Twa's eyes took on a faraway look.

'Did he tell you how he got that scar on his hip?'

'Oupa Harman said he was tossed by a wild buffalo when he was thirteen.'

'More than that. He was tossed and trampled and the bull ripped out half his hip before your grandfather killed it. If you don't hit a buffalo the first time, you better be far away. There isn't an animal as angry as him. Your grandfather missed, and if he hadn't had a second gun, your father would be with his ancestors. Anyway, I remember it, because he was bleeding, and shaking from shock, but he never cried. Even Twa will cry after landing on the horns of a buffalo. But not your father. He was too big for that. I only saw him cry once, when his younger brother Stefan died, after breaking his neck falling from a horse. Your father wasn't the same after that.'

'How do you mean?'

'His spirit changed. He went out into the veld by himself and sometimes stayed two or three days. Your grandfather would send me to go and look for him. He had no one to play with or talk to except the Koi-na children. He understood the land and its animals, even its people.' Twa paused to look at him. 'But he was never able to separate them. You're his son by courage and stubbornness. Not by nature. Your father was always brave, but his heart's not Sonqua.'

Roeloff looked at the horses over by the tree. They had drunk all the water in the hollow and seemed to have regained some of their earlier spirit.

'We must go, or we'll stand here and talk and the others will get away.'

From the top of the mountain the land stretched greybrown and broken before them, the sky meeting the end of the earth. A dark line moving slowly northwards pinpointed the raiders.

'Do you see them down there?'

'Yes.'

The hunters had their first inkling of danger when they felt the vibrations under their feet and saw the riders materialise out of bush and rock in the distance and race towards them.

'Koerikei, look!' someone shouted.

The men reached for their arrows, and Koerikei issued a spate of instructions over the rising panic.

The horsemen pressed forward in a rush of speed and four men stood with their arrows poised while women and children and sheep went bolting in all directions.

'Wait, wait! It's him! Eyes of the Sky! Don't shoot!'

'I said he would come,' Kabas said crossly.

'That's him, Limp Kao, the one we spoke about,' Koerikei said.

'He's grown like a tree, but that's Eyes of the Sky! Be careful, he has a gun. And be careful of that old lizard with him!'

Roeloff, too, had recognised the hunters and his spirit sank. He'd hoped it wouldn't be them. Twa had been right in his calculation—he counted eight adults and six children. He dismounted and threw his gun up to Twa to show that he was coming in peace, standing firm and fearless in front of the man he thought was in charge.

'You've stolen my father's sheep.'

Koerikei lowered his bow.

'Shoot over their heads, Twa, and get the sheep,' he said in Dutch.

The shot echoed over the plain and they jumped back.

'Well? Speak up! Don't just stand there.' He turned to Toma, 'Why'd you come back and steal our sheep?'

'Your father has many sheep.'

'They're his sheep, not yours. We've paid money for them, worked hard to keep them. You can't just come on our land and take them.'

Limp Kao studied him. Eyes of the Sky was indeed as the others had said: white hair stained gold by the sun, eyes rich as the sky. But there was anger, and something else. For someone so young, he seemed remarkably unafraid.

He came forward quietly.

'I am Limp Kao, Eyes of the Sky.'

'I am Roeloff Kloot.'

Limp Kao nodded.

'We wouldn't have borrowed your father's sheep, but the drought has taken our food, chased away the animals. Many of our old people and children have died.'

'The drought affects everyone, not only the Sonqua. It's that much harder for us, to find grazing land for our animals, to keep them alive. And you haven't borrowed, you've taken. You eat it up and it's gone and we don't get it back. Borrowing is when you have permission to take, and later you return it. What can you return? Tell me. Would it be all right for me to come here in the middle of the night and borrow one of your children? You took twelve sheep! I took a chance with my father when I cut Toma's bonds and let him go. I was a fool! You've taken advantage of me.'

'Sit down,' Limp Kao said gently. 'Maybe we can come to an understanding.'

'We will come to no understanding, you have nothing to bargain with. If my father were here, you'd all be dead.'

'We're sorry you're so angry.'

'You're not sorry at all. Tomorrow you'll do it again. That's Sonqua's nature. Sorry today, unrepentant tomorrow. You have short memories. No one else would've spared Toma.'

They hung their heads like naughty children. They didn't know why he was so angry. They hadn't done anything wrong.

'Did you take the other farmer's sheep, too?'

No one answered.

'Well, no answer's as good as one. Watch your backs with that farmer. With him there will be no second chance. He has no feeling for the Sonqua.'

'Does Eyes of the Sky have feelings for them?'

'Only anger and disappointment. They have proved themselves ungrateful.' He looked around for Twa and saw that he had collected ten of the sheep. 'Where's the other?'

'Behind those rocks,' Twa said. 'I'll get it.'

Limp Kao coughed politely.

'What if we promised to stay off your land, if you agreed not to interfere if we brought the other farmer's sheep past it?'

The others stared open-mouthed at Limp Kao.

Roeloff laughed and got back on his horse.

'You have courage, old man, but I cannot agree. I don't see eye to eye with that farmer, but it's not in me to betray him. And I don't need promises. If you come near our sheep now, it's over between us.'

There was a sudden commotion and heads turned as Zokho came running out from behind a bush.

'Zokho!' Toma said angrily. She'd been warned to stay hidden.

Roeloff forgot everything when he saw her. Zokho's skin had taken on a russet tone, and she wore only the tiny leather flap covering her private parts. She had grown tall, with long legs as strong as an eland's, the tips of her breasts glistening in the dying sun.

'Zokho …'

'Take me with you, Roff.'

'You will not go anywhere!' Toma came forward angrily.

Roeloff couldn't stop looking at her. The pouty lips, the slant of her eyes, the short hair decorated with chips of white ostrich eggshell. She was dusty as the veld, but even more beautiful than before, and everything he'd felt for her came rushing back. He'd missed the sound of her voice, and hearing it again, soft and childlike, made him realise how far he'd pushed her from his mind.

'I've missed you, Zokho.'

'I want to come back to Kloot's Nek.'

The others looked on in shock. They had never seen one of their own behave like this.

Toma glared up at him on the horse.

'She's mine.'

'So she is, Toma.' His first impulse was to snatch her up and ride off. But then what? Bring her back as a servant to Kloot's Nek and get himself embroiled in something that would only turn things upside down and invite the wrath of his father? The Karoo would be unbending if he broke the rules.

'It won't work, Kudu,' Twa's voice sounded behind him.

Roeloff leaned down from the horse and touched his hand to her face.

'Mijn Zokho.'

A murmur of voices rose up. They didn't know the word, but understood the gesture.

'Take me with you,' she begged him in the language he'd taught her.

'What will I do with you, Zokho? You know what will happen if you come with me.'

Zokho's eyes filled with tears. She stood still, not daring to look at the others.

The tribe watched in disbelief. Everything they'd heard about him was true. They watched him round up the sheep with the old hunter then, with a last glance back at the group, follow behind on the horse.

'He has wild blood in him,' Limp Kao marvelled.

'Yes,' Koerikei nodded. 'There was something between them. Things seem clearer now. Why Zokho behaves the way she does.'

A short distance off they saw one of the sheep separate from the group.

'What's he doing?'

'It looks like he's leaving one.'

Limp Kao shook his head in amazement.

'You were right about him, his heart's soft.'

'I feel sorry for Toma.'

'Toma beats his wife, Koerikei.'

'He's frustrated because Zokho won't lie with him. She's taken away his pride. And now, after this, I don't know what he'll do.'

'He'll learn, that's what he'll do. He'll learn not to be too anxious for life.'

By nightfall the women had erected shelters and were busy at their fires.

At Zokho's hearth there was no preparation of food. Toma was staring morosely into the flames, Zokho was lying on her side inside the skerm.

He crawled through the entrance into the shelter.

'I've made the fire, Zokho. Two nights now I've eaten with Koerikei and his family.'

'Why don't you ask his daughter to make your food? She'll be only too happy to do it.'

'Karees is not who I've chosen.'

'You should ask her to be your wife.'

'I don't know why I'm so stupid, Zokho, that I'm staying with you. You have made a fool of me in front of the others. How can I ask Karees to be my wife when I'm with you? The white boy has gone. He didn't take you. He doesn't want you, Zokho. You are of the lizards and the dust, not his kind. Why can't you see it? Don't you like me, even a little?'

'I like you.'

'What then?'

'I don't …'

'You don't what?'

'I don't want to be with you any more.'

He turned and crept out of the hut.

At his hearth Limp Kao, roasting sheep guts, saw Toma come out of the skerm. It was disrespectful to call out to someone at his own hearth, where he should have privacy, and he waited for Toma to look up, then waved at him to come and sit at the fire.

'I have too much, Toma. You must help me eat this.'

Toma looked at the roasted intestines and took the portion offered to him. It was hardly enough for the old man, but to refuse would be to insult him.

They ate slowly and finally Limp Kao broke the silence.

'Zokho is young, you must have patience with her.'

'For how long, old father? I am getting old waiting. It's many seasons now that we're mated. There are others who would be happy to cook my food and have my children.'

Limp Kao nodded.

'Karees, for instance. Koerikei has not found anyone yet for his daughter.'

'You are not interested in Karees.'

Toma picked up a stick and stirred the coals.

'Zokho's difficult, old father. Today like this, tomorrow like that. And stubborn.'

'One thing about this land, Toma,' Limp Kao leaned

back against the tree, closing his eyes. 'You know it's not going anywhere. The rain will come and give it life and we will eat, and the rain will stay away and every tree and blade of grass will suffer by its selfishness. In the end, it's still here with us. Generous. Stingy. Ours.'

Toma nodded.

'It's hard to be trapped between the teeth of the jackal and the favours of the gods,' Limp Kao continued. 'One who understands the soul of the veld knows he can't change it. He doesn't try. He fixes his bow. He watches. He waits.'

Toma sat while the flames grew smaller and smaller, until only a small pile of ashes remained. When a respectable time had passed, he got up and bid Limp Kao a peaceful night. With some feeling of relief in his heart, he returned to his skerm.

He lay for a few minutes in the dark beside Zokho, then slipped his hand between her thighs.

'What's this?' he asked, pulling his hand away. 'Why have you tied a branch to your genitals?' He felt around her waist, discovering the leather strap holding the contraption in place. 'What have I done to you that you are doing this? Why are you keeping me away?'

'I don't want to.'

'You are my wife.'

'My insides hurt. And you have woken me up.'

'Woken you up?' He pushed his hand between her thighs and pulled at the leather strap. 'You're disobedient. I will not take your stubbornness any longer! Come here, and let me come to you.'

Zokho pushed him away.

He hit her over the head with the branch, pulling her roughly towards him. 'Why do you think I chose you for a wife? Just to live with you?'

'My insides hurt, I said!'

'Your insides don't hurt, you are thinking of him!' He hit her again, his open hand stinging her face.

Zokho curled up like a ball. When he entered her against her will, hard and savage, doing his business with fast jerks, she cried silently, helplessly, while the voices of Tau and the others hummed pleasantly in the background.

In the morning, when Karees got up early to urinate, she saw Zokho come out of her skerm. She watched as her friend draped her kaross over her shoulder and walked from the camp. She said nothing to the others when Zokho's absence was noted and there was speculation that she had gone looking for food. She knew. Zokho had told her. When Roeloff had touched her, his eyes had spoken to hers.

Chapter Eight

Vinkie was in the kitchen with her mother when Sanna came in from outside with an armful of wood and said there was a wagon coming down the path.

'Who is it, ma?'

'I don't know,' Drieka said, tucking her hair under her kapje and going to the door. 'Sanna, go call the grootbaas.'

The wagon rolled up, and a tall youth in a dark jacket stepped out to help down a man with a cane. They looked at the house and the land, then focussed their attention on the woman and child standing at the door.

'We're told this might be the Kloot house.'

Drieka studied the man who had spoken. His stance, the bowed legs, the way he narrowed his eyes, all seemed faintly familiar. Their exhausted expressions and the tired horses indicated that they had had a long trip.

'Krisjan Kloot,' he said, answering her thoughts. 'And Pieter, my grandson.'

Drieka's hand flew to her mouth.

'I see the name's known,' the old man continued. 'I'm Harman's brother, Krisjan. We're at the right place then, I take it.'

'You're at Willem's house. I'm Drieka, his wife.'

'You're not …?'

'Lisbeth died long ago. This is Vinkie, our daughter. There are children from the first wife—two sons, David and Roeloff. One's with his father, the other's away looking for some of our sheep. We've been robbed. But come in, you must be tired. Where have you come from? Roodezand? Stellenbosch?'

'The Cape.'

'All the way from the Cape? That's a long journey,' she said incredulously, her eyes on Pieter who seemed most attentive to Krisjan Kloot, helping him up the steps. She'd heard him right, he had said *grandson*. How was it possible? She'd thought he was the old man's servant. 'How long did it take?'

'We stopped for a few days where we found water and grazing for the horses along the way. We also stayed a week with a family in Roodezand, another week in the Cederberg. In all, about two months.'

'Two months! That's a long time to be on the road, and in such unbearably hot weather. You must be tired.' Drieka's mind raced with the implications of the visit. If it had taken them two months to travel to the Hantam, they weren't coming for just a few days. 'I'm told it's hard to cross the Cederberg by wagon.'

'Very hard. And dangerous for such a small party.' Krisjan Kloot stopped on the top step to catch his breath. 'But Pieter is handy with a gun, and can turn his hand to many things. He and Karel did all the heavy work loading and unloading and dondering the oxen up steep hills, and repairing wheels when they broke.'

Drieka looked at the wagon. She hadn't seen anyone else.

'Karel?' she asked.

'Karel's been with me for ten years. His wife died two years ago. He jumped off when he saw some Koi-na near the dam. He went to make their acquaintance. Karel's Koi-na himself. He'll make his place with them while we're here.'

'Come in, please,' Drieka said. 'It's hot out here.'

Inside the house, Vinkie went to sit in her small chair alongside the hearth from where she had a clear view of the visitors. Pieter was the same build and height as Roeloff, but his skin was dark, his hair a strange combination of wire and silk—not clumpy like a Koi-na's, but not straight like theirs either. She wished Roeloff was there to see him.

'Where's Harman?' Krisjan Kloot asked.

Drieka realised with a start that he didn't know his brother had died. She was searching for the right words to tell him when a shadow fell in the doorway and presaged the entry of Willem Kloot and David.

Vinkie, watching her father, saw the colour change in his face.

'Oom?'

'Yes,' Krisjan said, getting up. 'You were twenty when I last saw you. My, how the time's flown!'

'This is indeed a surprise, after all these years! What brings you to the Hantam? Are you passing through?'

Krisjan Kloot laughed.

'Through to where, son? You people live at the end of the world. I thought I'd come and visit.' With two fingers he smoothed out his moustache which curled up at both ends like the horns on a buffalo. He had tremendous presence.

'Your father and I haven't seen each other since Emily died and I remarried. It's time the family settled things.'

The smile left Willem Kloot's face. He cleared his throat.

'I have bad news, Oom. I didn't know where to find you, and to be truthful—well, it doesn't matter now. Pa died some years ago.'

Krisjan Kloot leaned back in the chair and closed his eyes. When he opened them again, they looked glassy and tired.

'Some years ago?'

Willem looked sheepish.

'Six years ago, I think. Out here, we're not always—well, the years just run into one another. One loses track.'

'I said to Pieter something was wrong. Maybe I even knew, deep inside. What caused his death?'

'His lungs.'

Krisjan nodded.

'He always had trouble with his chest. Winter was bad for him. I'd have thought the dry air of the Karoo would be an expectorant, keep them clear.'

Willem looked at him. The word was one he didn't know. He took a chance.

'It can get cold in the Hantam during winter. People have the wrong impression of the Karoo. Stinking hot in the day, shivering at night. You can have a bad chest here, just like anywhere else.'

Krisjan Kloot nodded. 'Did he suffer?'

'Pa never spoke about his pain. Right to the end he pretended it was a cough. He said more to his grandson,

Roeloff, than to anyone else. If anyone knew what ailed Pa, he did.'

Krisjan smiled at David.

'Not me,' David said quickly. 'My brother.'

The old man studied David; he had been quick to distance himself.

'Yes, a grandchild can be a blessing. I have three children and twelve grandchildren. Pieter came to live with me last year after Emily died. I've lost both wives to the bladder. Of them all, he's the one—well, you don't want to favour one grandchild over another, but there's always one who has a little time for old people.'

Pieter looked down at his hands, which already had huge calluses on the palms and around the index fingers. He didn't say anything.

Vinkie watched her father and brother. Her father had not yet addressed Pieter, and David looked unimpressed. Were they as amazed by his looks as she was? Was that why no one spoke to him? Pieter's light grey eyes and dark skin looked strange, but he was handsome, and he had a nice way with Oupa Krisjan. She liked him.

Supper was a forced affair with Krisjan Kloot doing most of the talking, and Drieka falling over herself offering plates of potatoes and meat to the guests. After coffee, the tension eased up a bit. Krisjan Kloot talked about the journey: how the entrails of an ostrich they'd killed along the way kept a pack of wild dogs on their trail for several days, and how Pieter and Karel had had to take turns guarding the oxen at night as the dogs hung back during the daytime, waiting for darkness to attack. To get rid of them took the killing of one of the pack and leaving behind a slain eland. Then he spoke about life at the Cape, and they listened in awe to stories of travellers and explorers, and people who had enough money and time to be able to just idle about, doing nothing. He had Willem Kloot's full attention when the talk turned to farming and he mentioned the hardy merino sheep with their long, fine, silky wool, that were arriving in ships from Spain and other countries into the Cape. These sheep were sheared only once a year, the wool sorted and baled and then sent out on the ships to buyers overseas. Willem asked whether merinos had made their way into the interior yet, and Krisjan said he knew of a family who had left the Cape more than five years before with about fifty merino to settle in the drier regions north of Roodezand. He was sure that by this time they would have got there and increased their stock, but he didn't think farmers would part with the merinos easily, as disease was wiping out whole flocks and merinos were so hard to obtain. Because of their thick fleeces, it was particularly difficult in the hot months to keep them free of parasites and dirt. Some farmers docked the tails of the lambs to help control the problem and facilitate mating, as well as to put more fat on the body and less on the tail. It was all worth it, Krisjan said, as the wool fetched quite a high price.

The stories were entertaining and everyone enjoyed them, even though here and there a word was thrown in that no one understood, and no one queried. When the lamp started to flicker and the last of the coffee had been drunk, Willem said he was going to bed. He offered the visitors Roeloff's room while he was away.

Vinkie was lying awake on the cot in the room she shared with her parents thinking of the guests and everything Oupa Krisjan had said, when she heard her mother and father whispering.

'He's black,' she heard her mother's voice, 'your oom's grandson.'

'He married outside.'

'A Hottentot?'

'No.'

There was silence for a few minutes.

'What if the Retiefs or Steenkamps visit? People will talk.'

'Oom Krisjan won't stay long,' her father said. 'There's nothing for him here with his brother gone.'

Her mother was right about the talk. The next morning when she saw Kleintje, the first thing he told her was that the Koi-na were bristling with the news. They had seen Pieter. Karel had told them he was a Kloot. Kleintje's mother said Pieter was from the seed of a black man, there were black people in the Cape. Was it true? Was Pieter's mother or grandmother black?

Vinkie didn't know who to talk to about it, and wished Roeloff was there. The way her parents and David behaved, she knew they would be the wrong people to ask. She had also noticed the strain in the house. Her father was pleasant and respectful towards his guests and sometimes even started conversation with Oupa Krisjan, but there was an awkwardness between them that everyone felt. Oupa Krisjan came out on the stoep in the mornings to see her father and brother leave on their horses, and didn't see them again until dusk. They never asked Pieter if he wanted to go with them. Vinkie was anxious for Roeloff to return and wondered what was keeping him. He would have known exactly what to say to Oupa Krisjan and his grandson to keep them from looking so long-faced every day.

On the fifth morning after their arrival, Vinkie found Pieter outside spanning in the oxen, the cases with which they'd arrived waiting to be loaded onto the wagon.

'What are you doing?'

He looked up.

'Loading the wagon. We're leaving today.'

'But you have only just arrived. And Oupa Krisjan looks tired. My brother will come any day now. You'll like him.'

'Don't I like your other brother, then?'

'I don't know. But I know you'll like Roff. Everyone does.'

'Oupa wants to leave while he still has a tiredness in his bones. He feels that once he sits down and gets too comfortable, he won't feel like getting up again. We would also like to miss the rain on the way back.'

She watched him in silence for a few minutes.

'Are there many people in the Cape?'

'Oh, yes. They arrive in ships from all over the world. My grandmother came on such a ship.'

'Your grandmother? You mean Oupa Krisjan's wife?'

'His second one, yes, the one who died last year.'

'I didn't know we had family who came here on a ship.'

Pieter straightened up and smiled.

'You never even knew you had an Oupa Krisjan, so how could you know that?'

'My brother Roeloff's always talking about going down to the Cape. Oupa Harman told him stories when he was little. He says you have people living just across the road from you.'

Pieter laughed.

'That's true. But it's changed since then. There are buildings and churches and schools, and of course, the Castle of Good Hope. Under the Devil's Hill.'

'The Devil's Hill?'

'There are many mountains and hills in the Cape. The main one is the Table Mountain, which gets its name from the flat top and the clouds which gather at its peak. Then there's the Lion's Hill, which has the shape of a lion, and the Devil's Hill. If you stand on the edge of the Table Mountain you can see over the other hills, and the sea.'

'You've climbed it?'

'Yes. Below this mountain are gardens with beautiful avenues and all kinds of flowers and herbs and fruit trees.'

'Roff will be disappointed when I tell him! He would want to know everything.'

'Does he read?'

Vinkie brightened.

'He likes that more than anything. Well, not as much as his stallion because Boerhaan's like a person to him, but he reads his books over and over again.'

'I have a newspaper from Holland.'

'Really?'

'Also a book that I carry with me when I travel, but I only have two copies left.'

'You're giving him a book?'

'I don't know. Will he take care of it?'

'Oh, yes. He has a few books under his bed. No one's allowed to touch them. What is your book about?'

'Just some stories about the people in the Cape. Your Oupa wrote it.'

'Oupa Krisjan?'

'Yes.'

'Oupa Krisjan can write books?'

'Oupa Krisjan is well-known in the Cape.'

'I didn't know.'

'This will keep your brother happy for months. Tell him he must come to the Cape. I'll take him up the Table Mountain when he comes to visit.'

By noon the wagon was loaded with water and beskuit and biltong and a sheep Willem gave them for the journey. The family stood in a circle around the departing travellers, as Willem helped his uncle up onto the wagon.

'Travel safely, Oom.'

Willem handed him a folded blanket when he was in his seat. 'An extra one, for those cold nights,' he said.

Krisjan Kloot looked down at Willem, the reins in his hand.

'This is the last time we will see each other, Willem. I'm glad I came.'

'I'm glad too, Oom. I'm glad you made the effort to come all this way. All the best.'

They watched as Krisjan Kloot flicked his whip, starting his oxen on the long road home. As the wagon reached the huts, they saw Karel separate from a knot of Koi-na to join it. They watched in silence as the grey canvas top bobbed slowly down the track and disappeared between the boulders at the end of the road.

'I'm glad that's over,' David said, letting out a long sigh. 'Thank goodness no one visited.'

'Don't you forget who that is,' Willem Kloot shot him a stern look. 'What he does is his own business, not yours.'

The day after their departure, Vinkie and Kleintje were helping Sanna spread out washing on the grass when they saw dust rising in the distance. They ran excitedly to Willem and David, who were heading for the kraal.

'It's Roff and Twa, Pa, look!'

But Willem was too upset by the scene confronting him even to look up. They had heard a commotion and rushed outside, guns at the ready, only to find half a dozen bloodied lambs lying there ripped open. The baboons had gone straight for the curdled milk in their stomachs. Three ewes lay bleeding in the dust, with bite marks on their necks and heads. The bleating was deafening.

Willem sighed and straightened up.

'It's them all right. I'll be damned—he's got the sheep!'

David squinted.

'It doesn't look like all the sheep.'

'I didn't expect to see any.'

David opened his mouth to speak, then thought better of it. His father had chosen to forget the past deeds of his younger son.

'The Jouberts are coming for a meal,' Vinkie said. 'Ma says there's water for baths.'

'Are you sure? The rain hasn't been that plentiful,' Willem said.

'Yes. Ma wants you to hurry.'

Willem grunted. A bath was a luxury, requiring patient co-operation. Daily cleanliness was a wipe of the face; a full bath required privacy in the kitchen where the tin tub was set up in front of the hearth late at night while other members stayed politely behind their partitions. With the Jouberts coming for the evening meal and Roeloff arriving with two weeks' dirt on him, there would scarcely be enough time or hot water, and besides, Drieka would surely be upset about the kitchen being occupied at a busy hour. He would inspect the water level himself, to see if his wife had been correct. Water for the animals came before baths. Even drinking water was limited.

'Don't the two of you have anything to do?' Willem addressed the two children in front of him.

'Kleintje has done his jobs already. We want to wait for Roff.'

'Doesn't Kleintje have a mouth of his own?'

Vinkie turned to Kleintje. Kleintje looked back at her, his eyes wide.

'He can speak, but he's afraid of you, Pa.'

'Why's he afraid? He must only be afraid if he's done something wrong. Has he done something wrong?' Willem asked sarcastically.

'No, Grootbaas,' Kleintje said quickly.

'Tell your father to fetch the lambs, and to put these ewes out of their misery. Tell him to cut up the ewes and bring the meat to the house. The lambs are for you people.'

'Yes, Grootbaas.' Kleintje ran off to tell his father the good news.

Vinkie stayed behind to watch Roeloff and Twa come slowly over the rise with the sheep.

'Had any trouble?' Willem asked when they arrived.

'I knew them.'

'You knew them?'

Roeloff dismounted, looking at the carnage.

'Baboons?'

'Yes.'

'One of the thieves was the bosjesman I cut loose years ago,' said Roeloff.

'What? How did you know it was him?'

'I saw him again when they came for Zokho.'

'I thought Zokho ran away.'

'They came the night of your wedding and took her.'

'You didn't tell me.'

'I didn't want to spoil things. They came unexpectedly.'

David smiled. 'I said he knew more about that bosjesman girl. It was too easy, the way she just disappeared.'

'I knew nothing.'

'You know, if you hadn't set him free, this wouldn't have happened,' Willem said.

'They are not the only group out there, Pa. Why do you think they didn't kill us that night? It's because of Toma, because of what I did.'

'You know his name.'

'I know them, and they know me, and they all know each other. They split up during the year, and come together again when food's plentiful. If we killed one lot, another would come. It's better to reason with them. Setting Toma free gave us the chance to speak.'

'You can't reason with a bosjesman,' David said. 'He has no conscience.'

'I did, and here's the result. They gave back the sheep. No one got hurt. Now you know why I didn't want you along. You lose your head, and next week, next month, we lose more sheep. Maybe even our lives. Where will it end?'

'When we show them who's boss,' Willem said.

'No, Pa. As long as there's drought and no game, they'll come for the farmers' sheep. The best we can hope for is that it rains, or that they go somewhere else to find food.'

'Somewhere else is everyone we know. The Jouberts, the Steenkamps, the Retiefs, a few others.'

'We can't worry about the neighbours. They must take care of their own.'

'There are only ten sheep here. Where's the rest?'

'They ate it.'

'They killed two sheep in two days?' David asked incredulously.

'Didn't you say they were savages?'

'You probably gave it to them.'

Roeloff didn't bother to answer his brother. He was tired and dirty, and all he wanted to do was stable his stallion and go inside to sleep.

'Were they the ones who stole from Oom Jan?' Willem asked.

'No.'

'How do you know?'

'I asked.'

'And took them at their word.'

'They knew I would do nothing, whether they had stolen from him or not. They had no reason to lie.'

'Because you don't really care for Oom Jan, do you,' David accused. 'Not for any of the Jouberts, except maybe one who pays no attention to you.'

Roeloff looked at him, then gave a short laugh.

'What's that laugh for? It's true, isn't it?'

Roeloff started to unsaddle Boerhaan.

'She's with you because I won't have her.'

David came forward to strike him, and Willem stepped quickly between his sons.

'That's enough! For God's sake, what's the matter with you two? You haven't seen each other in weeks and the first thing you do is fight. The Jouberts are coming to have a meal with us. You know why they're coming—a special occasion. It's the engagement supper tonight. Go inside and clean yourself up, Roff. There's water for baths. You go first.'

Having the first bath was an honour. The water was hot and the tub clean.

'I'm too tired,' and he started to walk away with Boerhaan.

'Roeloff?'

It was seldom his father called him by his full name.

'Yes, Pa?'

'If we don't stand together as whites, we won't last. You can count on Oom Jan, no matter what his manner is. We're all in this together.'

'He's also one who goes into his Koi-na's huts at night.'

'What?'

Roeloff smiled.

'Take a look at the servant's baby. His hair's straighter than yours. They even call him Kleinjan.'

David watched with satisfaction. It was only a matter of time before his father lost patience with Roeloff.

But David was wrong. Willem's mood held. What Willem hadn't said was that he'd regretted sending Roeloff and Twa off on their own. He'd put Roeloff at risk, knowing the hunters' readiness with the arrow, and the disadvantage of a gun that needed reloading after every shot. David, by his stubborn strength, would survive in the veld. Roeloff relied more on instinct than strength. His courage was dangerous.

By evening, Willem and David, smelling of hair pomade and carbolic soap, sat stiff and grand with a half-naked Roeloff on the stoep drinking brandy, watching the Joubert wagon approach.

'Go wash yourself, man. I've told you three times now,' Willem Kloot said. 'You stink. Don't let the Joubert women see you like this.'

The sensibilities of the Joubert women were Roeloff's last concern. Sweaty and foul-smelling from the heat and grime of the veld, the fatigue of the journey had claimed him. Already the clouds dancing overhead made him want to close his eyes and just drift off.

'Did you hear what I said?'

Roeloff tipped the last drops into his mouth.

'Don't worry, Pa, I'll make myself scarce in a minute. I won't embarrass the family.'

David recognised the grumpiness. One more drink and Roeloff would grunt like an aardvark.

'More?'

'Yes,' Roeloff smiled, holding out his mug. Right then he was enormously fond of his brother, even though a part of him registered that David wanted him drunk.

'Don't give him more to drink. Here they come. Go on—get a move on, now!'

Roeloff grinned. The wagon was dancing crazily in front of him, making him dizzy. The brandy had had such an effect that tensing his facial muscles was an effort. He had a tremendous urge to urinate in front of the guests.

The wagon came to a halt. Elsie Joubert's thin lips moved in prayer when she saw Roeloff, dirty and in a state of undress, waver uncertainly on the top step of the stoep, not knowing if he should come forward, or turn back into the house.

'Hello, Roeloff,' Diena said, stepping up. 'So you got back safely, then.'

'Safely.' He gave a hollow laugh, nodding a greeting at Oom Jan and his wife. 'Soela.' His lips curved into a wicked smile.

Soela blushed and walked hurriedly past him onto the stoep where her mother ushered her into the house.

'Did you get the sheep?' Joubert asked.

'He brought them back, yes,' Willem Kloot answered when there was no response from his son. 'They got back this afternoon. Try some of this.' He poured brandy into a mug.

Joubert took a swallow and blinked.

'Magtig! This stuff's better than Retief's! What's the occasion?'

Willem laughed.

'David and Soela. The return of the sheep.'

'He didn't bring them all,' David said.

'How many were stolen?'

'Twelve. He brought back ten.'

'What happened to the others?' Joubert asked.

Roeloff went into the house without glancing at him.

'Don't take it personally,' Willem said. 'He gets like that. He and brandy don't mix. The bosjesmans ate two of the sheep. The important thing is, he got the rest back.'

'How did he manage to do it?'

'He reasoned with them, if you can believe that.'

'And they gave the sheep back, just like that?'

'That's what he says. Never lifted his gun.'

'You don't believe him, Pa, do you?'

'Of course I believe him.'

'Me, too,' Joubert said. 'He has a recklessness that takes courage. But you should trust a savage only as far as you can smell him.'

'That would be quite a distance, then,' David laughed. 'One of them was that thief he set free years ago. Remember him, the one Pa said you could have?'

'What?'

'Apparently, they met again the night of Pa's wedding. When they came for the girl.'

'They had the nerve to come back for the girl?'

'Yes.'

Joubert finished his drink in one swallow.

'Who would have thought the Karoo such a small place? But he did the right thing.'

David was taken aback.

'You're saying they have honour?'

'I don't think they have a straight bone in their bodies, but I think they'll keep their word to him. Are they the same ones who stole from me?'

'He says not, but I don't believe him. He lied about the tracks, because he wanted us to go in the wrong direction.'

Joubert turned to Willem. 'Willem?'

Willem Kloot raised his drink to his mouth.

'You don't know with Roff. He lied about the tracks because he didn't want us to go with him. I let him go. It worked out.'

'Maybe we should pay them a visit.'

'What good would that do? The sheep will be long gone. He's extracted a promise from them.'

'A promise?'

'They've agreed to stay off our land.'

'And you believe them.'

'I believe him.'

Joubert leaned back in his chair. Not every trekboer set much store by promises. Maybe David was right. He would talk to him about it again.

In the kitchen the women were huddled around Drieka, admiring six green-tinted drinking glasses on the table. Despite Willem's indifference, Drieka had transformed the sparse little dwelling into a cosy homestead, and the Kloot house was quite the grandest in the Karoo, with mats, a bench, and two riempie chairs in the front part of the house that served as the voorkamer.

'They're delicate, Tante Drieka,' Diena said. 'Where did you get them?'

Drieka waved her hand in front of her face like a fan.

'Tell us,' Elsie coaxed.

Drieka lowered her voice.

'Frederik Jantzen. He's with a group of men working together for the benefit of the farmer. He said the Karoo being such a hard place for women, it is wise to protect a son or husband, just in case. A small payment every six months would ensure that there was money for burial, and a little left over to help for a few months.'

'I've never heard of such a thing.'

'I told him that money was just as scarce as water—as if he didn't know that—and that bodies went free into the ground. If a woman couldn't manage a few Hottentots after her husband was gone, she might as well dig a hole for herself and join him. No amount of money would fix that.'

'What did he say?'

'That's when he took out the glasses. He wanted me to speak to my husband. A husband would know what he meant, he said. He would come back in a month, and if I could get Willem to listen, the glasses were mine.'

'What did Willem say?'

'I haven't told him. You know how he is. To get him to sit down long enough to listen to anything—well, it's almost impossible. I thought I'd use the glasses tonight, and give them back when Jantzen comes.'

'I'd be afraid to use them, Drieka,' Elsie said. 'What if one of them breaks? You'd be forced to make a payment then. And Willem will ask about them tonight, in any case.'

'If he notices. What does he notice except sheep? And now that he's heard of merino, he talks of nothing else.' She remembered that she hadn't told Elsie about Krisjan Kloot's visit, so she returned quickly to the subject of the glasses. 'He won't notice anything.'

'Glasses like this? Of course he will. We don't have any. Neither do the Steenkamps or Retiefs.'

'Well, I'll see how far that brandy has mellowed him. Maybe I can talk to him, with all of you here tonight.'

Out in the yard, Soela pulled the shawl about her shoulders and went briskly in search of Vinkie. The sun had gone down, taking with it the heat of the day, and there was a nip in the air. The dark clouds meant rain. Tante Drieka had asked her to call Vinkie in for supper, and she saw her playing with the Koi-na children at the far end of the kraal.

'Vinkie!'

Vinkie was too far away and didn't hear, or heard but paid no attention. Soela had already noticed the girl's wilfulness. Vinkie listened to no one except Roeloff. Wherever he was, there she lingered, with Kleintje, fetching and carrying for him, pestering him.

Soela walked quickly down the hill, past the barn. A noise from inside made her stop. She had seen Roeloff take the kettle from the hearth and walk to the barn with it. Had she come to look for Vinkie in the hope of seeing him? There was no need to lie to herself, her engagement was a lie. She'd done it to get Roeloff's attention, and hadn't thought it through. It was Roeloff who stirred her feelings, but Roeloff didn't know she existed. She'd heard talk of his fondness for the runaway Bushman girl, a stinking little creature with woolly hair. She didn't believe it. He would never be interested in something like that. And who else was there in this wilderness for him but herself? Not Johanna Steenkamp. Johanna had a hole in the roof of her mouth and lived with her hand in front of her face. Diena? Soela didn't really think so.

She remembered the incident in the foaling barn, how Roeloff had touched her, then pushed her away. It had been the most humiliating experience of her life. She'd hated him, but she couldn't stop thinking about him. She kept telling herself that if he hadn't liked her at all, he wouldn't have done what he did. He liked her and wanted her, but he had denied himself out of respect for her. That she understood. It was the cold, indifferent way in which he acted that had hurt. And when she saw him that afternoon on the stoep—half-naked and browned from the sun, his long hair soft and white, unlike the grizzly thatch of his brother and father, the eyes that sent tiny darts of pleasure throughout her body—the thrill of his closeness was too much. She turned to see if anyone was watching. There was no one in the yard, so she walked quietly to the back of the barn.

She stood at the half-open door and watched him step out of the tub, naked and dripping, with a fearsome erection.

'Come in, Soela,' he said.

There were no words, no preliminaries, only the hurried lifting of skirts, and a gasp as he stood her up against the door. She cried out once, then clung to him as he rammed her back and forth.

The sight of his brother and his betrothed jerking at each other like dogs struck David like a thunderbolt as he peered through a hole in the barn wall. From the kitchen window, he'd seen her enter the barn and followed to tell her to come inside for the meal. Nothing had prepared him for what he saw. He felt sick. She'd pledged her love and asked him to wait for the wedding night. Those words, uttered under the pomegranate tree, putting the seeds of the fruit, one by one, into her mouth, letting the scarlet juice stain her lips— they were lies. She was no different from any animal. He prepared himself to confront them, but all feeling drained from him, and he walked slowly back to the house.

David wasn't the only person in the yard. Willem Kloot, remembering, as he sat talking with Joubert on the stoep, that he'd seen Twa's horse limping, had left his guests briefly to check on the mare. He too, saw Soela enter the barn. He paid no attention, until a few minutes later when he saw David looking through a hole in the wall. He still wouldn't have given it any further thought if he hadn't seen David leaning, his forehead in his hands, against the barn wall. He waited for David to leave, then went to the same peephole in the barn door. What he saw made him choke: his younger son and Soela Joubert committing a sin. He couldn't believe his eyes. Soela was David's, their engagement was being celebrated that night. How could Roeloff do such a thing? To his own brother? And Soela? What was going on in her head? Wasn't it David she wanted?

They came separately into the kitchen; Soela first, with Vinkie, and Roeloff a few minutes later.

'Roff?' Vinkie asked as he passed them in the kitchen. 'Did you see what I left on your pillow?'

'No.' He remembered vaguely that she'd been trying to speak to him all afternoon.

'Go and look.'

Both families were seated at the table.

'We're just waiting for you,' Diena said.

'Yes,' Drieka added. 'Hurry up.'

'I'm too tired to eat, I'm turning in.'

'Come and join us, man,' Joubert said. 'We want to hear more about those bosjesmans.'

'Let him go,' Willem Kloot said. 'He won't add anything to the conversation.'

Roeloff said goodnight and left them. Had he heard an odd tone in his father's voice? He found the newspaper and book on his bed, and wanted to ask Vinkie where she'd got it, but he didn't want to go back to the kitchen. He leafed through the newspaper, amazed at the headlines, then picked up the book. The writer's name jumped out at him. Krisjan Kloot! He couldn't believe it. Oupa Harman had spoken the truth. He fingered the fineness of the paper, and the cover, then opened the book. An index listed the contents and he saw that it was a book about travellers to the Cape. He settled himself on the bed to read, but was so tired that his eyes closed and he was asleep before he'd finished the first page.

A short while later Sanna walked behind the reed partition carrying a plate of food for Roeloff, only to find him asleep on the bed, wearing only his pants. The book had fallen on the floor. She picked it up and smiled. She knew about the gift from the young grandson. This book would be read over and over again. It had started to rain, so she pulled the blanket over Roeloff. She touched his hair, still damp from the bath. It reminded her of when he was young, when his mother had bathed him and she had dried him off. He was still beautiful, but he was no longer a child. Was it true about him and Zokho? Of course it was. The girl had had foolish notions, and Roeloff had been led by his tail. It was better that she had gone away. Roeloff had in him something which attracted girls like bees to a honey hole, then, when he got his hands sticky, he didn't know how to beat them off without breaking their wings. She knew from the glow on Soela's face and the way her eyes followed Roeloff that the two of them had been together. She also knew from the twitch at the corner of David's mouth and his forced gaiety at the table that he had seen them. She'd come to bring Roeloff something to eat and to warn him.

The liquor had its effect on the entire family, and no one remembered when the Jouberts left, who locked up, or at what time everyone went to bed.

At dawn there was a frenzied knocking on the back door.

'My grootbaas, kom!'

'What is it, Hennerik?'

'Ooo, Basie, ooo …' and he bolted down the hill like a frightened animal.

Willem pulled on his pants and followed. Seeing a group of nervous, fidgety Koi-na outside the barn, he was gripped by a horrible foreboding. Then he saw the congealed pool of blood at the door.

'What the …'

He took a deep breath to calm himself. He didn't want to go in. He couldn't. Not one of his horses—not Boerhaan!

He braced himself and stepped into the barn. A ribbon of pain shot across his chest. Boerhaan's stall was spattered with blood, and the horse lay on his side, his throat slit and his eyes open in death.

'Get Roeloff and David!'

Hennerik scampered up to the house.

Roeloff arrived first. 'What's wrong?!' He looked at the blood, then entered the barn. The words died in his throat.

'You promised you would look after him,' Willem hissed.

Roeloff looked at his father in confusion.

'What do you mean?'

'You were drunk last night.'

'Are you saying I did this?'

'I'm saying there's blood leading out of this stable. Hottentots don't wear shoes.'

Roeloff was stunned by the accusation.

'You think I did this to my own stallion?'

'Someone did! Someone who's sick in his head!' He looked at the frightened faces of the Koi-na. 'I want to know who committed this crime. Did you see or hear anything last night, or this morning?'

The Koi-na looked at one another.

'Speak!'

'It's not us, Grootbaas,' Sanna spoke on their behalf. 'That's a devil horse. He would make a noise if we came near him. You have to be strong to kill him.'

'We should search the premises,' David said, coming up behind them. 'Two or more of them could have done it.'

'Why would they want to kill Boerhaan?' Roeloff asked.

'Don't ask me. You're the one who knows what goes on

in their heads. Maybe it's you, Roff. You came out here last night.'

'What?'

'Didn't you?'

'He went straight to bed,' Willem said.

'No, Pa. He got up in the middle of the night to relieve himself from all that drinking he did. I saw him come out here myself.'

'That's a lie and you know it!'

'And where were you if you saw him?' Willem asked.

'In bed. He woke me up with the noise he made.'

'Did you come out here, Roff?'

'You think I could do such a thing, Pa?'

Willem Kloot looked at Roeloff. There was a lot he could say—what Roeloff had done with Soela in the barn had spun round and round in his head all night, and still plagued him. To remind Roeloff would be to embarrass his other son. David could maintain his dignity if he thought no one else knew, and Willem wasn't going to give anything away. But if Willem Kloot was stunned by one son's behaviour, he was confused by the other's. David had given no indication that he'd seen the girl he was to marry in the sexual act with his brother, and David wasn't one to restrain himself.

'Hennerik, you and Kupido search the barn. Sanna, check the huts and everyone's clothes for anything that looks strange or out of place. You look around the grounds,' he said to David. 'Roeloff and I will check in here.'

There was no word between father and son as they examined the straw and the surrounding area for evidence.

Roeloff was outraged by his father's readiness to accuse him. Did he not know his own children? Had he no inkling of their character? He found nothing in the stall, and turned his attention to the stallion. Boerhaan's coat glistened like alabaster in the morning light. He drew the eyelids over the open eyes, wrapping an old rag around the horse's head to keep them closed. The crusted blood and the presence of insects in the nose and ears told him Boerhaan had been dead a long time.

'He was killed at least eight hours ago.'

There was a commotion behind them, and they turned to see Hennerik in the doorway, holding something. The other Koi-na hovered nervously in the background.

'We found it in the barn, Grootbaas.'

'What is it?'

Hennerik put it down at his feet.

Willem looked at the bundle. It was the rag they used for the horses, caked with blood, wrapped around something.

'What's going on?' David came up.

'Open it,' Willem Kloot instructed Hennerik.

Hennerik kneeled down and unrolled the rag. There was a murmur of disbelief—everyone knew what it was and who it belonged to. A soft sigh escaped Willem's lips.

'It's the knife Oupa Harman gave you for your twelfth birthday, Roff.'

Roeloff looked at it. He couldn't believe it.

'David did this, Pa.'

'How dare you!' Willem struck him across the face. 'To lie and then blame someone else!'

Roeloff got up from behind the stallion where he'd fallen

when he lost his balance after his father's blow. There was blood on his lip, the horse's blood on his hands.

'Tell Pa why you did it!' he shouted at David.

'You're drunk. Why would I kill his horse?'

'*My* horse,' Roeloff charged. 'You killed him because you saw me with Soela! And left the knife, so I would know you saw us, and so Pa would think it was I who did it!'

David punched him in the face.

Roeloff grabbed the whip from the hook on the wall and snapped it over his head. 'You want a fight?'

There wasn't enough room in the barn, and the whip caught David on the cheek.

David felt at the blood on his face. 'Bastard!' He came straight for Roeloff, the momentum hurtling both of them to the ground.

'Stop it!' Willem roared. 'It's your knife with the stallion's blood on it, Roeloff! What more proof do I need?'

'It's my knife, but I didn't do it!'

'I entrusted him to you. I asked you to look after him.'

The words were a death knell. Then it came to Roeloff, how to prove he hadn't done it.

'Why don't you check our boots? That should tell you who was in here last night.'

'Get their boots from the house, Hennerik. Hurry!'

'Tell him, Hennerik,' Sanna elbowed her husband in the ribs.

'Tell me what?'

Hennerik looked at David. David glowered back. 'Nothing, Grootbaas,' Hennerik said, and ran up to the house.

Twa had heard the commotion and came up. He nodded

sadly when he saw the stallion in a pool of blood. 'There will be trouble now.'

'Did you hear anything last night, Twa?' Roeloff asked him. He knew it was pointless to ask. Twa, exhausted after the journey, had gone straight to his hut after eating the plate of food he had received from Sanna. Roeloff had also given him a mug of brandy.

'I didn't hear anything.' Twa was almost embarrassed to admit it. Usually he was the one who sat at the fire all night and hardly slept.

Hennerik came back with the boots and placed them on the ground in front of Willem. Roeloff knew from the way Hennerik avoided his eyes, that something was wrong.

Willem picked up David's boots and inspected them closely. Except for some dried dirt in the cracks, there was nothing suspicious. Then he picked up Roeloff's boots. A look passed between them that Roeloff would never forget.

'It's better you take your things and get off Kloot's Nek,' Willem said.

Roeloff picked up the boots his father had dropped to the ground. There was blood on the soles.

'I didn't do this, Pa.'

His father turned and left the stable.

'Pa!'

Willem walked, stone-faced, up to the house.

Roeloff felt hot and cold at the same time. He looked at his brother. The hate in David's eyes told him all he needed to know: that that was for Soela, for what Roeloff had done to his leg. They would never be brothers again.

'Kleinbaas,' said someone behind him.

He turned. It was Kupido, Hennerik's eldest son.

'We all know you didn't do it.'

Then Vinkie came running down from the house.

'Roff, what happened? Pa says Boerhaan's dead!'

'Yes. He says I did it. That I killed my own horse. He chucked me out.'

'But you didn't, Pa's wrong!'

'He *is* wrong,' Sanna said. 'Tell him, Hennerik. Tell him what you told me.'

Hennerik opened his mouth to speak, then saw David walking towards them with a shovel in his hands. David barked some orders at the Koi-na, and Hennerik left.

Roeloff started for the barn, the women and children following him.

'Hennerik saw something last night,' Sanna said, walking alongside Roeloff. 'Your brother was with Soela in the barn. She was crying. That's why Hennerik looked through the hole and listened. David was pulling at her clothes, and when she wouldn't let him, he hit her. He said, 'You like it with him, you like it with me.' Then he did it. Afterwards, Hennerik said, Soela went back to the house and your brother stayed behind in the barn.'

'Hennerik saw this?'

'Yes. You must go in and tell the grootbaas. We'll all tell him what Hennerik said if Hennerik's too scared to talk.'

The Koi-na nodded.

'It's no good, Sanna. He's made up his mind. And Kloot Nek's too small for David and me anyway.'

Vinkie started to cry.

'You can't go away, Roff. I'll miss you. And Pa doesn't mean what he says. Who will I have when you're gone?'

'You'll have your mother and Sanna.'

'I can't do without you. And where will you go, anyway? To the neighbours?'

'I don't know. Vinkie, you mustn't worry about me. I have too many things in my head right now. Pa threw me out, and I can't think of anything else.'

'Did you find the book and the newspaper I left in your room?'

'Yes.'

Vinkie wanted to tell him about Oupa Krisjan and his grandson, but it was not the time to talk of such things, and anyway, all the excitement had gone out of it.

'I am ready.' Twa appeared at Roeloff's side with his kaross and quiver of arrows.

'Ready for what?'

'For our journey.'

'There's food for you here, you must stay.'

'I've lived before without food. I know this land. You need someone to watch over you.'

Roeloff was touched by the offer.

'I have nowhere to go.'

'You have. We will go that way,' he pointed north.

'There's nothing up there—except rock and sand and the bones of dead animals. And it's too hot.'

'But we'll come to a river with trees, and animals coming right up to our feet. It's the place where I was born. We can live there, Kudu, you and me.'

'This is no time for imaginings.'

'You're right. It's the time of your freedom. You're lucky that this is happening when you are young.'

'He's talking nonsense again,' Sanna said. 'Don't listen to him. Your father doesn't mean what he says. He shouts now, tomorrow he forgets. Stay a few days, Roff, and wait for him to calm down. You can't go out there to nothing. Twa's used to eating lizards, you're not.'

'Go up to the house, Sanna, and fetch my clothes, my blankets, and my books. And make us a parcel of food.'

'You are sure this is what you want to do?'

'Yes.'

Vinkie had tears in her eyes as she stood there, then, not trusting herself to speak, she ran after Sanna and buried herself in her skirts.

'We'll need things for the road, Twa. Get my knife, then come to the barn and help me.'

'Your brother took it.'

'Get it from him.'

'Not me,' Twa shook his head. 'He has the devil in him—he looks ready to kill. Everyone knows he did it, and he knows that we know.'

Roeloff took his sling from the wall and fitted a large stone into place. Twa followed him to the stable where David and three workers were trying to remove the dead stallion.

David winced when he saw the sling. He still limped from the time Roeloff had used it on him.

'You wouldn't dare!'

'Give me my knife.'

'Why don't you take it,' David challenged.

'I said, give it to me.'

David looked at the blue eyes, dark with fury. He knew Roeloff wouldn't hesitate to use the sling. He kicked something at his feet.

'Over there.'

Roeloff picked up the knife and wiped it clean on his pants, then tucked it behind his belt. He walked away without looking at his brother.

Sanna and two other Koi-na women arrived with the clothes rolled up in a blanket, a parcel of food, and several books.

'He said to give you this.'

'I want nothing from him.'

'Take it,' Twa said. 'We will need it.'

Roeloff took the gun.

'Is Dorsbek ready?' he asked Twa.

'Yes. But how will we carry all this? The horse will carry the books and we will walk? Or you will ride and Twa will carry the books?'

Roeloff looked at the old hunter. He was clearly excited at the prospect of travelling.

'All right. I'll only take two books and leave the rest. Sanna, give this to Vinkie to keep for me.'

Sanna started to cry.

'When will you come back, Roff?'

'When he's dead.'

'Dead? That's very hard. You mustn't be hard like him.'

'I'm of his making, not so? Ready, Twa?' and he tucked the blanket roll firmly in place, balancing the load on the mare.

'Where will I sit?'

'You'll sit behind me, or run if you don't stop asking me questions.'

Twa looked towards the people seeing them off.

'We haven't left yet, and already he's ordering Twa around.'

Someone gave Twa a piece of tobacco; another, a special stone for good luck. Then Roeloff hugged the woman who had looked after him all his life.

'You must take care of Tinktinkie.'

Sanna wiped the tears from her face with a corner of her dress.

'Come back, Roff. Kloot's Nek won't be the same without you.'

The women cried openly as they rode off, the children running after them until their figures got smaller and smaller and eventually blended into the bush and rock.

Back at the house, Willem sat at the table, trying to close his ears to the commotion in the yard.

Vinkie came to stand at his elbow.

'He didn't do it, Pa. Hennerik knows what happened. Why don't you ask him? Hennerik's scared of David, that's why he won't talk. Stop Roff before he goes. He's not going to come back if you let him go.'

Willem got up and went to his room.

Vinkie turned to her mother, who was busy piling wood on the hearth.

'Ma? You heard what Sanna said. You have to tell him.'

Drieka pursed her lips and stirred the fire vigorously.

The day was long. Roeloff was brooding and silent,

and Twa wisely held his tongue when they passed the same cluster of rocks for the second time. Towards evening they stopped under a kareeboom and struck camp for the night.

'You have lost your spirit, Kudu. Sleep. Tomorrow, a new day will come.'

Roeloff slumped with his back against the tree, his hat pulled down over his face. The shock of betrayal sat like a stone in his chest. Brothers fought and had disagreements, but blood was blood, one didn't cut the breath of the other. David had got him removed from Kloot's Nek. His father had condemned him. He was banished, his life reduced to a tongue of flame on the open veld and the clothes on his back. Where would he go? How would he live? He'd been falsely accused and cast out. His father had thought him capable of a heinous crime. Nothing would lessen that pain. If his father were to prostrate himself before him and pour out a thousand words to express how sorry he was, Roeloff might be obliged, as a Christian, to forgive him, but he would never forget what his father had done. He looked at Twa lying next to the fire. Roeloff wished he could be like Twa and just throw himself down anywhere. Twa had no worries. For him, there was no tomorrow. Were the Sonqua the true owners of freedom?

'I've decided what we will do, Twa. We'll go south and look for work. When we have enough money, we'll buy a wagon and travel down to the Cape.'

'Who will give us this work and this money? And have we left one farm to make ourselves slaves on another?'

'We can't do anything without money.'

'We don't need it if we turn around and go up to the river.'

'I can't live forever with my arse in the wind.'

'You have lived with your arse in the wind, what're you talking about? You're one of us. But your spirit is low today. It'll come back, you'll see. The world will be all yours again.'

The day broke with a wave of heat, and by noon they were walking alongside the mare carrying their belongings as Dorsbek had developed a sore under the saddle. The night rain had done little to change things, and the earth was parched, with no trees or cover in sight.

'We're not making much progress,' Roeloff wiped the sweat from his neck. 'We'll have to stop soon to look for something to eat. There are only a few pieces of biltong left.'

Twa looked around him.

'We'll be lucky to find a dassie in this heat.'

'Do you know how to catch them? They're fast.'

Twa smiled. 'You're talking to Twa. If there's a dassie anywhere among these stones, Twa will find it.'

The next day was slower because of a steep mountain and Twa's refusal to cross it on an empty stomach, and they stopped early to pay serious attention to obtaining a meal. Roeloff felled a bird with his sling, saw too late that it was a vulture, and refused to eat it. Twa chopped off the head, took out the guts and threw it, feathers and all, onto a fire. When he couldn't entice Roeloff with the roasted meat, he finished it off himself, licking his fingers and rubbing his belly to show he was whole again.

The third day, coming down the kloof, they found water in a deep hollow in the rocks, and replenished their dwindling supply. By noon the temperature was unbearable, and Roeloff was stripped to the waist, his long hair tied back with a leather thong.

'This land's so flat, you can see to the end of the earth. Not even a hill in front of us. Nothing. We could have been far away by now if the mare didn't have this wretched sore on her back. I should have checked that saddle before I put it on her. Our weight on it made it worse.'

'Kudu, look!'

Roeloff looked behind him to where Twa was pointing. He couldn't see anything on the kloof they'd descended.

'Someone's following us!'

'What?'

'Yes. By all that's good in me, it's Smoke in the Eyes!'

'Zokho? Are you sure? What's she doing out here?'

'She's walking with a purpose.'

Roeloff watched in amazement as the figure materialised out of the heat shimmer. Zokho saw him, and came running. The next moment, he felt her warm breasts against his chest and his arms went about her instinctively.

'I left you just a few days ago. What are you doing out here all by yourself?'

'I ran away.'

'You ran away? Why?'

'To come to you.'

'To me?'

'Yes.' Her head had been shaved and the new hair was just coming out, making her look like a boy. 'I saw in your eyes that you wanted me to come to you.'

Roeloff released her.

'I'm the son of the man who killed your people.'

'You are Eyes of the Sky.'

He looked at the small, delicate head, the sensual mouth, the sun glistening on the tips of her breasts. There was something that he liked about Zokho, much more than her physical beauty and her innocence. He turned his eyes to the horizon beyond, to the road he must travel. What did it matter now? he asked himself. He was what he was and Zokho was what he wanted.

'What will you do with me, Zokho?'

'I will go where you go. Be your shadow.'

'You like me, is that it?'

'Yes.'

'It will not be easy. People will not accept.'

'*You* accept, Eyes of the Sky.'

'I'm still Roeloff Kloot. Never let that be far from your mind.'

Twa walked up towards them, shaking his head at the silliness of young people.

'And now, Kudu? Now we are *three* without food.'

Chapter Nine

Wynand Roos was resting his foot on the shovel, wiping the sweat from his brow with the back of his hand when he saw the horse and three strangers in the distance.

'Looks like we have visitors.'

Neeltje stopped what she was doing and put her hand to her brow under the brim of her kapje, to look. Neeltje, a sixteen-year-old girl of great common sense, with a straw-coloured plait down her back, had been raised by her father to do the cooking and cleaning and pasture the sheep when there was no one else to do it. She had no friends except a one-eared mongrel called Boet who had been left behind by a trader, and although her father had paid for lessons for Neeltje from a travelling teacher, the closest she had come to a kinship with someone her own age was with one of the Hottentot children. But the year had been bad on the farm, money was scarce, and the Hottentots had all gone somewhere else.

'One be an Africaander and two bosjesman.'

They watched in silence as the small party drew up.

Roeloff took off his hat, grateful to be finally at some destination. They had spent a gruelling week crossing the red-stoned Cederberg mountains, taking their chances with snakes and wild animals, but there was more chance of securing a meal in the mountains. The farm, nestled unobtrusively in a kloof, had only been spotted because of the smoke spiralling up from a chimney. It was sheltered from the wind, and there was a good deal of green land on either side of the dwelling. He had noticed the change in terrain as they travelled south. Hope surged in his breast.

'We saw the smoke from the kloof. I am Roeloff Kloot.'

'Wynand Roos,' the farmer greeted. 'This is Neeltje. Her mother's dead.'

Roeloff noted the calluses on the young hands, the clean eyes. She reminded him of Vinkie.

'This is Zokho and Twa. We're looking for work. I see you've had some damage here to your fence. Jackals?'

'Elephants. Two of them. They pass through every year. I hit one of them in the trunk, but he charged off as if nothing happened. They've ruined everything as you can see, eaten all the mealies and pumpkins. Completely flattened the tobacco plants.'

Roeloff looked around at the devastation.

'A stone wall would keep them out.'

'It is costly. There're no bricks.'

'There's a lot of stone in these mountains. It would take time to cut enough, but it's not impossible if you have the right tools. Still, if they only pass through once a year, a guard with a gun is perhaps all you need. A stone wall would be better, though. Protect the animals a lot better, too.'

Wynand looked at him. He had already measured Roeloff's character: upright, used to work. He'd probably built just such a wall where he'd been before.

'What kind of work do you have in mind to do?'

'Anything. Build a fence if you want. Till some of this land. Twa can pasture the sheep and set traps for the jackals. He's good at trapping.'

'A jakkalsjagter.'

'A bit of everything. I also have knowledge of reading, writing and arithmetic, if you have children you want taught.'

'Neeltje's my only child. Where do you come from?'

'Ten days north. We could have come faster on the mare, but there are three of us, so we walked. The mare also had a sore on her back. My father's Willem Kloot. Perhaps you've heard of him.'

'Herman's son?'

'You knew my grandfather?'

'My father did. He talked often of how they travelled together from the Cape. My father didn't want to go as far north as the others, so he broke away and headed for Stellenbosch. We lived there until his death ten years ago. I came here for the land. I thought it would be better.'

'There are trees here, at least, and grass for the sheep.'

'Yes. I believe it's much worse where you are. Who are these bosjesmans, then?'

'Twa's been with my family since long before I was born.'

'And the girl?'

Roeloff looked at Zokho standing next to him, wearing one of his shirts over her small leather flap. The rigours of the journey had narrowed the gap between them, brought them closer.

'She's with me.'

'It's the old one's daughter, then.'

'I mean she's with me.'

Wynand looked at him intently.

'I see.'

Neeltje wiped her hands on her apron and looked away.

'I should tell you as well, so you know, that I'm accused of a crime I didn't commit.'

Wynand studied Roeloff's face, then he took off his hat and turned his gaze to the land made untidy by the marauding elephants.

'There's work here, much more than I can pay for. And them I can't pay anything. Food and shelter, and clothes for the girl. You, very little.'

'How much?'

'A few ryksdaalder.'

'We'll stay half a year.'

'I'm not a man to be taken advantage of,' Roos warned.

'Me, neither.'

'There's a buitekamer round the back from the last knecht, and also a hut. Share it however you want. Drinking water's in the barrel. The sluits are dug, so rain water runs right from the top of the hill into the mealie field. Even when it rains there's no waste.' He turned to his daughter. 'Neeltje, light the fire and start supper. I'll finish here by myself.'

Neeltje had regained her composure.

'What will we eat tonight, Pa? There are only twelve potatoes and one cabbage.'

'You're good with potatoes and cabbage. Boil it in a little salted water. Better still, kill one of those old cocks.'

'It'll take hours to boil one of those cocks, and we only have five chickens left.'

Wynand was already bent over his shovel, ready to resume work.

'Twelve potatoes, five chickens. Ever since that teacher and his timetables, it's two of this, six of that. Kill one of them, I said.'

Roeloff smiled at Neeltje.

'It's all right. Show me which chicken and I'll do it.'

Neeltje straightened her dress and walked quickly up to the house, mumbling under her breath.

Roeloff turned to the farmer to thank him.

Wynand spat on his hands, rubbed them together, then started digging.

'Someone's out there, chopping wood in the rain. At this hour. The oubaas isn't back, is he?' Roeloff got up from the bench and went to the door to look out.

Zokho lowered her eyes to the work in her lap. Roeloff had been restless ever since the oubaas had gone on his horse and left him in charge, worried about the girl left alone in the house for three days. What was he worried about? She, Zokho, had slept alone under the stars. Heard the cough of a leopard. Seen the night eyes of hyenas. Women were afraid of other things, not silence. They were afraid of a man not coming back. Of losing him. Neeltje had courage. The problem wasn't the emptiness of the house. Zokho knew what ailed her.

'It's Neeltje chopping out there. That be one stubborn girl, to be out in weather like this.'

Zokho watched him pull on a jacket and go out. She took her time sewing on a button the way Neeltje had shown her, straining her eyes in the dim light. The farmer had given them a lamp, but there wasn't much fuel and the small flame flickered like an old man unsure of his step. She got up and watched for a moment from the doorway. She couldn't hear what was being said, but the continuing crack of the wood signalled determination. She closed the door and sat for a few moments watching the shadows on the wall.

Roeloff stood outside, his boots in the mud, watching the axe smack into the wood. Neeltje knew he was there, but she didn't look up. Her long hair was plastered down her back, and the wet dress outlined the strength of her arms.

'It's storming, Neeltje, why are you doing this now?' There was something annoying in her wilfulness.

'There's no wood for the fire; the house is cold.'

'You'll catch your death in this rain. Why didn't you tell me this afternoon? I've told you before that there's no need for you to chop wood—Twa or I will do it. And your father's asked me to watch over things.'

'My father's left me before for a week. Three days is not a long time.'

'He's left you here by yourself for a week?'

'How else would he trade with other farmers?' She was soaked to the skin, but continued chopping.

'Here, let me do it. Go inside.'

'I'm almost done,' she broke her momentum to move the chopped wood out of the way with her foot.

He stepped forward.

'I said I'll do it.'

It was the authority in his voice, the touch on her arm. She let go.

'Tomorrow I'll chop enough wood for winter.'
She threw down the axe and walked off.
'Neeltje!'
Inside the buitekamer, Zokho sat naked on the coir bed, hearing him call out the name. The chopping had stopped and there was only the drumbeat of rain on the hard ground outside. She went to the door and saw Neeltje walking to the house in that determined way she had. Roeloff following with an armful of wood. It was the game of animals, she thought. A lion circled and sniffed, and circled and sniffed. Eventually the pull was too great and the female succumbed. Living with him, she'd come to know something about herself. She liked Toma—he was one like her, after all—but hadn't wanted to be his wife. She wanted Roeloff, but feared the differences between them, differences that had widened. She was caught between conflicting feelings. She liked Neeltje, yet feared her. Neeltje had shown her how to make teewater and coffee and darn clothes, and she had taught Neeltje how to look for roots and berries and honey in the veld. She would have welcomed the white girl talking to her about Roeloff the way Karees had, but Neeltje asked and said nothing. The girl didn't know her own power.

The chopping started again, harder, faster, and she got into bed, pulling the sheepskin up to her chin. How long would he stay out there? Where would his concern end?

When he came in, dripping water into a puddle around him, she got up and peeled off his clothes, holding her body next to his to warm him up.

'Mijn, Eyes of the Sky?'

He kissed her mouth and moved so that they were both under the heady warmth of the sheepskin.

'Yours, Smoke in the Eyes.'

Zokho fitted snugly into his arms, but there was unrest in her heart. He spoke the truth as he knew it but, he, too, like the oubaas' daughter, didn't know all about himself.

'Elephants!' Twa came limping down the row of tobacco plants. 'Two of them by those rocks near the stream!'

Wynand looked at Roeloff.

'That's them, the ones I told you about. They've come back. What were you doing out there, Twa? That's quite a distance from here.'

'Looking for ostrich,' Roeloff said. 'He has a mood for wild meat. We don't have to wait for the elephants to show up; Twa and I can steer them the other way. I haven't had any experience with elephants, but it's better than just waiting for them to get here.'

'I agree.'

They left on Dorsbek and arrived downwind of the beasts. There were two of them: a majestic bull with tusks reaching almost to the ground, and an emaciated cow with loose, wrinkled skin and deep hollows above the eyes. An old wound in her trunk was dripping pus. Wynand's gun must have done its work, Roeloff thought, because she was riddled with infection, dying.

The plan was to fire over the heads of the elephants and frighten them so that they headed north, but Roeloff was touched by the bull's loyalty to his mate.

'Kill it!' Twa whispered.

Roeloff knew he would do the cow a kindness if he were

to shoot her, but he couldn't. And the bull also knew they were on the boulder.

As they watched, the cow got progressively weaker. Then the bull did something that surprised them. He attempted to mount her in a mock mating ritual, not really doing anything. This went on for an hour, with the cow offering no resistance, until finally her struggle against the poison ended in a rumble that shook the earth as she collapsed, raising a cloud of orange chalk to the air. A snort of defiance rolled out over the hills. Then the dust settled and the silence of the Cederberg returned.

Roeloff and Twa sat quiet as vultures. The beast was intelligent: he'd shown feeling, stayed with his mate. He could have knocked them off their boulder and trampled them to death. Instead, with a sorrowful air, he inspected the fallen cow, then worked his trunk and tusks under the body, trying to prop her up. The weight was too great and there was a loud crack as the carcass dropped to the ground, snapping his left tusk close to the lip, and trapping it under the cow.

'Kill him, Kudu. Kill Broken Tooth!'

'No.'

The elephant had lost his mate and now his tusk, leaving a bloody pulp in its place, giving him a lopsided appearance. Roeloff watched as the bull collected a trunkful of dry grass and stuffed it clumsily into the cow's mouth. When this failed to revive her, he stood near the carcass mourning. Quietly, forlornly, the formality impressive in its silence. Roeloff was moved by his grief. Finally, the bull uprooted a nearby bush and placed it on top of the cow, sprinkling dust everywhere.

Roeloff didn't want to look at the little hunter for fear of being laughed at. Twa laughed at everything, especially someone else's discomfort. Roeloff remembered once, out in the veld, when he'd forgotten to shake out his boots in the morning before putting them on. He'd slipped in his foot and been stung by a scorpion that had taken refuge there. Twa had held his sides as he laughed, watching the foot and ankle swell up. When he'd finished laughing, he had removed the scorpion's tail at its base, using the tip to make a series of overlapping cuts over the site of the sting. Taking the decapitated body, he'd mixed it to a pulp, and applied it to the puffy wound. The swelling went down and the pain drained away, but not before Twa had had his amusement.

'Sun's going down,' Roeloff said. 'Let's go.'

'What about him?'

'He's not going anywhere.'

'The oubaas wants us to kill him.'

'He won't come to the farm. I think he'll look for a herd now.'

'Bulls like this don't move in a herd. I know about elephants. There were many at the river where I lived. Kill him—we are wasting time. He'll be in a rage when he comes.'

'No. We'll guard the fence. I'll come back in the morning for the tusks. The scavengers will have cleaned up by then.'

'You're feeling sorry for him.'

'He's too grand to be touched.'

'Grand?' Twa shook his head in amazement. 'There would not be one of us left if we considered the grandness of animals. We don't kill animals for no reason, only when we have to eat, but the oubaas will be angry if this bull comes to the farm. You're not a true hunter, Sonqua.'

'If you say so. And I'm not Sonqua.'

Twa noticed the change in Roeloff's mood.

'You mustn't take notice of everything Twa says. You've fed us from the accuracy of your gun, of course you're a hunter.'

Wynand was glad to hear that his gunpowder hadn't been wasted, but none too pleased at Roeloff's decision to leave the bull alone, when it was so close by.

They took turns guarding the fence, but the night passed without incident. In the morning Roeloff picked up a pumpkin and set off by himself for the hill. The bull was still there, standing solemnly near the carcass. The scavengers hadn't been allowed near, and the sky broiled with vultures, the squawking of jackals and hyenas jockeying for position, testimony to the clamour-for-carcass warfare of the veld.

He walked slowly up to the bull and, ten feet from the massive animal, placed the pumpkin on the ground. It was a foolish thing to do, he knew; the elephant had wounded feelings, but something in the beast's demeanour told him he was safe.

The black eyes turned to look at him.

Roeloff's heart pounded. He was close enough to see the nicks and tears along the edges of the ears. A side swipe could catapult him clear across the veld, and no gun would save him if the bull attacked.

The elephant's trunk reached out and sniffed at the pumpkin. Cracking the shell with a delicate pressure from his foot, the bull curled his trunk around the pumpkin and lifted it to his mouth. Then the trunk unfurled and reached out, and Roeloff's heart froze in his chest. He would be seized by that powerful cylinder of muscle and flung to the ground. He waited for the attack, feeling the rush of blood in his ears. It came, in a wave of rotten breath as the hairs at the tip of the trunk brushed gently over Roeloff's face. Stunned by the gesture, he opened his eyes. The trunk was poised over his head. Then the bull gave a low rumble, and showered himself with a spray of dust. Fanning himself with his great ears, he raised his eyes to the distance and swayed majestically past Roeloff in the direction from which he had come.

The harvest had been good, and a tired Wynand sat at the table waiting for Neeltje to serve up his food. The work of the day was behind him, and he sat with his arms resting on the table, wondering what his daughter had concocted for supper. Supper was a surprise every night; sometimes a stiff porridge with two soft-boiled eggs on top, other times, mealies and cabbage, or beans and rice. Sometimes she took so long fiddling over the pots that he was asleep before the food came. But he was wide awake this evening, his thoughts on the pumpkins and tobacco he would trade with other farmers in Roodezand. There was no doubt that Roeloff had helped to change their luck.

His eye was caught for a moment by the glittering beads on Neeltje's dress. He'd seen her and Zokho talking and laughing in the kitchen, heads bent over ostrich eggshell beads they were sticking onto things with tree glue. He hadn't known his daughter cared for such things, but then, there were other things he hadn't known about her, things he started noticing soon after the arrival of young Kloot; the high colour in her cheeks, her neatly brushed hair left loose on Sundays and, once, he'd seen her looking out the window at Roeloff washing beside the barrel when he'd thought he was alone. Wynand had said nothing; things had a way of working out. But Roeloff's half-year was up and that was foremost in their minds. Neeltje didn't want him to go. Wynand didn't want him to go. What the boy did with the Bushman girl after he closed his door at night, was his own business. He did a good day's work and he was trustworthy. The rest was unimportant.

'I'm spanning in for Roodezand tomorrow,' Wynand said.

'I saw you getting things ready. How long will you be?'

'No more than a week.'

'We need a good stock-up, Pa. We're almost out of sugar, coffee, flour, beans—everything with Stoffel not showing his face. I don't know what's wrong with him, staying away like this. We ran out of rice weeks ago.'

Wynand smiled. It was strange that a girl who could shoulder a gun and put her weight behind a shovel, hadn't worked it out. The smous with the soft lips and the stutter was confused. He'd seen Roeloff on the premises and lost his nerve. Had Stoffel asked, he would have discovered that Roeloff was with someone else, but he hadn't.

'I also need some cloth, Pa.'

'Cloth? What for?' She'd never made such a request before.

'I've worn the same dresses now for three years. I've let them out and let them out, but I've grown. There are patches on the elbows, and the hems are in tatters. I need at least one dress that fits. For special.'

Wynand looked genuinely surprised.

'For special? What special occasions do we have?'

'Well, Pa, maybe not for special, but for every day. Here,' she plonked his plate down in front of him.

He looked at the food on his plate.

'Where did this meat come from?'

'Roeloff shot an ostrich. Twa cleaned it, Zokho cooked it. I fried four potatoes in that bit of chicken fat we had left.'

'Everyone has his hand to my supper now?'

'No, Pa, but I thought it was good of them to consider us. If you like it, there's more for tomorrow.'

He tore off a piece of meat and put it in his mouth. It had been roasted dark brown on some sort of spit, judging by the ash still sticking to it—too wild-tasting for his liking, but tasty. Neeltje was at his side, waiting for the verdict.

'It's good.'

She relaxed. 'It's not bad, is it, Pa?'

'No.'

She sat down with her own plate and started to eat.

'If we can eat this, maybe we can eat other things and save the chickens. One gets tired of pumpkin and potatoes all the time. Zokho says tortoise is good. And you can use the shell afterwards.'

Wynand looked up from his plate.

'Don't put anything that drags its belly on the ground on my plate, Neeltje.'

'I'm just mentioning it, Pa.'

'Mention it. Just don't go thinking on it.'

They ate for a few minutes in silence.

'What's this cloth you want? Maybe we should just ask Faan's wife to get it and make you a dress.'

'We want to do it ourselves.'

'Yourselves?'

'Me and Zokho. I said I would show her how.'

'That girl's from the veld. What does she know about armholes and sleeves? And you've never made a dress. Don't go wasting the cloth.'

'I have never made a dress, but I have fixed my own many times. Taking it apart, putting it all back together again. Look at this,' she stood up. 'It's almost new if you don't look under the arms.'

Wynand looked at his daughter turning before him, showing off her handiwork. Affection welled up in him. What would he do without Neeltje? She was his right hand, his life. His late wife, Sara, lived on in that headstrong way she had. But Neeltje was grown up, and growing away from him, he could feel it. It saddened him that her first affections should be for one unable to reciprocate.

'And enough decoration on it too, we couldn't miss you even if we wanted to. You're wasting a lot of time, the two of you. I don't see you outside any more.'

'You don't need me so much, Pa, now that he's there. We work inside. You're eating every night at the same time. Didn't you notice your pants have all been fixed? I can do all these things now.'

He studied her for a moment.

'You know they won't be here forever. In two weeks, his time's up.'

She looked down at her plate.

'You can ask him to stay.'

'I can do that. I can pay him more money, he'd like that. But what good would that do? If he stayed?'

'What do you mean?'

'He's not alone. He came with that girl.'

Neeltje turned red.

'Pa!'

'I'm just saying. It's like what happened when Stukje died and Stoffel brought you that dog. Remember? How you felt about him?'

'About Stukje or Stoffel?'

'Well …'

'I don't know why you're talking to me about these things,' she got up, her cheeks flushed. 'This meat's not good for you, we won't have it again.'

He watched her disappear behind the partition in a huff. His head lolled sleepily, and a few minutes later, it had fallen on his forearms.

Roeloff was sitting on a rock at the far end of the kraal, throwing stones for Boet. He hadn't used his sling for a long time, and he'd gone out to give the dog exercise and to be alone with his thoughts. Things had gone well in Wynand's absence—he was expected back at any time and Neeltje was all right. All that remained was to decide what he would do now that his time on the Roos farm was up. He looked at the sun sunk halfway into the land, the sky a ribcage of purplish pink. He thought of his half-sister, Vinkie. Had she forgotten him? Was she watching the sun go down, too? He was reminded of other times, other sunsets. His beloved

Oupa Harman. What advice would he have given now? To stick to the plan or call on the alternative? 'Sometimes you have planned for you one thing, Roff, and the Almighty has planned another. Don't waste time regretting what could've been. Call on the alternative.' It had sounded easy when he'd said half a year to Wynand Roos. The half-year was over, but they weren't ready. Another year would swell his purse and, with the proceeds from the tusks, help give him a start, with the purchase of a wagon and supplies. They could then live in the wagon while they searched for land of their own.

'Kudu?'

He turned.

'What is it, Twa?'

'Zokho's bringing up all her insides. She looks bad.'

Roeloff walked back with Twa. Zokho was on her knees at the back of their quarters.

'What's the matter, Zokho?'

She answered with another bout of vomiting. He scooped a cup of water from the barrel and gave it to her.

'You ate too much of that meat.'

She shook her head to indicate that it wasn't so, and put her hand on her belly.

'What?'

'Yes.'

'How do you know?'

'I know.'

'Zokho, you cannot possibly know about growing babies. Do you realise what you're saying?'

'I've had one before.'

'You've had one before?'

Twa watched the exchange.

'What's the matter, Kudu? You thought potatoes would come from all your lying with Zokho?' He laughed, and left them to sort things out themselves.

'You've had a baby?'

She looked at him with watery eyes, realising she had made a mistake.

'Yes.'

'You never told me. When?'

'After Toma fetched me.'

'It was Toma's?'

She was unsure how to answer. She'd thought he would be upset that she was having a baby, not that she'd already had one.

'No.'

'Whose?'

'Your brother's.'

It was as if she had hit him in the face.

'My brother's? What are you talking about?'

'I should lie to you, Eyes of the Sky? Remember the time in the stable? When you found me crying, with my dress torn?'

'You never told me. Why didn't you tell me you had a baby by him?'

'Look what it's doing. And when should I have told you? When you came to our camp? When we met each other out there?'

'When we talked about Toma. When I told you what happened between me and my brother, why I left. Before now, Zokho. Before this.'

She looked down at her feet. He'd never been angry with her before.

'Where's the child?'

'He didn't live.'

Roeloff turned away.

'Don't walk away from me,' she pulled at his arm.

He jerked himself free.

'That was then, this is now!' she shouted after him.

Roeloff paid no attention and walked on.

Darkness came with a thickness of breath, a moonless night on the mountain. Zokho waited patiently for the crunch of his boots on the path and, when it looked like he wouldn't be back, she pinched out the flame of the lamp and went to bed. She hadn't heeded the words of the old people. *Never tell the one that feeds you everything.* She had thought she knew all about a woman's fears. She didn't. A woman could also lose a man to the past.

When she heard Roeloff come in, towards morning, she closed her eyes.

'Zokho, are you awake?'

She stirred, as if in a deep sleep.

'Zokho, Zokho,' he pulled her towards him, his hand exploring the smoothness of her skin. 'I'm sorry. We'll have this baby and forget the other. It wasn't your fault.'

Zokho curled herself up in his arms and cried quietly into the sheepskin.

In the morning he got up to light the fire to make coffee. He was warming his hands over the kettle when Zokho came rushing out, her hand covering her mouth. He listened to the retching behind the dwelling. It hadn't taken hold of him yet, the reality of becoming a father, of what he had done. He'd rinsed his blood with hers and there would be a child. A baster. One who would carry his name.

'I feel bad,' she said, coming round the corner.

He handed her a mug of coffee.

'Drink this, it will make you strong.'

'It was the smell that did it. I don't want any.'

He took the mug back for himself and followed her inside.

'I'll talk to Wynand Roos about staying on another six months, or a year. We're not ready. Especially now, with the baby coming.'

'You like it here?'

'We have somewhere to lay our heads. And he keeps his thoughts to himself. It might be different elsewhere.'

'And his daughter?'

'Neeltje?'

'You have feelings for her?'

He was surprised by the question.

'Feelings?'

'I've seen how she looks at you. You do things for her.'

'Doing things for her is not bad, Zokho. She's alone.'

'She has her father.'

'Her father's her father, that's all. She has no one to talk to. I feel sorry for her.'

'Sorry will lead to other things. Next time you'll feel sorry she has no husband. What then? I have no husband either.'

'I don't know you like this, Zokho. I thought you liked Neeltje.'

'I like her, but she has powers. It will come between us.

You can't see this. Why do we need this farm? We can live out in the world. We will eat, sleep, and live like all my people.'

'You're talking foolish things now. If we had a wagon, it would be different. And where would we get oxen without money? The farmer has four and they are hardly sufficient for these mountains. When I said we would go to the Cape, I wasn't thinking of the hardships of such a journey, only of the adventure. This isn't an adventure, Zokho. Look at us. We can't just drift around. I have nothing. You're going to have a baby. We need money.' He sipped his coffee, and came to sit next to her on the bed. 'As for Neeltje, I see her as a sister. It's not necessary for you to worry about that.'

'She's not your concern.'

'You're making it my concern, the way you're talking. Stop now, or you'll spoil the thing that separates you from others. I have chosen you, Zokho. Above everyone.'

'You do not wish to play marriage with her?'

'No. But I have feeling for her of a brother. She be an Africaander like me.'

Wynand rested his foot on the shovel and turned his face into the rain. The weather had turned suddenly in the afternoon, and dark clouds hung grape-like above them.

'It's going to be a bad one this year. No use working on in this rain, let's go in. I want to talk to you about a kraal I want to build for the sheep.'

Roeloff wiped the wet hair out of his face.

'There's something I want to talk to you about, too.'

They found Neeltje seated in front of the hearth with some handiwork in her lap, and Boet lapping at the water dripping from the roof into an old bucket near the door.

'I smell coffee,' Wynand rubbed his hands together for warmth. 'Come in, Roff.'

Roeloff stood awkwardly at the door, waiting for someone to invite him to sit down. The house was not half as grand as the one he came from. Reed partitions divided the rooms instead of walls and doors, but there were no draughts, it was warm, and there was the same sense of wellbeing. It occurred to him that he could live with such a kitchen: the barrel of potatoes and onions, biltong hanging from the wall, the table where Wynand cleaned his gun and ate his meals, the unspoken communication between father and daughter. Theirs was a close kinship, and he longed, at that moment, for the same.

'I knew you would come in early. Sit down, Roff.'

Roeloff didn't have to look at her. She'd had a bath, and a smell of something moist and feminine still lingered in the air. He'd never seen her like this, so soft and unguarded, the firelight dancing on her damp hair. A real woman, his grandfather would have said. One who had stamina, strong nerves, and beauty that didn't show itself immediately, but unfolded over time like a caterpillar into a butterfly.

'Did Pa tell you he was thinking of moving the sheep?'

'Yes.'

'What do you think?' She got up and set out three mugs for coffee. 'He wants to clear the bush and stone at the back and move them there.'

'That's right,' Wynand said, taking the first mug offered. 'The land is higher there. That way, when the rain comes, they're not standing in mud.'

'I told Pa it would take too long to clear it all away. The

time would be better spent building a shelter for them where they are. We need some protected place anyway, for the ewes when they're lambing, and to keep them out of the rain.'

Roeloff felt trapped in the middle.

'Well, both plans make sense, but perhaps we should first take a look at the land at the back to see if it isn't better suited to cultivation, and then perhaps leave the sheep where they are.' He turned to Wynand. 'Sheep will be sheep, and in the end, even on a hill, will still stand in the mud.'

'Perhaps so.'

'It would be better, of course, to have them under shelter. We lost twenty last year to exposure.'

Wynand nodded.

'I just thought the land at the back was more suitable. I bought six merino sheep. They're not like the vaderlandse schaapen. All sorts of things get into their fleece.'

'It's too steep at the back.'

'Maybe you're right. Building a shelter where they are now is easy enough, we have the wood. We need a bigger barn anyway, for storage. How big do you think the kraal should be, assuming we leave it where it is?'

'I'd say about eighty by twenty. We would need at least thirty poles, six feet long and six inches thick, five hundred feet for rafters, ribs and ridges, frames and doors wide enough for a wheelbarrow to pass through to remove the manure.'

'That kind of wood would be hard to find.'

'We'd have to go to Stellenbosch; I've heard they have wood there. I've a suggestion also for the barn. Instead of having the hay take up half the floor space, why not have a grain loft above it?'

They discussed the pros and cons for some time, then there was nothing more to be said and they sat for a few minutes in silence, listening to the wind rattling the door.

'Now, there was something you wanted to talk to me about?' Wynand asked.

'Yes.'

Neeltje sensed that this was of a personal nature and excused herself.

'It's about our employment on your farm.' Roeloff had his hat on his knee and he fidgeted absentmindedly with the brim as he spoke. 'I said we would stay for half a year, but I've worked out what we have. It's not enough to buy what we need to take us over these mountains. If we could come to some new arrangement, and if you needed us, we could stay for another half-year.'

'I was hoping you'd change your mind, Roff. We'd like you to stay. This is what I can do. I'll pay the same as before, but I'll give you a start with twelve sheep …'

'Twelve sheep?'

'And a piece of land to build up a flock of your own.'

It was more than Roeloff had expected. He picked up his mug, found it empty, put it down again.

'That is very generous of you.'

'There's a condition: you'd have to spend two years here. It's a fair trade. As a bijwoner you would be in charge, but have sheep and land of your own. The land is yours to work as you wish as long as you stay. If your flock's grown sufficiently and you wish to leave at the end of your time, well, that be it then.'

'Two years will give us some time, and who knows what there will be at the end of that period.'

'It's agreed?'

'It's agreed.'

They shook hands.

'We'll see about getting the wood,' Wynand said. 'Also, if you wanted to extend the buitekamer or move closer to where you'll have your land …'

'There is one thing I will need, within a month. I will need a dominee.'

Somewhere behind the partition, something crashed to the floor.

'Neeltje, are you all right?'

'Yes, Pa.'

Wynand turned his attention back to Roeloff.

'I am going to marry Zokho,' Roeloff said.

Wynand ran his hand through his hair. He let a full minute go by.

'You've thought this through?'

'There's nothing to think about.'

'There will be consequences if you go down to the Cape. Here you can hide something like this. There, it'll be different. Everyone has slaves. A wine farmer I know has more than twenty working for him in Stellenbosch. Even Stoffel travels with one.'

Roeloff waited for him to come to the point.

'Bosjesmans are at the bottom of the heap. They have no

status. It won't matter that you're the grandson of Harman Kloot. When you marry Zokho—and don't get me wrong, I like the girl—you'll set the course for the rest of your life. People won't look at who you are, only at what you have done. Barnard Brink married his Hottentot servant in 1796. They wouldn't allow him in church or at nachtmaal. Sure, after a while they bought his wheat again and he carries on, after a fashion, but he's a lonely man, without friends. And when the children come, it's too late. It's none of my business what you do, but I ask you to think very carefully before you do anything.'

Roeloff shifted uneasily in his seat. By making the request, he'd invited the lecture. It's what his father would have said, or his late grandfather, or even Twa, who was Sonqua himself. Roeloff got up and stood respectfully at the door.

'There's no right way for Zokho and me. I will raise the anger of my people if I take her, and kill my spirit if I don't. Also, it's no longer a question of what I want for myself. There's a child coming.'

Wynand looked at him. These were strong words for one so young. If he'd doubted Roeloff Kloot's conviction before, he no longer did. He hoped Neeltje hadn't been listening.

Chapter Ten

'Soela! When are you coming out of that room?'

Soela rocked the baby in her arms, trying to get her to stop crying. She could hear David pacing in the kitchen, and Sanna offering to dish up his food. He wouldn't take it, she knew, refusing to let anyone else but her serve his meals. His work was outside, not in the house, and his wife, not the servant, had to see to his needs. Any moment now he would storm in and start a row.

She put her sore nipple to the infant's mouth and looked around helplessly, she didn't know for what. Drieka and Willem had gone to visit Soela's mother who had broken her leg a few weeks ago, and had not yet returned. Only Sanna was in the house, and she stayed out of David's way.

'Soela!'

'I'm coming.'

His footsteps sounded outside the door and his grizzly bulk filled the doorway.

'How long must I wait for my food? You've had all day to take care of the child.'

'She's crying, I can't help that.'

'Put her down and get my food.'

Soela carried the baby into the kitchen where Sanna was cutting up pumpkin. 'Sanna, hold her for me, please.'

Sanna took the screaming infant to her bosom. Despite her earlier dislike of Soela, Sanna had come to feel sorry for her, and found some goodness in the girl whose actions, she knew, were responsible for the trouble between the brothers. She was privy to the exchanges, had seen the blows and the bruises as they came off the back of his fist. Soela was paying threefold for her sin. Sanna held Bessie up against her breast, and patted her. The baby let out wind, then settled against the fleshy bosom.

'Take that child and put her down inside!'

Soela recognised the cruelty in his voice and quickly took the baby from Sanna.

'We'll never know, will we, Soela?' he followed her into the room.

'What?' She put the baby on the bed.

'If it's his or mine. Will we?'

He'd never said it out loud, yet, here it was, flung in her face, the unspoken devil between them.

'*Will* we?'

There was no one in the house to protect her, and she braced herself for the fight.

'How can you say that? She's yours.'

The flat of his hand caught her across the face and she fell back on the bed.

'She looks like him! Like *him*!'

Soela curled herself up in a ball.

'Get up!'

She sat up slowly, holding the side of her face.

'*That's* what's wrong! What's always going to be wrong. *What* you did. *How* you disgraced me!'

'Why did you marry me, then? You should have left me alone.'

He laughed.

'Left you alone? You're going to pay, Soela Joubert. You'll have my children and wash my clothes and serve my food, and do it with a good heart or your father will hear what you did with that horse killer. Now, lift up your dress.'

'I'm bleeding.'

'Lift it up!' he pressed his groin in her face. 'And take off my pants!'

Her hands fumbled with the buttons and he pushed her back on the bed. He threw her skirt back over her head, and reached for her bloomers.

'Take away this thing!'

She lay, her face smothered under the calico, and reached nervously for the sling between her legs.

He was heavy, his hands rough, and she closed her eyes to the humiliation. She would not give him the satisfaction of tears. She was dried up, dead inside. He could do it until she lost consciousness, it wouldn't matter. A few minutes later he was done. He lifted himself off her and left the room.

Outside the door, Sanna listened to the distressed cries of the infant and wondered whether she should interfere. She knocked. There was no answer. She knocked again, then slowly opened the door. Bessie lay, red faced and screaming, on the blanket that was stained where Soela crouched on the edge of the bed. A blood-soaked cloth, the kind white women wore, lay ugly and exposed on the floor.

Soela burst into tears.

'You have to tell his father, Kleinnooi. You cannot go on like this. Look at your face. He will kill you one of these days.'

'I did a bad thing, Sanna, I can't tell his father.'

'No, Kleinnooi, you didn't do a bad thing. I know what you did.'

Soela looked up.

'Sanna knows everything. You went into the barn with his brother. You forgot yourself.'

'Yes.'

'Everyone forgets themselves with Roff, even that bosjesman girl that was here. He does that to people.'

'I thought he cared for me.'

'I know. And you didn't do anything wrong. You had feelings for him, you couldn't help it. But you must forget him, Kleinnooi, he's gone. You must do something now about this.'

'He'll tell my father.'

'What is worse? Let him tell your father and let it rain one time on your head. What can your father do? He will shout for a day, then return to his sheep. It cannot be worse than what the kleinbaas is doing to you.'

Soela allowed herself to be comforted by Sanna, the sourish smell rising up between the huge breasts reminding her of the woman who'd looked after her and Diena as children. That had been a happy time, before her father's transgressions and her mother's silences. The big arms enfolding her alleviated some of her fear.

Willem Kloot and Drieka arrived home after everyone had gone to bed.

The next morning at breakfast, Willem enquired after his grandchild.

'Sun's up and everyone's still sleeping. What's happening to this household? Where is everyone, Sanna?'

'The kleinnooi's not well.'

'What's wrong with the kleinnooi?'

'I don't know.'

'It can only mean something is wrong if you say it like that,' said Drieka.

'What is it?' Willem asked again.

'Grootbaas better ask himself. Come, Vinkie, I kept this crust of bread for you. You like it when it's hot.'

'Where's David?' Willem asked.

'Gone. He doesn't want her to come out.'

'What do you mean?'

'He told her to stay in the room.'

Willem exchanged looks with his wife.

'I don't like this. Go and see what's going on, Drieka.'

Drieka knocked on the bedroom door, then went into her niece's bedroom. The room was in darkness, and Soela was lying on the bed with the baby in her arms.

'Soela! What happened to your eye?'

Soela had never complained about David's ill-treatment because she thought she deserved punishment for her sin, but this time David had gone too far. Grateful for the chance to get it off her chest, she told Drieka the whole story.

Drieka listened, then went out and told Willem.

When David came in that evening, Willem was waiting for him at the kitchen table.

'Sit down.'

David looked from his father to his stepmother.

'Is something wrong?'

'You know very well what's wrong. What did you do to Soela?'

'Who said I did anything? Did Soela say …'

'Stop that. What did you do to her?'

David's jaw tightened in defiance. 'Nothing a man can't do with his wife.'

'You hit her,' Drieka accused him.

He looked at his stepmother and smiled.

'Who asked you?'

'What did you say?' Willem Kloot demanded, shocked by his son's rudeness. 'Is that how you speak to my wife?'

'Your wife, not mine,' David got up. 'I'll do as I please with mine.'

Willem got up, facing him.

'She's someone else's child, and this is still my house. You'll behave yourself in it, or …'

David smiled.

'Or else what, Pa? You'll throw me out like you did your other son?'

Willem's fist caught him right between the eyes, and he fell to the ground.

David got up.

'You're getting old, Pa,' he sneered. 'I would watch where I put my fists if I were you.'

Willem snatched a mug from the table and threw it at David. 'Shut up!' David caught the mug and threw it back at Willem. It caught him on the shoulder, hard, and he sat down, stunned by what had just happened.

'Well,' Drieka said when David had left the house, 'he's raised his hand to his own father. What's next?'

Willem didn't answer. His thoughts had wandered far away, to another morning, a dead stallion, a wronged son. Perhaps he'd known even then that Roeloff hadn't done it, but he had been too angry about what Roeloff had done with Soela in the barn. He'd gone along with the evidence, but he'd known, deep inside, that Roeloff wasn't capable of such a deed. His anger had stood in the way of reconciliation; that, and Roeloff's refusal to punish the bosjesman who'd stolen his sheep. He'd protected one son at the expense of the other. He shouldn't have considered David's feelings. Soela hadn't loved David, and here was the result—everyone suffered, especially the child, who bore no resemblance to his eldest son.

Willem was filled with despair. David and Soela's unhappiness had brought discord to Kloot's Nek, and he missed Roeloff. Where was he? Was Twa looking after him? Willem was not a praying man, but he asked God to protect Roeloff and the old hunter, and to bring them back to Kloot's Nek.

When Elsie heard what had happened, she sent word with one of the Hottentots that she wanted David and Soela to come to the Joubert farm right away. They arrived the next day, in time for the midday meal. After the initial shock of seeing what his daughter looked like, Joubert came straight to the point.

'We heard that there's been trouble between you.'

David rested his hands on his knees. His manner had changed from what it had been the previous week. If he had little respect for his father, he certainly didn't trust Joubert. Soela's eye was swollen and bruised, ample evidence of his ill-treatment.

'It was my fault.'

Soela stopped eating. She'd never heard him admit to doing anything wrong before. Elsie and Jan looked at each other.

'I lost my temper. I admit I took my hand to her. It won't happen again.'

The surprising confession took the wind out of the Jouberts.

'A man can make a mistake.' If there was one thing Joubert did know about the Kloot brothers, it was that you could predict the actions of the younger one by the way he was bent; the other, no manner of indication was enough. David had never struck him as being one to confess. 'What did Soela do?'

'I don't want to make it worse by telling tales.'

'Tell us. If she did something wrong, we want to know what it is so we can make sure it doesn't happen again. A man shouldn't lift his hand to his wife for no reason.'

'That's why I'm sorry. I would never have done such a thing, but I was greatly grieved. I thought ...'

'Grieved?'

Soela stood up.

'You're going to tell? After all you have done?'

'Sit down,' Joubert ordered.

'See? I can't talk to her. Ever since that night.'

'What night?'

'I don't want to say.'

'Soela?' Elsie spoke for the first time. 'Is there something we should know?'

Soela lowered her eyes and said nothing. She understood now why he'd been so ready to confess his wrongdoing.

'Will someone please tell us?' Joubert asked, in exasperation.

'It was the night of our engagement, when you all came to supper. Soela was with him in the barn.'

Elsie wasn't sure she understood what he meant.

'Yes? With who?'

'She was in the barn with Roeloff,' David repeated.

'Well, what were they doing in the barn?'

'Never mind,' Joubert interrupted, his face red. 'Soela, is this true? A daughter of mine, raised with the Word of the Lord? You were in the barn with his brother?'

Soela looked down at her veldskoene. She would have to make a new pair of laces, she thought. David's boots shone for the visit. If one judged him by his feet, one might have a good opinion. They were a decent size, unlike the rest of him. Should she tell what she knew? Should she kill it between them for good?

'But I care greatly for Soela,' she heard David continue. 'I married her all the same. I kept my promise.'

'Is what David's saying, true?' Joubert asked again.

'Yes.'

There was a long pause.

'Well, this is a fine mess. If I hadn't heard it myself, I wouldn't have believed it. I don't know what to say except that we're sorry for the shame brought upon you,' Joubert said.

Elsie turned her attention to David. The colour had drained from her face.

'You've been very kind then, haven't you, David, to protect my daughter's honour?'

'She's disgraced us,' Joubert said.

'I'm talking now. My daughter has broken God's commandment. Who here will judge?'

The sisters looked at each other. Their mother seldom spoke, but when she did their father didn't dare oppose her.

'I think Soela should stay here for a few days. Until she's recovered. She needs help in any event, with the baby.'

'I can't be without her,' David said, uncertainty creeping into his voice for the first time. 'Drieka and Sanna are there to give her a hand. She doesn't need more help than that.'

'He's right,' Joubert said. 'He's sorry for what he's done. And Soela …'

Elsie shot him a look.

'Soela what? She deserved it? Soela will stay here for a week. It will give her time to gather her strength, and it might be that, after that, David will have forgiven her. From what I can see, she's still paying for her sin.'

David looked at the flinty eyes of the stern-faced woman in the chair opposite him. He hadn't expected the encounter to turn out this way, with Soela not getting a proper upbraiding, and Elsie Joubert effectively telling him that he was going home without his wife.

'My father will wonder what's happened. I've kept this from him.'

Elsie gave one of her rare smiles.

'Then now is the time to tell him. So that there's nothing standing between you when she returns.'

David waited for Joubert to come to his aid, but the farmer said nothing. For the first time, David saw who was really in charge. He put on his hat and got up.

'I will be back in a week.'

'We'll be here,' Elsie said. 'Go in peace.'

For the first few days, Soela stayed studiously out of her parents' way, ashamed of the embarrassment she'd caused them, but also relieved that she no longer had to live in fear of being found out. Sanna had been right: her father had shown his disappointment for a day, given a lecture on morality in marriage, and then warmed gradually to forgiveness, enchanted by having his grandchild in the same house. Soela's mother never mentioned the incident.

After a few days, Soela got used to living at home again and to being with her sister, enjoying Diena's stories of the new knecht, Lourens's clumsy attempts at courtship.

A week later David arrived, bearing a barrel of butter and ten bars of soap.

'I've come for Soela,' he said to his mother-in-law who was sitting on the stoep shelling peas. 'My father sends his regards, and this butter. The soap is from me.'

'Thank you. Come, sit down,' she pointed to a chair on her right. 'Was the ride uneventful?'

'Yes. I've promised my father we'd be home before sunset.'

'Soela's decided to stay.'

'What do you mean?' he asked, a flush rising fast and hot up his neck.

'She doesn't want to go back.'

All the niceness melted from his eyes.

'But she can't just decide that. Who will care for my child? I won't be parted from Bessie.'

Elsie looked at him.

'She says you've said otherwise, that Bessie's not yours.'

'I was angry. I said the first thing that came into my head, to hurt her. Where's Oom Jan? I'd like to speak to him. Is Soela in the house?'

Elsie settled the cushion more comfortably behind her back.

'Jan's away until tomorrow evening. Soela and Diena are lying down with the baby, this hot weather makes everyone sleepy. You can wait if you wish, but Soela won't go with you. The matter rests with me, and I've told her she can stay.'

David suppressed his anger.

'You're encouraging her to stay away from her husband?'

'That would be wrong. I'm encouraging her to consider herself.'

'Herself?'

'Her feelings. And her feelings, right now, are not good. She doesn't have warm feelings for you. She needs time.'

'I won't come back again, if I leave.'

'You'll come back because you need a wife, and she needs a husband.'

He was confused.

Elsie continued. 'If you're sincere about changing yourself and …'

'There's nothing wrong with me.'

'… and changing towards her and the baby, I'll talk to her.'

'It's too much to ask.'

'What's too much? You've been without her for one week, you can manage without her for another.'

'I beg your pardon, but that's for her to decide. I would like to hear from Soela herself that she wants to stay here.'

Elsie looked straight at him.

'You've lost already, David, both of you have. You can't continue the way you've begun. If she goes with you now, it will be only a matter of time before there's trouble again.'

'A week will make a difference?'

'A month would be better, but you wouldn't agree to that. You both need time to think. Soela might even come round on her own to thinking of returning to Kloot's Nek, and it would be better, wouldn't it, if she wanted to return?'

'A man cannot be without a wife for so long.'

'A woman cannot be with one who thinks he is God.'

He couldn't enter the house uninvited, and couldn't call to Soela from the stoep. If Oom Jan had been there, he might have had a chance. He forced himself to be civil for a few minutes longer, then made his farewells and left.

Elsie watched the wagon roll slowly down the hill, then called to one of the servants to check if her daughters were up. She'd already decided that Soela would go back to Kloot's Nek. She needed a husband with that baby, and Elsie couldn't take the chance of the new knecht losing interest in Diena. Besides, David had learnt his lesson, and one day he would inherit Kloot's Nek.

'David will come for you next week,' she said when Soela came out onto the stoep.

'He was here?'

'Yes.'

Soela sat down next to her mother.

'You should have called me, Ma. I wanted to tell him I'm not going back. I've never loved him. It's no use.'

Elsie put down the bowl of peas.

'Do you think I loved your father when I married him? My father arranged it. "He'll put a roof over your head," he said, "parents aren't there forever." Your father's a hard man, not one I would have picked on my own, and I cursed my father for negotiating my future as if I were a brood mare, and my mother for allowing it. I thought there was more to being a wife, I thought I would feel things. By the time you and Diena arrived, we had amassed all this land and the responsibility it brings. You get used to things, and then almost nothing matters. You were still on the breast when my mother developed a blockage in her pipes and died. My father died eight weeks after that.' Elsie put the bowl back on her lap. 'I was glad then that I'd married. I would have been alone.'

'You want me to go back to David.'

Elsie looked at her daughter.

'If you think he will have learnt from this. It's hard to raise a child by yourself, and besides, Diena will also be getting married.'

Soela looked down at her hands clasped in her lap.

'Did you come to love Pa, eventually?'

'What is love? I had you and Diena. He holds us all together. If that is love, then I have come to it.'

'And your feelings, Ma?'

Elsie laughed softly.

'Feelings are there for you to like yourself. Remember that. The other kind gets in your head and promises the impossible.'

Soela returned to Kloot's Nek. David, true to his word, never once mentioned the incident. One afternoon, he came in, with three daisies in his hand, took off her kapje in front of Drieka and put the flowers in her hair. Soela was stunned. It was totally out of character, and implied feelings she hadn't thought he possessed. Perhaps she had misjudged him after all, she thought.

The following afternoon, still suffused with the warmth of his gesture, she put her daughter to bed for a nap and inspected herself in the mirror. The heat sat in hot little pockets between her breasts and she wiped it with Bessie's cloth, rubbing herself with the fragrance of violet flowers. If it was unbearable in the house, it would be sweltering in the veld. She would take a beaker of water down to the men. The flowers had been a sort of peace offering. She would do something nice in return, show that she was appreciative of his efforts. At first it had pleased her that she could get into bed and know her sleep wouldn't be interrupted, but as the weeks passed, aware of his hardness and her own urges, she'd wondered if she'd lost her appeal. The night before, she had left off her undergarments and had even turned towards him, but he fell into bed and went to sleep instantly.

She checked her appearance one last time. Her breasts were filled with milk for the baby, and she didn't like the way her dress rode up in her waist, but her hair was still her best feature, silky gold down her back, and she had brushed it until it shone and left her kapje off. She went into the yard with the beaker, filled it with water from the barrel, and left for the sheep kraal. She was at the barn when she saw Willem Kloot come out, shaking the dust from his clothes. People said he had changed since the banishment of his younger son, working numbing hours, smoking like a Bushman to render himself insensible to what he'd done. But she'd come to know his other side, and to like him. The father was nothing like the sons. Both sons had betrayed her.

'I was just bringing down water for everyone. Is David still down there?'

'He was when I left a few minutes ago.'

Soela continued down the path, past the huts, to the end of the kraal. She looked out over the veld to where the sheep were, but there was no sign of him. She was about to turn back when she saw Katrijn, the heavily pregnant kitchen servant, walk quickly around the far side of the giant boulders in the direction of the dam, looking furtively behind her. Soela watched her disappear around the corner. She wondered where Katrijn was going. Something told her to stay where she was. A few minutes later she saw David emerge from the barn and walk in the same direction. The beaker fell from her hand. This explained everything. She felt sick.

Sanna was in the kitchen when Soela came in and she knew from the grimness around Soela's mouth that David's secret was no longer a secret. Sanna had spoken many times to the girl, telling her to leave the kleinbaas alone, but Katrijn wouldn't listen. Sanna shuddered at what was to come.

David came in for supper a few minutes later in good spirits.

'What are we having?' He took a wet cloth from Sanna to wipe his hands and face and sat down.

'Pumpkin and rice,' Vinkie said.

'I was at the dam this afternoon,' Soela said suddenly. 'I came looking for you, to give you some water. I thought I saw you, but I must have been mistaken. It was Katrijn. Every time you look for her, she's lying under someone. Heaven knows who's fathered that one in her belly.'

Willem Kloot stopped with his spoon halfway to his mouth. He looked at his son. The humour had gone from David's eyes.

'Well, isn't anyone going to eat? Dish up more food, Sanna,' Soela said. 'Give the kleinbaas an extra helping. He needs his strength.'

Sanna looked at her from the fireside, her eyes begging Soela to stop.

'Don't you?' Soela looked at David directly.

David said nothing. That night he didn't come to bed.

Two weeks later, Sanna informed them that Katrijn had given birth during the night and would have the day off. Soela tried to concentrate on her work, but she couldn't get Katrijn out of her mind. In the afternoon, she went to the hut. She found the servant lying on a coir mattress in the dark, the infant at her breast. Katrijn was not the ugliest Hottentot Soela had ever seen, but it was perhaps the girl's cunning that repulsed her. Still waters hide wild undercurrents, and despite being so young, she already had two children.

Katrijn was surprised to see Soela enter the hut. Quickly she pulled the blanket over the infant's head. Soela leaned forward and pulled it back. The baby's colouring and straight hair screamed out at her. She looked at the girl on the mattress and ripped off the blanket.

'Out!'

Katrijn lay there with her breasts and belly exposed. She struggled to her feet.

Soela smacked her across the face, then beat her about the arms and head.

'No, Kleinnooi, no …' Katrijn cried.

'Get out, and don't come back!'

Katrijn stood trembling with the child in her arms, fending off the blows, blood dribbling down the inside of her legs.

'What's going on here?!' David's voice boomed behind them.

Soela stopped with her hand in the air.

'You slept with this slut!'

David's fist smashed into her face.

'You want more?'

Soela looked at him with a dazed expression. Her face numb. He had struck her in front of the servant. She couldn't see through the tears in her eyes, and the taste on her lips was her own blood.

'I hate you!' she screamed.

His fist came straight for her eyes, breaking the bone of her nose. Blood gushed from her mouth. Soela collapsed in a heap on the floor. David grabbed her hair and pulled her through the entrance like a sack of potatoes, dropping her outside. Her head fell back with a thud in the dust, a red pool of blood collecting under her ear.

'You're on Kloot's Nek now, Soela Joubert. Your mother can't help you here!'

Chapter Eleven

Neeltje sat with her back against a rock, soaking up the warm sunshine. She'd taken off her boots and set them to one side. She liked exploring the hooks and hollows of the mountain after rain. This was one of her special spots, out of the wind. She was telling all her secrets to Boet. Boet did not understand the words, but wagged his tail at the tone of her voice.

'A boy or a girl, Boet? What do you think it will be?'

Boet opened his eyes, then closed them again.

She smiled, content to just sit there and feel the heat draw into her toes, spread up her legs, travel all the way to her heart. She felt good. Perhaps it was the swell of new vegetation, perhaps the quickening of her pulse when she saw Roeloff bare-chested and lean, his pants held up by leather thongs wound twice round his waist, working her father's land. He still wore the same pants in which he'd arrived and Zokho hadn't thought to patch the knees. Soon he would rub through them and stand naked before them in his boots.

A shadow fell across her and she opened her eyes.

'Zokho! You startled me.'

'Your father fell from his horse. Roff wants you to come.'

'What?'

'He says you must hurry.'

Neeltje pulled on her boots and ran off, leaving Zokho, in her last month of pregnancy, to follow at a more leisurely pace. She arrived at the house to find her father on his bed, and Roeloff bent over him.

'What happened?'

'We were riding along and I turned to speak to him, when there he was, lying on the ground.'

'Was the horse frightened by something?'

'No. One moment we were riding side by side, the next he was down. He just fell off.'

'He's very still.'

'I've checked his bones. Nothing's broken, but his breathing's weak.'

'What if it stops?'

'It won't.'

'But what if it does? What if he doesn't wake up?'

'I don't think we should worry about what *could* happen.'

'How can I not worry? There are just the two of us. Nothing must happen to Pa.'

Roeloff wanted to still her fears, but he said nothing. He wasn't sure what had happened to Wynand, and he didn't want to say too much, in case he was wrong. He was also confused by other feelings. Feelings he'd thought belonged only to Zokho. He didn't know how this could be. His feelings for Zokho were strong; for Neeltje it was a need to be part of her life and to protect her. He wanted to ease her fears. He knew that she was affected by him. How he knew, he didn't know, but was careful in his dealings with her now, much more than in the past.

'He has the sleeping sickness,' Zokho said. 'He will sleep for a few days.'

'Do you know a cure?'

'There's a plant that we use, but I haven't seen it here.'

'Buchu?' Neeltje described the plant and its medicinal properties.

'I know that plant. It won't help with this.'

They took turns sitting with Wynand, wiping his face with a cool cloth, trying to get him to wake up. In the evening his eyelashes flickered and it seemed he might come out of his sleep.

Zokho was with him when it happened. It was cold in the evenings and she had refused Neeltje's clothes, finding them too uncomfortable in her condition, and greatly upsetting Roeloff in the process, because he didn't like her walking around with her stomach and breasts exposed. That was partly why she did it, to anger him. It wasn't anything he'd said or done, just a feeling she had that things had changed. She wanted the oubaas to recover. If he died, it would overwhelm Roeloff with pity for the girl. She went into the kitchen to tell Neeltje the news.

'Your father's stirring in his sleep.'

Neeltje was cooking food for the three of them and for Twa. She left what she was doing to go behind the partition. She saw her father lying in a slightly different position, and burst out crying.

'Don't do that, you'll anger the gods,' Zokho said. 'And he'll think he's sick if he wakes up.'

Neeltje dabbed at her eyes with the hem of her dress.

'Pa? Can you hear me?'

The eyelids opened, then closed again.

'He heard me. He heard me, Zokho. Where's Roff? We have to tell him.'

'Here,' Roeloff said coming in behind them. 'It looks like the worst is over.'

'Do you think so? There's a doctor a day's ride away in Jan Dissels Vlei. His name's Otto Lieberband, he's German. If my father doesn't improve, we could get him to come and take a look. He'll do that for Pa. Pa knew him when he was younger.'

'Perhaps your father will be well enough in the morning to tell us himself what he wants.'

'I hope so.'

'I'll stay with you, if you want,' Zokho said. 'I can sleep on the floor.'

'You need your bed, Zokho. It's any day now, isn't it?'

'Yes.'

When Neeltje got up the following morning, her father had his eyes open, and was looking around the room.

'Pa? You're awake.' She sat on the side of the bed. 'You fell off your horse yesterday. You've been asleep ever since. Can you talk?'

Wynand couldn't. His limbs seemed crippled, his tongue stiff in his mouth.

'Don't worry, Pa, you're getting better. Yesterday you were in a deep sleep, today you're awake. I don't want you to worry. Just rest. I'm going to ask Roeloff to get Oom Otto. He'll tell us what to do.'

When Roeloff and Zokho came into the house, she told them that her father had woken up.

'That's good news, Neeltje,' Roeloff said.

'But he can't talk, he can't move his legs.' She noticed Zokho standing with her hand on her belly. 'Are you all right, Zokho?'

'Yes. I ate too much last night, my stomach's cramping.'

'Are you sure?'

'Yes.'

'I think we should get Oom Otto, Roff. Pa can't move his arms and legs. Do you think you could go?'

'Where is he?'

'Jan Dissels Vlei.'

Roeloff looked doubtful.

'I don't know where that is. I didn't travel anywhere else in this area before coming to this farm. And,' he looked down at Wynand in the bed, 'I think we will need help with your father. Is there anyone living near here who can help us? He'll need washing and turning around.'

'No one. We're the only ones out here in the Cederberg. But there is the widow Reijnhardt. Tante Marta. Persistent as a mosquito after Pa. She's in Jan Dissels Vlei too. She would come right away.'

'I must go to Jan Dissels Vlei, then. You'll have to tell me the way.'

Neeltje's brow was furrowed in thought.

'Tante Marta won't travel alone with you.'

'You'll have to go with me then. I know it's not proper, but we have no choice. How long would it take?'

'We could leave at dawn and be back the day after tomorrow.'

Roeloff looked at Zokho.

'You must go,' Zokho said.

'What about the baby?'

'It won't come yet.'

Roeloff turned to Wynand Roos. 'Do you want us to fetch the doctor, Oom?'

Wynand blinked.

'We'll also get the wid …'

Neeltje kicked his foot.

'Don't tell him that,' she whispered. 'He'll get worse. We'll leave at dawn, Pa. Zokho will stay with you in the house. Twa will look after things.'

'He's handy with a gun,' Roeloff added. 'We won't be away long.'

That evening Neeltje put a few things together for the trip.

'You'll be all right by yourself, Zokho, you and Twa?'

'Yes.'

'There's soup in the pot. Give Pa the soup in the morning. You and Twa take the meat.'

'Your father won't open his mouth if he knows what it is.'

'Don't tell him.'

Zokho watched her wrap a few strips of biltong and bread into a cloth.

'You'll be back by sunset tomorrow?'

Neeltje looked up.

'The day after. Why, are you afraid?'

'No.'

'What then?'

'I'm thinking that—I'm thinking it will be quiet around here.'

'That's not it, Zokho. What is it?'

Zokho looked down at her hands.

'Something will happen on this journey.'

'What?' Neeltje came to stand in front of Zokho and put her hands on her shoulders. 'You're talking strange things, Zokho. What will happen?'

'I don't know. I feel it in here, under my heart.'

Neeltje laughed.

'You're feeling the baby. You've said yourself he was kicking your insides. What can happen on this journey? I've been over these mountains twice since I was born.'

Zokho said no more.

Roeloff and Twa came into the kitchen.

'I've asked Twa to have my horse saddled first thing. We'll have to go on one horse, the mare's getting ready to foal. The oubaas's horse will stay in case Twa needs it to go after the sheep. I told him to keep an eye on things. He and Zokho are in charge.'

'That's all right with you, Twa?' Neeltje asked.

Twa's face wrinkled into a smile.

'Twa will do it.'

The next morning, Zokho was up early to help Roeloff and Neeltje get under way. She watched them ride off on one horse into the darkness of dawn. Her heart was heavy. The journey for the doctor would bring change.

Neeltje had said to keep the house warm and to give her father soup. She entered the kitchen and went to the hearth. She bent over to pick up some wood, and a pain shot across her belly. The baby had dropped lower, and a cramp was working itself up her leg. When it subsided, she went behind the partition to tend to the oubaas. He was still asleep, but opened his eyes at her approach. She looked at him in the half dark, helpless, at her mercy. In his own bed she could put a sack over his face and smother him. Hold her hand over his nose and mouth the way Tau had done with her baby. Zokho had seen her do it, but pretended it hadn't happened. It would be over by the time his eyes rolled back in his head. She could take his sheep for her people. They would forget her past and welcome her back.

Boet got up from where he was dozing at the foot of Neeltje's bed, and licked her ankle. She bent down to touch him, ashamed of her thoughts.

'You're ugly, hairy one,' she rubbed his fur. 'You can see in Zokho's heart?'

The dog licked her with a slobbering affection. She was surprised, amazed as always by white people's feeling for animals. Boet was Neeltje's dog, and she treated him almost like a human, feeding him from her plate. Roeloff had had two dogs on Kloot's Nek, and shared Boet's affections with Neeltje.

'You are stupid, Zokho,' she chastised herself. 'Why are you crying, you foolish girl? He's waiting for you to empty your belly so he can feel you again. Be strong. He is yours.'

She gave the oubaas his soup, then settled his blankets, and went to her own quarters and climbed into the bed Roeloff had vacated less than an hour before. She stayed there all morning, whimpering in her sleep. A dull ache woke her in the afternoon. She got up and went to the barrel outside for water. She hadn't yet reached the door when a knifelike pain cut across her belly, bringing her to a halt. She recognised it; the first of the pains. She looked around the room she shared with Roeloff—the small trestle table, the powder horn, the extra gun, his clothes and books neatly stacked on a ledge in the wall. His presence was everywhere in the room. But where was he? Where was he when she needed him with her? He was crossing some mountain with the oubaas's daughter, and she was by herself. She had said he could go, and had wanted him to so that the oubaas could recover, but she had also expected more concern for her and for the baby that would come. Who was there to help her? She, Zokho, was alone. As she'd always been. At least with her people, Tau had come to her aid, and the others were there as support. She missed them. Karees with her questions—she'd enjoyed talking to her. Was Karees with Toma now? And Limp Kao? Was he still there? And where were they? Behind the Hantam, or in the land of great dryness below the yellow river? It was far, far away. She started to cry, slowly at first, then sobbing desperately into her hands with the longing for familiar smells and family fires. A sudden contraction drove her back to bed.

The ride to Jan Dissels Vlei was quick and uneventful. They stopped once along the bank of the Olifantsrivier to have something to eat and stretch their legs. Roeloff talked a little about his sister, Vinkie, his life on Kloot's Nek. Neeltje told him how lonely it was without brothers or sisters in the Cederberg. Otherwise their conversation was strained. Both seemed aware of the other's presence.

Neeltje knew the way to the widow Reijnhardt's farm, a

lonely little house in a dusty bowl of bush and rock in the valley. When they arrived there, they were informed by a Koi-na servant that the widow had left a day before to visit relatives. She was not expected back for a few days.

'We have come all this way for nothing,' Neeltje said forlornly.

'Never mind. There is still the doctor. Hopefully, we will find him in.'

Otto Lieberband was home when they arrived, and came limping out with his wife to greet them. Visitors were always a welcome change, although he got more than most because he was a doctor and people showed up unexpectedly for his help.

'Neeltje! What a surprise! You've married then, since I saw you.'

Neeltje blushed.

'No, Oom, I've not married. This is Roeloff Kloot. He's a bijwoner on the farm.'

Roeloff greeted the doctor and was introduced to Johanna, his wife.

'Come in, come in. Kloot, hey? I met a Kloot from the Cape. What brings you here in such a hurry? Johanna and I saw the dust in the distance and said whoever it was, was coming on a matter of importance.'

They followed the couple into the house, where Johanna put on the water for coffee.

'My father fell off his horse and lay for a day without opening his eyes. He's woken up now, but he can't move and talk, and his face is skew. The lip's up on one side. We've come here hoping to take you back to the farm.'

'I would, but it's impossible with this leg. I can't make any long trips. Martinus dropped a beam on my foot and I can't sit for long on a horse or in a wagon. But, I think I know what's wrong with your Pa. He's suffered a seizure, but the danger's over by the sound of it.'

'Do you think so?'

'I've seen cases like his. The first few days are the ones to worry about—whether he comes out of the sleep. Was he aware of it when it happened? Was anyone with him?'

'I was,' Roeloff said. 'I don't know if he was aware of it, but I was riding with him when suddenly, there he was on the ground and his heart was beating very slowly.'

Lieberband nodded.

'And now he's come to.'

'Yes.'

'That he's come out of it so soon is good news.'

'His right side also seems stronger than his left.'

Otto Lieberband turned to Neeltje.

'Your father's working too hard, that's his problem. I told him long ago that loneliness is a hard thing for a man out in those mountains. Eventually it puts you in the ground. You need womenfolk, children. Children bring life to a home. You married, son?'

'He's not,' Neeltje said before Roeloff could answer. 'Are you saying there's nothing to worry about? That Pa will recover?'

'He's out of danger. I'll give you medicine to make him strong and ointment to massage into his skin, but what he needs most is rest. He must forget about his farm worries for now. He'll probably regain his health and strength eventually. I'll tell Stoffel to bring me up to date after he's visited you in a month's time. He was here recently. He said he hadn't been to your father in a long time but that he was going out there.'

'He stayed away for no reason.'

Otto looked at Roeloff.

'He must have had his reasons. Anyway, regarding your father, he will walk again, and be able to go back to his old way of life. I'll try to get to see him when my leg's better.'

'Thank you.'

'Now, you must take your evening meal with us and rest so that you can start out early in the morning.' He turned to Roeloff. 'I met a Kloot once in the Cape, about ten years ago. Treated his daughter for snakebite. I remember him because he couldn't find anyone to come to the house, but I don't think there's a connection.'

'My late grandfather has a brother in the Cape, Krisjan.'

'Krisjan?'

'Yes.'

'This is a coincidence. The old man's name was Krisjan, but it can't be your relative. You see, the reason he couldn't get help was because he'd married a slave, and his daughter was dark-skinned. Not a caffre, mind you. Her hair was straight, you couldn't stand a pin up in it, and she had features like yours and mine, but black as the night nevertheless. A handsome woman.'

'Krisjan Kloot's wife was a slave? Are you sure?' He remembered Oupa Krisjan's visit to Kloot's Nek in his absence.

'That's what they said. From Ceylon, came to the Cape

on a ship. What set the others against him wasn't only that he'd taken up with this woman and had children by her, but that he'd abandoned his own Christian teachings and followed her strange practices. But, as I said, that was ten years ago, there're many Kloots in the Cape, and Krisjan's a common name.'

'Was he known for anything in particular? Was he a farmer?'

'He was a man of letters, I believe. Wrote books.'

Roeloff started to laugh.

'Roff?' Neeltje looked at him with concern.

'It's all right, Neeltje,' he said, still laughing. 'I think we should do as the doctor suggests, and turn in now for an early start.'

The elephants shuffled slowly along, stopping as one at a cluster of rocks. The cows, agitated and weary from having to outrun their pursuers, stopped further away, their calves trumpeting hoarsely as they tried to keep up. Three bulls watched, particularly interested in a young female in oestrus. They grazed patiently on the branches of a few scraggly trees then, without warning, one of them broke away, making straight for the young cow. The cow saw him coming and bolted, stirring up clouds of orange dust as she galloped flat out for open ground. Faster than the male, she put distance between them, then slowed down and walked rapidly in a circle to meet up with her family who came rumbling up, trumpeting, locking tusks and rubbing their heads affectionately against her. She had hardly had a chance to rest when she was chased by another bull, and so the game continued with different bulls taking turns, the distances getting longer, and the cow managing each time to outrun her pursuers.

Roeloff and Neeltje had stopped earlier on the other side of the rocks to rest the horse and to have something to eat. They watched the game from their hiding place.

'They have strange rituals,' she whispered. 'Look at that. The bulls are all on one side, the cows on the other. That young cow knows she's safe for the time being.'

Then suddenly there was a low rumble from somewhere to their left and they noticed the excited behaviour of the cows and the alarm of the bulls. The sound drew nearer, then a sharp, acrid odour was upon them and minutes later a towering bull, in full rut, appeared through a gateway of rocks, a viscous fluid oozing down the sides of his massive head, his sheath covered in scum, leaving a trail of urine behind him. His left tusk was broken, and he came trampling towards them with flapping ears, making straight for the cows.

'Broken Tooth!'

Neeltje stiffened beside him.

'Don't be afraid,' he took her hand. 'We're downwind.'

'You know him?'

He could feel the pulse in her hand throbbing into his.

'He's the one we let go, Twa and me.'

'He seems very excited.'

They watched as the cows jostled and rumbled and rubbed their heads against the bull's hindquarters, urinating profusely to welcome him. Broken Tooth had no interest in them, and headed straight for the young cow. Now the cow acted differently. She started to leave the group, running with less determination than before. Broken Tooth picked up speed, his penis dropping from its sheath, until it was only inches away from scraping the ground. He caught up with her, reached his trunk over her back, and she came to a stop. Moving his head and tusk over her hindquarters, he placed his front feet on her rear, and leaned back so that most of his weight was on his hind legs. His penis changed from an arc to an S-shape and, finding the vulva, he hooked it in, thrusting up, jamming four feet of muscle into the cow's vagina. They stood locked together for a time, then he disengaged from her in a gush of sperm.

The cow gave a deep bellow and her family came rushing up, waving their trunks in comfort. She smelt the sperm on the ground, then emitted a series of rumbles. The females rallied round to calm her down, then she left the group to stand alongside the bull.

Standing with her hand locked in his, Neeltje was suddenly aware of the throbbing of Roeloff's pulse, the power of his body. Then the pressure of his grip changed and he turned to look at her.

'Neeltje …'

'It's not necessary to say it.'

'I must, I want you to know how I feel. I've developed feelings for you, but I'm promised to Zokho. I've feelings for her, too, and she will bear my child. I would be your husband if I could. You need a husband, Neeltje, someone to care for you, to give you children.'

Neeltje had dreamt of such words, but never thought she would hear them.

'You wanted me to know you had feelings for two?'

'I wanted you to know how I felt. That I care greatly for you. The two of you mean different things to me.'

'Different things? A man can want two women?'

'Not at the same time. But he could be with one, and want another.'

'It would have been better not to have said anything.'

'I just wanted you to know. Zokho and I have been together on Kloot's Nek, we …'

Neeltje could listen to no more. Without thinking, she ran from their hiding place out into the open. Her scent drifted on the wind and there was a loud trumpeting as the matriarch of the herd sounded the alarm and one of the young bulls broke loose.

'Neeltje!'

She ran blindly on.

Roeloff grabbed the gun, feeling cold fear in the pit of his stomach. He fired a shot in the air, and the elephant, already on Neeltje's heels, turned at a lumbering speed. For a moment he thought it was all over for him, then the bull joined the herd and they stampeded off in a hurricane of dust.

'You could have been killed!' he shouted. 'Don't you know how dangerous that was?'

She realised the stupidity of her actions and, shaking with fright, she turned so that he wouldn't see her crying.

He looked at her trembling back, the plait of hair reaching down to her waist. He threw down the gun and spun her around.

'Neeltje.'

Neeltje spluttered all over his face and buried her face in his shoulder.

'Neeltje, Neeltje, oh God ...'

He stood there with her for a long time, stroking her hair, feeling the curve in her waist, the strength of her shoulders. Then Zokho's face, glistening and catlike, flashed before him.

'I'm sorry. I had no right.'

Neeltje trembled under the most intense feelings she'd ever experienced. Roeloff's sudden withdrawal left her feeling cold and rejected. She watched as he turned and resaddled the horse.

'We have to get back. Your father's waiting for us.'

She stepped meekly into his cupped hand and mounted. Roeloff got on after her and sat in front. Burying her nose in the sweat of his back, she cried soundlessly into his shirt.

Chapter Twelve

Twa was squatting at his fire in front of his hut heating a tin mug of water to make coffee when he saw Zokho come out of her quarters clutching her stomach. He was about to shout after her when he noticed her slow and limping walk as she headed for the bush at the back. Was she having the baby already? He'd had a feeling that it would happen when no one was there. She'd slept all day, giving him nothing to eat when he knew there was meat for him in the kitchen pot. He wondered if she'd checked up on the oubaas in the house. He was reluctant to do so himself. Whatever it was that had caused the oubaas to turn into stone, he didn't want his disease.

Lately, after squatting, Twa had to walk slowly for a while before settling into his regular rhythm. He got up, rubbing the kinks out of his leg.

'You're getting old, thin man. Soon you'll join your ancestors.' He chuckled. 'And what will happen to Kudu? He wants to be fair to the hare in his trap while wanting him for his supper. When will he learn one's got to be sacrificed for the other?'

A sudden bleating in the kraal made him look up. His first thought was baboons. He picked up the gun and fired a shot in the air, limping slowly towards the kraal. But everything was in order. Looking at the lambs, he had an idea. What did they expect, anyway, leaving him dependent on someone like Zokho to fill his belly? He would starve if he had to depend on her laziness. The oubaas had many sheep, and Roeloff wouldn't notice right away. He selected one of the lambs and led it out of the kraal to a spot far from the house. He dug a hole in the ground, and holding the lamb over it, pushed the knife deftly into the vein in the neck. Soon the soft-fleeced animal was lying on its side. He hacked and sliced, buried the entrails, and returned to his hut with the meat draped over a stick. There he scooped out a shallow pit and made a fire. He laid out half the meat on the coals and hid the rest. Three hours later, drowsy with dagga, his stomach distended, he was fast asleep in front of his hut.

The next morning he was awakened by a pain in his leg, and knew the moment he opened his eyes that something was wrong. It was too quiet. He felt for the gun next to him and hobbled quickly over to the kraal. He was not prepared for the shock. The gate was open and all the sheep were gone except for an old ewe, lying dead on its side with half a dozen arrows sticking out of the stained coat. He couldn't believe it. The whole kraal! They'd left one to show their audacity. An urgent need to defecate reminded him of his own crime. He would have to get rid of the bones. But what was one lamb in the face of so many? If only he could get back the sheep.

He remembered the oubaas alone in the house. Had they killed him, too? Zokho? Why hadn't he seen her? Where was she? He didn't know what to do first.

He ran to her quarters and banged on the door.

Zokho took several minutes to answer. He saw immediately from her decreased size that she had given birth.

'Something terrible has happened!'

'With me, too,' she moaned softly.

'What?'

'There's no baby.'

'No baby?' He had big things to worry about, he didn't have time for her nonsense. 'What do you mean there's no baby, where is he?'

Zokho sat down on the bed. 'He's dead.'

'Dead? I don't believe it.'

'I've lost him,' she started to cry. 'I know from in here,' she pointed to her heart, 'he's not mine any more.'

'What're you talking about?'

'Eyes of the Sky. He's not coming back.'

'You're talking nonsense, you foolish girl. Of course he's coming back. Where else should he go? And what does the baby have to do with it? What do you want? Isn't it enough that you live with him?'

She cried louder.

'Stop it! Where did you put the child?'

'I don't know.'

Twa had never struck a woman, but before he knew what had happened, his hand slapped her face and she fell off the bed.

'Where?'

She was instantly alert.

'At the back.'

'Show me,' he pulled her up, the sheep momentarily forgotten.

Zokho was naked except for the duiker flap, and went out with him in the cold to the back of the house. They came upon the infant wrapped in a scrap of sheepskin, near the stick in the ground marking the grave of Neeltje's mother.

Twa went down on his knees and unwrapped the sheepskin. The umbilical cord was still attached to the afterbirth, and the child was stained with dry blood. He lifted the infant, and put an ear to his heart. The sheepskin had protected it from the cold.

'You're lucky he isn't dead, his heart's still beating. Your callousness didn't kill him.'

'It's bad luck to bring him back from the dead.' She stood back, wanting nothing to do with the child.

'He wasn't dead. Take him now and cut his cord.'

'No.'

'I'm not telling you again.'

Zokho took the baby from him and quickly bit into the umbilical cord, clamping the severed end with an antelope strip she peeled off her arm. When she was done, she put the baby down on the ground.

'He needs your milk.'

She hesitated.

'I'm warning you, Zokho.'

She picked up the infant and reluctantly put him to her breast.

Twa breathed a sigh of relief. He was exhausted.

'Now, there are other problems. Did you hear anything in the night? All the sheep are gone.'

'I heard nothing.'

'When last did you check on the oubaas?'

'Yesterday.'

'Yesterday? What if he's dead?'

Zokho looked at him in defiance.

'What, Zokho? They left us in charge!'

She started to walk to the house.

'I'll check on him now, then I'll leave.'

'Leave? What are you talking about? How can you leave? You have no place to go to. Your place is here with him and the child.'

'He doesn't want me. I told him I didn't want to stay, but he didn't listen. Now, look what has happened.'

'What has happened? He went to fetch the doctor.'

'He wants her.'

'I swear, Zokho,' he limped along, trying to keep up. 'I don't know how he puts up with you. You make up things in your head. You have brought it all on yourself. Did you really think he would marry you? Just because you carried his child? You are stupid on top of everything else. And wait till he hears what you did.'

'I don't care. I will go.'

'If you go,' he stepped in front of her, 'you won't take his child. You'll leave him with me.'

'I don't want him. She can have him and his child. I've seen how she looks at him. He thinks I can't see how he changes colour in her presence. She can bring the baby up. He doesn't look like me anyway. I'll go back to my people.'

Twa looked at her in disgust.

'Not even a snake crawls away from what's his. You are despicable, Zokho. And what kind of people are they, to take you back every time you have the notion to run away? You behave like a child. Perhaps it's a woman he wants.'

It was all Zokho could bear.

'Go to the oubaas yourself now. I won't go.'

Twa looked on in anger as she returned to her quarters. He gave up and headed for the house, hoping he wouldn't find the oubaas with an arrow stuck in his throat. He opened the door and looked around the kitchen. The fire hadn't been lit since the previous morning, and the house was cold, with a terrible smell hanging thick and heavy in the dank air. He stood still for a moment to let the atmosphere speak to him, noting the pot in front of the fire, the crumbs on the table, the potatoes spilt on the floor where the dog had probably knocked the pot over. He braced himself.

'It's Twa,' he called out so Wynand Roos could hear it was him. He stepped behind the partition, and was both sickened and relieved. The oubaas was alive, his blankets and bedclothes crusty with urine and excrement. Twa's first reaction was to run from the room, but the man in the bed looked so helpless that he felt sorry for him. Pinching his nostrils together, he stood back from the bed to survey the mess and to think. When he had worked it all out in his head, he came forward gingerly. He started at the feet, peeling off the stained clothing, rolling Wynand Roos on his side, then pulling out the soiled sheets. He dumped them in a bucket outside and took a wet rag to the oubaas, going out several times to throw water from the barrel over the rag to rinse it out, cursing Zokho and all her ancestors.

'Now what, you old fool, where will you find blankets? The man's shivering like a dassie.'

He found blankets on Neeltje's bed, settled the farmer as best as he could, then went to the kitchen to light the fire. When the water had boiled, he made coffee, propped Wynand Roos up in bed and held it to his lips, spilling half of it on his shirt. When Wynand looked a little better, Twa returned to Zokho's quarters.

She was annoyed by the disturbance.

'I'm sleeping. What do you want?'

'I can see that you are sleeping. And that baby's still crying. Haven't you fed him?'

Zokho didn't answer him.

'I went to look at the oubaas. He was lying in his own mess. What will you tell them when they come back and find out you've left him like this? When he can talk and say what you've done? I cleaned him up. His blankets are in the bucket. Wash them so they can dry before they come tonight. You're in charge now, I'm going.'

'Where are you going?'

'To look for the sheep. If I'm not back when they come, tell them what happened.'

'You'll leave me here by myself?'

Twa laughed.

'You've been with the devil, Zokho, what are you afraid of? Be afraid of Eyes of the Sky and of what he will do when he finds out that you tried to kill his son. And I will tell him if you don't do as I say. Go in there and give the oubaas his food. And make sure you take care of that baby.'

Zokho challenged him with her eyes.

'I mean it, Zokho, don't disobey me. Twa's old, but he'll find you. You will wish then that you'd been found by a lion.'

He was fond of Zokho, more than she knew. Looking at her was like looking at his sister, Shy Little Tortoise. The same spirit and naughtiness. Zokho was hurt, she wanted revenge. He understood. But he understood the other also. What would Zokho say if she knew who he was? She, who sometimes forgot to feed him and had answers for everything?

Roeloff knew the moment they came within sight of the house that something looked wrong. It got dark quickly on the Cederberg mountains, and it was just at that twilight time when he could still see the outline of the dwelling, but not make out people or animals.

'There's no smoke in the chimney. I hope everything's all right.'

'It looks too quiet.'

They arrived at the empty kraal and saw the dead ewe.

'We've been raided!'

Neeltje felt suddenly cold.

'Oh, my God, Pa! Come with me to the house, Roff.'

They passed Twa's hut and stopped.

'Look at this. Bones.'

Roeloff had already seen them.

'Twa!' he called to the hunter.

There was no answer.

They arrived at the buitekamer where Roeloff had his quarters. Neeltje waited at the door while he went inside.

'Neeltje!'

She went into the dark room, and looked to where he was pointing to something on the bed.

'She's had the baby …' Neeltje whispered.

Roeloff opened the kaross and they looked down at a pink-skinned infant. His navel was raw and his face was wet, as if he had cried himself to sleep.

'A son,' he said hoarsely. 'I'm a father.'

'He's beautiful, Roff. Look at his hair. It's the colour of a moon, almost silver.' She put her finger into the tiny hand. The hand tightened around it immediately. She leaned down and picked him up.

'Where's his mother?'

'She must be in the house with my father.'

Roeloff went to the little hollow in the wall where Zokho kept her beads and antelope strips. There was nothing there. 'Her digging stick's gone.'

'Zokho wouldn't just walk off and leave her baby.'

'She has.'

'Let's go to the house and see if she's there. I hope nothing's happened to Pa.'

'We can't tell him anything about the sheep, Neeltje. We don't know ourselves. It will set him back. What about the baby?'

'I'll take him and dress him in something warm. Do you think Twa could have done that—to make it look like we've been raided, and taken the sheep?'

He stepped in front of her.

'Never say that about Twa, Neeltje. He's not like that. And where would he go with the sheep? I thought you knew his character.'

'What about the bones at his fire?'

He let go of her arm.

'I don't know, but he'll have to answer for that. It's

possible he's gone after the thieves. Twa's never stolen from me. I'll check the spoor.'

They entered the kitchen. The house was cold and smelly. The fire had gone out, and no one had cooked or cleaned, or attended to anything. Roeloff lit the lamp on the table and they went behind the partition.

'Pa!'

Wynand closed his eyes in relief.

'We're back, and we have good news. But, first, are you all right? It looks like you are. Oom Otto says you'll get better. He cannot come now because of his leg, but he'll come soon to see you. He gave us medicine to build up your strength.'

She noticed her blankets on the bed. There was much effort on her father's part to speak.

'Are you all right?'

He blinked.

The baby started to cry.

'You're wondering about this baby? That Zokho, I'll wring her neck when I find her. Where is she? Did she feed you?'

He shook his head to say that she hadn't.

'Who changed your blankets?'

He looked to the window.

'Twa?'

Her father nodded.

'He gave you something to eat?'

The effort to communicate was too much, and Wynand Roos closed his eyes.

'The doctor says you're to rest and not to worry about

anything,' Roeloff said. 'Twa and I will manage. Oom Otto says he's seen this before. You have to believe that you'll be your old self again soon.' He turned to Neeltje. 'I'll start the fire, the baby's hungry. My, my, listen to him!'

'Check the cow in the barn, Roff. For milk for him.' She didn't want to voice her fear in front of her father that the milk cow too might have been taken.

Roeloff was glad of the time alone, to grasp fully everything that had happened. A son. Zokho. The sheep. If Zokho was gone, he'd caused it. She'd warned him, begged him to take her away. Her fears had been right: he had cheated on her with his thoughts. But that hadn't been so when they'd talked. Now, she had drawn the line between them, and her actions were beyond his experience. A mother leaving her own child. Nothing could justify that, but it was possible that she had been captured. He had to know.

He found the cow, heavy with milk, standing uncomfortably in the stall. She hadn't been milked, and mooed gratefully at his approach. He was glad that the barn had been overlooked by the raiders and that at least they had milk. Drawing the bucket underneath the huge udder, he set to work. A thick froth quickly filled the container. When the stream thinned to a trickle, he patted the cow affectionately and led her out of the barn to the back of the house where there was grass.

He took the milk into the kitchen. Neeltje already had warm water in a basin and was washing the baby, who was crying at the top of his lungs. He watched while she dried and wrapped him in soft flannel cloths, fashioning something to wrap around his little bottom from an old towel she'd torn in half.

'Tomorrow I'll think of how to dress him so that he doesn't kick everything off. Did you get milk?'

'Yes.'

'What will we put it in?'

The thought occurred to him for the first time: they had milk, but nothing to put it in to feed the baby.

'Do you have any medicine bottles?'

'We bought druppels last year from Stoffel. I'll have a look.'

'Do it quickly. Look at him, his face is red with his efforts, he's hungry. I'll fit something over the bottle.'

'What?'

'Something that can stretch over the mouth of the bottle, with a hole in it.'

'You have something like that?'

'I'll make it out of a piece of soft hide. In the meantime, let's see what you have.'

Neeltje disappeared behind the partition and came back with several small bottles. He selected one and examined the cork.

'I'll make a small hole in this. Just make sure it's on properly, otherwise the milk will seep out onto his face.'

'It's too hard, it will hurt his mouth.'

'I can't do anymore tonight. Tomorrow he'll have a proper bottle. Neeltje?'

'Yes?'

'I would be grateful if you could keep him here for the night, if it's not too much trouble. I must look for Zokho.'

'Don't worry, I'll be happy to look after him. What will you call him?'

'Harman.'

She looked down at the child in her arms.

'Harman,' she tried the name out. 'Harman's a good name for him. Strong.'

'It's the name of my grandfather. You will look after him, then, tonight?'

'Yes.'

He looked at her one last time with his child in her arms. It was what he wanted, only not this way.

'Good night, then. Here's the bottle. Don't make the milk too warm, and mix some water with it.'

She smiled.

'Don't worry.'

The baby had fallen asleep, tired from crying, and she put him down while she prepared something for her father. She had just finished feeding her father when the infant woke up. She picked him up and sat down with him on her bed, putting the bottle to his mouth. The cork didn't feel the same as a nipple, and he turned away, crying, the milk dripping onto his face. She didn't know what to do. What if she couldn't feed him? In desperation, she opened the front of her bodice. Her breasts were small, the nipples erect. She was willing to do anything. She stuck one in his mouth. He sucked greedily, and the suction caused strange sensations in her belly and breasts. She could see that the baby would soon discover that the breast was dry, and she let a few drops from the bottle trickle down onto her breast towards the nipple, where his lips sucked them up. She didn't know if it would help, if it would be too little or too much, or if he would choke. But it worked, and she sat with the bottle poised over her breast, trickling just the right number of drops over her breast. Finally, Harman's eyes closed, and he slept. She looked down at the soft hair, the small mouth still fastened to her breast. She'd never held a baby in her arms before.

'You are beautiful, Harman,' she said softly. 'One day old, and already you have stolen a heart.'

That night she had little sleep. She did not know where to put Harman—next to her, on top of her, under her arm. And he was awake several times, crying for milk.

Next morning, she was hanging out washing when Roeloff came towards her leading his mare.

'Did you find her?' Neeltje asked.

'I found her tracks. But there's no good news about the sheep. The raiders divided the flock and went off in two directions to confuse us and to move faster. Twa went north-west after one lot. I told you he would have gone after them. A smaller party went east. Of course, they could have doubled back and be right here in the vicinity.'

'Which way are you headed?'

'I'll go after Zokho, then north. How's your father?'

'He drank some soup this morning. I think we'll hear him talk before the end of the week.'

'That's good. And Harman? I hope he wasn't too much trouble. How did the feeding go?'

She blushed.

'Not well?'

'He wouldn't take the bottle.'

'What did you do?'

'Well—I—you will have to make something to fit on the bottle when you come back. I managed. He has a little swelling and redness around his navel, but he slept well. He's hungry every few hours.'

Roeloff smiled.

'He sounds greedy. He has his mother's mouth, yes? And her eyes?'

Neeltje turned back to wringing out clothes and spreading them over the branches of a tree.

He realised he'd said the wrong thing.

'Neeltje?'

'If she wants to return to her people, why do you want to bring her back? Perhaps she's not happy here.'

'I want to know why she left and why she left Harman by himself. It's also possible that she was captured.'

Neeltje dried her hands on her apron.

'I never thought of that. How long will you be?'

'I don't know. When I find the sheep.'

'Come in, and I'll give you some food to take with you.'

He followed her into the house. Harman was wrapped in blankets, and lying on a pile of folded clothing on the kitchen table. Roeloff looked at the sleeping infant, marvelling at the miracle he and Zokho had created. His own flesh and blood. Who would the baby take after, his father or his mother? Would there be in him something of the man whose name he bore?

'How much food should I pack?' Neeltje cut into his thoughts.

'Enough for three days. Maybe four.'

'As long as that?'

'If I find the sheep—you know how long it will take to walk them back.'

Neeltje stood in the doorway to see him off. Her life had changed since Roeloff's arrival. She was no longer satisfied.

Out in the veld, Roeloff headed in a northerly direction. It had been easy at first to follow the tracks, but by noon he had lost them over stony terrain. He spent the afternoon riding around trying to pick up the trail, but it was useless. Either he'd missed something, or Zokho had fooled him and was even then watching him from some hiding place, laughing at his ineptness. He could take the easy way and tell himself that he'd done what he could, let her go, then simply look for the sheep and head home. But he couldn't. He wanted to see her eyes when she told him why she'd done what she had; he wanted to hear it from her own lips. He wanted to know that he had not made a mistake.

He thought of Neeltje. Headstrong, but soft-hearted. Looking after his son. How had all this happened? What force had steered him towards the Cederberg and the Roos farm? How could he have feelings for both of them? He'd grown up with Zokho, but Neeltje was the one who understood his Africaander heart.

He decided not to waste any more time in the area. He would travel towards the Hantam, his own birthplace, and look for the Sonqua behind the mountains. If Zokho was going there, he would find her along the way; if not, he would find out from the Sonqua if they knew anything about who might have taken the sheep.

He rode steadily throughout the day, setting the horse out to graze once in the afternoon. There was nothing slowing him down, and by nightfall he had covered quite a distance. He camped near a clump of trees, built a fire, and sat down to a supper of biltong and water. It felt strange in the inky silence without Twa, the sounds of nocturnal predators his only company. Presently, he fell asleep with his back against a tree, the gun between his knees. He woke up once to see four pairs of eyes glowing in the dark, and threw a stone in their direction. The onlookers scampered off and he closed his eyes again, kicking wood onto the fire.

On the second day, late in the afternoon, he reached the Hantamberge. Smoke was furling through a patch of trees, and he realised that he had arrived at a camp. The sound of his horse's hooves on the hard ground would alert them and send them hiding, so he got off the horse, covering the last mile by foot. Twa said you could be almost on top of the Sonqua and not know they were there, so naturally they blended with their surroundings. As he drew nearer, he heard chanting and clapping. He hoped it was the right tribe.

But he was not as careful as he thought he had been, for one of the children, playing on the perimeter of the camp, ran back to camp and warned them of his approach. The music stopped and a hush fell over the group.

'Eyes of the Sky!'

He had come to the right place.

Those who had never seen him watched in awe as a tall figure clothed in the same sun-baked colours as the Karoo, white hair flowing off broad shoulders, came striding towards them.

He came upon the skerms suddenly in a clearing behind a clump of trees, to find the largest group of yellow-skinned hunters he'd ever seen. He recognised some of the faces.

Koerikei detached himself from the group.

'Eyes of the Sky. We are honoured by your visit.'

Roeloff greeted him and nodded to all those around him.

'You are wondering why I am here.'

'We have no sheep. We kept our promise to stay off your land.'

'I know.'

'What brings you here, Eyes of the Sky?' Toma came forward, not as patient as the others to wait for the visitor to speak.

Roeloff looked at the young hunter.

'I'm looking for Zokho.'

It was the last thing they expected to hear.

'Zokho? Why are you looking for her? She ran away long ago.'

'She came to me.'

The voices rose up as one.

'To you?' Koerikei asked.

'There's a child. She left him by himself, scarcely a few hours old.'

They looked at each other in disbelief.

'The two of you? A child?' It was all too incredible.

'You're brave to come here after taking one of our own,' Toma said.

'I didn't take her. She came to me, of her own free will.'

'And left you too, the same way. That is Zokho.'

An old man came limping away from the group. Roeloff recognised the bent figure of Limp Kao.

'You remember Limp Kao?' Koerikei asked. 'He's blind, but he sees farther than most of us. He tells us, old father, that Zokho has been with him. There is a child. Now she's run away.'

Limp Kao nodded.

'Come, we'll sit,' Koerikei said. 'The day will be long. We will talk.'

Roeloff noticed that they had been standing in a circle around someone lying on the ground. He looked more closely and saw that it was a young girl, several months pregnant, with a man dressed in skins, vines wound around his legs, bent over her.

'I've interrupted something.'

'A healing ceremony. It is over. This girl is Toma's wife. She's possessed by bad spirits. Toma has not been lucky with his wives. This one also has her head filled with devils.'

Roeloff looked at Toma.

'Was the ceremony successful?'

Toma didn't respond.

'We will know tomorrow, if the healer takes on her sickness,' Koerikei said. 'If not, we'll try again with the new moon. Come, let us sit with Limp Kao at my fire. You have come on a good day; we have killed an eland.'

The arena cleared quickly and people returned to their hearths. He sat with Koerikei and Tau and Limp Kao at their fire and shared the meat the hunter handed him on the end of a stick. The leg was roasted to perfection, falling off the bone. He was so hungry, he would have eaten pofadder if it were offered. He noticed the manners of his host, the calm of the others. Koerikei offered first, taking the smallest piece for himself. Roeloff wondered at the harmony of these people, living so closely together. He had questions, but felt it intrusive to speak. After the meal, Tau handed around an ostrich egg container and they each had a swallow of muddy water.

'I haven't eaten this well in a long time,' Roeloff said, meaning it. 'Thank you.'

Koerikei busied himself with the small branches of wood at his hearth and tried not to show how much this pleased him. They were sitting on opposite sides of the fire. Roeloff studied him. His feet were cracked and dirt-ridden like Twa's, but Koerikei was many years younger, his finely-muscled body glistening in the firelight. Roeloff was impressed by his modesty. Koerikei had kind words for his wife, and seemed to weigh things carefully in his mind before speaking. A good trait, his grandfather would have said. *A man who blusters along like the wind makes a lot of unnecessary noise, but one who measures his words is sure to have something important to say.*

'You have given us much to talk about around our fires, Eyes of the Sky,' Limp Kao said at last. 'We have not met anyone like you before.'

Koerikei smiled. He agreed with the old father.

'We talk always of the one with the wind in his eye and the rain in his heart; how, after everything that had happened, he still left us one of his father's sheep. We said he was clever. And just. The white man has not treated us kindly. Every day he pushes us farther and farther to the sun. We are not selfish about his taking a piece of our land, but he wants the fruit of the soil, and the animals on it, and doesn't want us to have anything. Look how high up we are. This was all ours before he came here with his guns. Where does he want us to go? The gods bring water, they bring animals, but they are not growing any more land. Soon we will fall off the edge of the earth.'

Roeloff took out a piece of tobacco and crumbled it on a dry leaf which he flattened and folded. He lit it and passed it to the old man.

Limp Kao drew the smoke deep into his lungs.

'We're a people with nothing, and ask only to live in peace. We wouldn't survive without understanding. Sharing. If you have a buck, I eat with you. Tomorrow, when you have nothing, you eat with me. You said once that borrowing is taking with permission. Afterwards, you give it back. We have talked about this among ourselves. I ask you, Eyes of the Sky, who is the true lender of things? Who takes it back? It's easy to talk with a full belly, but what would you do, if *you* were the owner, and we the intruders coming to rob you?'

'I would be true to myself.'

Limp Kao considered this. 'To be true to yourself with a gun pointed at your heart, is dangerous.'

'It is, but you can't change who you are. My grandfather spoke to me once about freedom. He said to beware of one who says he can give it to you. When he says that, he's talking only of a new way to put you in chains.'

Limp Kao nodded.

'He was wise, your father's father. Freedom comes from in here,' he touched his chest. 'Without it, you die.' He took a last pull on the tobacco, and handed it back to Roeloff. 'Now we must talk about Zokho. You have come a long way. What will you do when you find her?'

'Ask my question and leave.'

'What is your question?'

'Why she did it.'

'The answer will not please you, Eyes of the Sky. Zokho has lost favour with the gods, her spirit is tainted. But if she did it, she did it to protect herself. Our way is hard for others to understand. A mother who gives birth to two must choose between them if one's to survive. A child with a deformity, is buried to spare him. The law of the veld demands it.'

'What would justify leaving a child while his father is not there to protect him?'

'Nothing. I don't know why she did it. A jackal doesn't understand the laziness of a python, but he stays out of its way nevertheless. Forget it, and forget Zokho. Take your father's father's advice.'

They sat for a long time in silence. By some unspoken agreement, several people got up from their hearths and congregated in the centre of the circle of huts to build a fire.

'They will put on a show in your honour,' Koerikei said. 'The hunters will entertain us with their stories. Toma and Gau killed this eland, they will be first. You will hear how Toma almost got pierced by his horns. He's the best storyteller, and has many scars to prove it.'

Roeloff sat with his hosts at the fire, caught up in the merriment. The tales were acted out with dancing and drama to mimic the frightened animals, hunters throwing themselves flat on the ground, writhing in agony. The festivities continued into the early hours of the morning with children running back and forth between hearths.

The next day he woke up with the heat on his back, lying between Limp Kao and Koerikei.

'I have to thank you, Koerikei and old father. I must go before the sun gets too high.'

'You will not join in the hunt?' Koerikei asked.

'I have people waiting for me. But, I have one last question.'

The hunters waited.

'Do you know who might have stolen sheep ...' He calculated quickly the distance on foot to the Cederberg. '... about five days that way?' he pointed south.

'Our people are between the Hantam and the big river. It is not us.'

'I know. But do you know where I might look? Are there Sonqua down in that area?'

Koerikei's face pleated into a warm smile.

'Sonqua is everywhere, Eyes of the Sky. Sometimes you're standing right in front of him and don't even know that he's there.'

Roeloff knew the hunter's concern.

'I won't harm them, Koerikei. I've never harmed your people. I just want the sheep back.'

Koerikei looked down at his feet, then looked up slowly.

'We know of a group on the red mountains.'

Koerikei was referring to the Cederberg mountains. Roeloff felt hope surge in his heart.

'The mountains are many, and long. It would take days to find them.'

'You have to go right to the end. When you look down

from the top and see grass and trees and the land changing, you will know that you have found them.'

Roeloff got on his horse.

'Thank you.'

'You are sure you will not stay longer? We have seen springbok not far from here. With your gun we can kill one and have food for many days.'

Roeloff smiled.

'I'll come again, and we'll hunt. If I find anything on the way out, I'll shoot twice to let you know I've killed one.'

Tau handed him an ostrich egg container.

'You can spare it?'

'Yes.'

Roeloff knew she was lying, but took it out of respect.

'Go safely, Eyes of the Sky. If you see rain, tell it to come this way.'

'Thank you, and thank you, old father.'

Then he was gone, galloping quickly over the veld. The visit had refreshed him, rested his horse, and he was eager to find the sheep and then go home. An old route he'd once taken with Twa came up on his left, and a feeling of longing welled up in him. He was less than an hour from the place where he was born. His thoughts went for a moment to his family, the people on Kloot's Nek, then he forced them out as he'd done so many times in the past.

It was late afternoon when he stopped near a clump of thorn bushes to rest and have something to eat. What had attracted him to this particular spot he didn't know, but he found a recent upheaval of sand, as if something had been unearthed and reburied. He looked more closely and saw that someone had squatted there, the heels dug deeply into the sand, the footprints narrow and small.

He got down on his knees and started to burrow with his hands. Minutes later he lifted out an ostrich egg from the sand, warm from nestling in the baked earth, with a tiny hole in it and a wad of dry grass stuck in it to stop it up. The hunters had ostrich eggs with water buried all over the Karoo for passing travellers.

'So you've been here, and had a drink.'

He reburied the egg and got to his feet. He was tempted to leave there some memento of his presence, but decided against it. They would think the water poisoned, and it wasn't his intention to thwart a lifesaving tradition.

Where are you, Zokho? Are you near?

He walked around, inspecting the ground, and found tracks leading to a clump of bushes hardly two hundred yards to his left. His heart hammered against his chest.

'Zokho!'

There was no answer, only the soft swoop of a lone vulture overhead.

He walked towards the spot where he thought she was hiding. It was different from the time he'd found her alone in the veld. Then there was wild expectation and Zokho had run to him. Now there was distance and guilt.

He reached the bush and went behind it. She wasn't there. He went to a second, smaller bush, and found her crouched with her head between her knees. If he hadn't been looking for her, he would have gone right past, so well did she blend in with her surroundings.

'So. This is where you have run to.'

She got up and, without acknowledging him, started to walk. The kaross was tied around her waist, and there was no sign in the taut belly to show that she'd recently given birth, except for the breasts, large and pearlike, streaking milk.

He came up alongside. 'I'm talking to you.'

She continued walking.

He stepped in front of her.

'Why have you run away? Left our baby?'

She scratched at something in the sand with her stick.

'I'm talking to you, look at me!'

The digging stick dropped from her hand and she looked up. Had she been angry or hurt, it would have shown feeling, but she looked at him as if she was seeing him for the first time.

'You have nothing to say?'

She took the kaross from her waist and threw it over her shoulders to cover her breasts, closing herself off to him.

'I told you I didn't want to stay on the farm.'

'That's why you left our child by himself?'

'That and other things.'

'What other things?'

'You know very well what other things.'

'You had our baby. You left him unattended. Anything could have happened to him. What kind of mother does that?'

Defiance crept into her eyes.

'What is your complaint? You want the white man's daughter, you can have her now. Zokho wasn't good enough to marry.'

'If you were angry with me, that's one thing. Didn't you care about him?'

'I don't want him! And I left him the night he was born. Under a tree for the jackals! Your cripple saved him from death!'

The words struck at his heart and he flinched. 'Jackals? What are you talking about?'

'Ask Twa. He'll be happy to tell you how he brought the baby back to life the next day.'

Roeloff looked at her. He was stunned. The Zokho he knew was playful and innocent, there was no evil in her. He got on his horse. What there had been between them died there in the veld, by her actions, her words. What she'd done amounted to the same as stopping his heart beating with her hands. No law could make it right. Not the Sonqua's, not anyone's. She was out of his hands. Even if any part of him felt sorry, he could not do anything.

'I've hurt you now. Are you satisfied?'

He was too stunned to respond.

Zokho pulled her kaross about her and stepped past him to continue her journey.

He sat in the saddle and watched her, a solitary steenbok who knew her way in the veld. That was the difference between them. Not that she was Sonqua, that her gods were not his, but that she could walk away. Unhurried. Free. The old father was right, he didn't understand. He didn't want to.

'Goodbye, Smoke in the Eyes,' he said softly to himself.

The kaross grew smaller and smaller in the distance. When she had become one with the veld, he turned and rode steadily into the wind, letting it dry his eyes.

Chapter Thirteen

Neeltje waited six days for his return with the sheep and ten more for him to emerge from his quarters after a sickness that bore no physical evidence other than silence. She knew from Twa, who had come back two weeks before, that Zokho had left and wasn't returning, but she didn't press for details. Twa knew more than he was saying, having met Roeloff on his way back from the Hantamberge, and she could see for herself that Roeloff was torn by some private pain.

She was in the kitchen holding Harman, keeping an eye on her father who was sitting in a chair near the door cutting out a pair of veldskoene for himself out of animal hide. The paralysis had weakened his limbs and he couldn't stand up for long, but he had regained his speech and had recovered all his strength in his arms. He was using this time to make shoes, oil his guns, mend the tears in the wagon's canvas top, and generally to fix things for which he had no time when he was up and about.

'Pa, are you strong enough to hold Harman? I see Roeloff out there, I want to talk to him. I also want Twa to slaughter a chicken for supper. Our chickens have increased, we have more now than we have sheep. I can put Harman down if you don't think you can manage.'

'I can manage.'

She put the infant in his arms and watched for a moment. She had not thought her father so soft-hearted; what with Harman a baster and not even family.

'Tell him I want to see him.'

'Not now.'

'Why not?'

'He hasn't even come to see his own son. I want him to come when he's ready.'

'I want to talk to him about the sheep he's lost.'

'It will have to wait.'

'Zokho's not coming back?'

'I told you.'

'What about Harman?' he looked at the child in his arms. 'Will he grow up without a mother? When's his father coming to see him? He looks just like Roeloff. There's nothing of Zokho in him.'

'There is. His mouth and his eyes. The eyes are slanted like hers.'

'His hair and colouring's a Kloot. He'll be strong, this boy. The way he cries, he wakes up the devil.'

'You're sure you can manage, Pa? I'll come in soon to take him.' Straightening her apron, she tucked the loose strands of hair into the side of her kapje, and went out. Her father didn't have all his strength back, but there was nothing wrong with his mouth except for a slight slur. He could talk, and he had many questions. She had had to tell him about the raid when Roeloff and Twa came back separately with forty of the sixty sheep. They'd never found the party going east; only the band Twa had gone after and the ones Koerikei had said would be found at the end of the red mountains. She'd also had to tell her father about Zokho, why Harman was in the house with them and why she was looking after him. But she had no answers for why Roeloff hadn't come to see his son. She knew from Twa that he asked after Harman, but that was all.

It was the beginning of summer, and she caught a whiff of the scent of flowers growing down by the stream. It was late for sowing, but it was a beginning of sorts to see him out there. She'd only caught glimpses of him during the past week.

She walked down to the kraal and stood with her foot on the wooden post of the gate as she studied him, planting seeds a few hundred feet away on the other side. He had grown thinner, his gait telling of his grief. Presently, sensing someone behind him, he turned.

She waved.

He waved back, then continued with his work.

She was disappointed and walked slowly to the henhouse to choose a chicken for supper. Then she became angry. She walked to where Roeloff knelt, tamping down seeds in the field.

'Roeloff Kloot.'

He turned.

'You have been back two weeks and you haven't come once to see your son, or ask about him. Is it that you don't care now that his mother's gone?'

He was surprised at the confrontation.

'I hear he's doing well in your care.'

'He needs his father, and his father needs him. His father

must snap out of whatever it is that's holding him back from living his life again. What's perished is perished.'

'His father doesn't need reminding of his responsibilities.' He returned to tamping and stamping, harder than before. 'And watch you don't hasten your own fate, Neeltje Roos,' he said darkly.

'My fate doesn't scare me.'

'No?'

There was silence. Suddenly she realised what he meant.

'Prepare yourself. Before winter I will come to you.'

The colour rose in her face.

'You will have to go to Roodezand for supplies,' she said hurriedly, in an effort to cover her shock. They needed supplies, but it wasn't what she'd come to talk to him about. 'We're down to the last salt and rice. I also need needles and thread and cloth. If I cut up any more of my clothes for Harman, I'll not have a dress left to stand in.'

He smiled a thin smile, the humour not reaching his eyes.

'That's perhaps not so bad. It is said that a woman with too many layers of calico suffers the same fate as one who lives with his head in the sand. And we mustn't forget that Harman's a baster.'

Neeltje raised her chin in defiance.

'He's one if you make him so.'

'No, Neeltje, his heart be half bosjesman, that be who he is. You have to be sure of your feelings. How you will feel when he looks at you with his mother's eyes.'

'He be your son, he be mine.'

Roeloff got up. His eyes looked deeply into hers and she felt dizzy under his gaze.

'I'll go to Roodezand in two weeks. When I return, I'll come and see you.'

'There won't be any memories and spectres claiming your soul?'

'No living thing will claim me. You have feeling for me, Neeltje? You have taken Harman. Will you take me?'

Neeltje wanted to cry with happiness. Only that morning she had tossed in her bed wondering when he was going to get over grieving for Zokho; now he was coming for opsit in a few weeks' time. What more did she want?

'I have feeling for you, yes.'

'A little?'

'More than a little. Look!—that dust cloud near the caves. It's a wagon. Someone's coming. It must be Stoffel.'

Roeloff squinted his eyes.

'It's not the trader, it's a woman.'

'The widow Reijnhardt. Oh my. She came.'

'What's wrong? Your father doesn't like her?'

'He's amused by her spirit, but she's not to his taste, you'll see.' She saw Twa talking to some of the Sonqua who were from the same band who had stolen the sheep, and who had later come asking for work. She called to him. 'Go to the house, Twa, and wait for me there.'

The wagon drew up in front of them. Marta Reijnhardt stepped down in a cloud of skirts and petticoats, onto the back of a young slave kneeling on his hands and knees. Her figure was ample, with huge breasts decorated by a rainbow of hankies tucked in the front of her dress; her eyes were flinty, inquisitive, and there was a prominent fuzz on her lip. The bonnet matched her outfit, and her hair, heavily pomaded, had two flattened crescents of curl on her forehead.

'Neeltje!' She tapped the slave with her cane to indicate he could get up. 'It's wonderful to see you. Otto's right, you *have* grown up. He's my doctor, too, you know. When I heard you had come looking for me and went to see Otto Lieberband, I went immediately to see him. He told me about your father.'

'How are you, Tante Marta? This is Roeloff Kloot.'

Roeloff came forward and extended his hand.

Marta Reijnhardt looked at him, and for a moment Neeltje thought she was going to tap Roeloff with the cane.

'Otto's told me about you. I believe you have family in the Cape. Not married yet? Neeltje?'

Neeltje blushed.

'He's the bijwoner, Tante Marta. He looks after things for Pa. You've had a safe journey?'

'Yes. I have a new driver, Agt. He understands Dutch and was able to follow instructions.'

'Agt?'

'Agt tenen. He has eight toes. The two big ones were cut off when he ran away from a previous owner.'

Neeltje tried not to look at the slave's feet. She had seen black people before, but not one with as polished a sheen as this young boy. And he was handsome. She'd thought slaves had thick features and woolly hair. Agt was as fine-featured as any white person, only his skin was black. She wondered how Marta Reijnhardt could come on such a long and perilous journey with only a child to protect her.

'I'll tell Pa you're here. Roeloff will help you with your things.'

'How's he now?'

'Almost recovered. I'll see you inside, Tante Marta.'

Inside the house she took Harman from her father and wrapped him in a blanket, handing him to Twa.

'Keep him in Roeloff's quarters. He's fed and changed, so he'll be all right.'

Twa took the infant and left.

'Marta Reijnhardt's here, Pa. She's come to visit.'

'What?'

'Otto told her about the accident. We also stopped at her farm at Jan Dissels Vlei when we were there, but she wasn't home.'

'The news of my illness will reach all the way to Graaff-Reinet, just you wait. Of all times to have to be civil! Why are you sending Harman with Twa?'

'She'll ask too many questions, and I don't want to answer them now.'

'Why not?'

'There's something I have to tell you.'

'What?'

'Later. In the meantime, it's better if she knows nothing.'

'What do you want to tell me?'

'Here she comes. Try to look a little friendlier, Pa.'

Marta Reijnhardt stepped inside and filled the kitchen with her scent.

'Wynand!' She came gushing towards him. 'I heard of your illness. How are you? Can you talk?'

'I can talk, Marta, well enough, and it's not my hearing

that's affected. What's that smell of death and flowers you're wearing?'

Neeltje blanched at her father's unkindness.

'You haven't changed,' the widow laughed heartily, leaning over to embrace him. 'I can see it won't be necessary for my remedy, a man with your spirit. But I've brought you dried peaches and beskuit. You enjoyed them last time.'

'I'm going out to talk to Twa,' Neeltje said, heading for the door. 'I need a chicken for tonight's supper. Make yourself comfortable, Tante Marta. I'll be in soon to make coffee.'

'How many times are you going out there to ask him about that chicken?' Wynand asked.

Neeltje smiled. She knew that although her father complained about the widow, he enjoyed their verbal sparring. Marta Reijnhardt was not to his liking physically, but she was funny and good-natured, and the only woman who stood up to him. Her father needed a little company.

'It's Sunday, Pa. We have chicken on Sundays. And Tante Marta's here.'

She returned to where Roeloff was helping Agt unload the wagon and wondered how long the widow was going to stay and what there was in all those bundles lined up at her feet. She didn't mind Tante Marta. The widow never came visiting without having something for her. She still had the brush and comb from the last visit.

'I've sent Harman to your quarters with Twa, Roff. You'll have to look after him yourself for a few days. It's time you two met, anyway. I'll still feed him and change him, but until I've told Pa, and while the widow's here—do you understand?'

'Yes. When will you tell him?'

'When she's gone. Before you leave for Roodezand. He'll want things, and so will I. I've made some clothes for Harman out of some of my old dresses, but I will need cloth and pins and extra things for him.'

'Do you think he'll agree?'

She looked at him in surprise.

'Pa looks on you as a son. You've done a lot on his farm.'

'There's Harman. His mother's Sonqua. People will know what he is.'

'You haven't seen Pa with him. Pa was upset that I sent him to the back with Twa. You would think it was his grandson.'

Roeloff put his hand on hers.

'You'll not regret your decision to take me, Neeltje. I have no earthly possessions, but my hands and heart will be yours.'

Chapter Fourteen

'My God, that child doesn't stop crying,' David said angrily. 'People can't hear themselves think. Keep her quiet, can't you?'

Elsie looked at her son-in-law. David had had a headstart drinking witblits with Jan in the barn, and was unceasing in his bullying. The flour on Soela's face hadn't camouflaged the yellow and green bruises under her eyes.

'Give her here,' Joubert said. 'Let's see what's ailing my grandchild. Come to Oupa.'

Soela handed Bessie to him.

'Not over the food,' David bellowed.

'I'll give her to you after we've eaten,' Soela brought the infant back to her own lap.

Elsie looked at David. 'Perhaps you should have something to eat to calm your nerves.'

'I would, but it looks like we're waiting for someone.'

'We are. Lourens.'

'The knecht is eating with us?'

'Yes.'

'Aah,' David grinned, turning to Diena next to him. 'Lourens is the special guest. Pa, would you have a knecht at your table at Christmas time?'

'Stop it,' Willem Kloot said. It had been an unpleasant

journey travelling to the Jouberts, with Soela bruised and wounded and not saying a word, and David saying too much. He felt trapped between his son's obnoxiousness and his daughter-in-law's suffering.

'Am I misbehaving, then?'

'You've had too much to drink.'

'It's your other son, Pa. He's the one who can't hold his liquor. Remember him? What he did?'

The room went quiet.

'My word, it seems I've said the wrong thing again.'

'I would stop now if I were you,' Willem Kloot warned.

Drieka recognised the tone in her husband's voice. The day would end in chaos if David persisted in his bullying behaviour.

There was a knock at the door.

'Come in, come in,' Joubert said, grateful to turn the conversation. 'You know everyone, Lourens. Sit down. Take a seat there, between Diena and Soela. We were waiting for you.'

Lourens took off his hat. His long hair, dark and straight, fell in his face.

'I was just finishing off. When I looked again, the sun was behind the kopje. I've barely had time to make myself presentable.'

'You look fine,' Elsie said, noting the drops still on the beard where he must have hurriedly dipped his head in the barrel. She looked across the table at her daughters. Diena's cheeks were flushed, even Soela had brightened slightly. She could see the attraction of young Lourens. He was a bachelor. There were no bachelors around, except for Pietie

Retief's half-witted grandson, Hennie. Lourens also took an interest in women's things, having recently enquired about a quilt he'd seen Diena tack and embroider. He was keen to have one like it for his mother. And a man who had thought for his mother ... that was the best measure of his character. Diena said he would be coming soon to speak to Jan.

'Well, now that we're all here—you comfortable there, Lourens?' David asked.

Lourens, unaware of the trouble between the Kloots, was talking to Diena, and only caught the end of the question.

'Sorry?'

'I said, are you comfortable there? Next to my wife.'

Lourens looked at the other faces.

'Yes.'

'Good. What part of the pig do you want?' He had the knife poised over the roasted haunch.

'Just carve it,' Willem said curtly.

Bessie, startled by the angry note in her grandfather's voice, started crying all over again.

'I'll take her, Soela. You eat,' Elsie said. 'You look tired.'

'We will not inconvenience anyone during supper,' David said. 'It's Soela's child. She'll look after her.'

'You take her, then,' Soela blurted. 'Do something instead of just issuing orders.'

Everyone looked down at their plates. They had never heard Soela answer her husband like this before.

David's eyes narrowed. 'You have spirit,' he smiled. 'Why don't you try that when we're alone?'

'That's enough,' Willem said. 'I'll not listen to any more. What's the matter with you?'

'Nothing, Pa—is there?'

Elsie took Bessie from Soela and sat down. She felt bad for Willem. His son had embarrassed him, she knew at what cost. David was unpleasant and was harassing his wife and being rude to the knecht on purpose. Asking him what part of the pig he wanted. Who did he think he was? He was a pig himself. David felt her stare and looked up. The poisonous look she gave him left no doubt that whatever tenuous link had been established between them was gone.

The meal was a sombre affair, with long faces and awkward talk, not the celebration the Jouberts had had in mind when they invited the Kloots and slaughtered a pig they had specially bought and fattened for the occasion. It wasn't only Christmas they were celebrating, but also the changes Joubert had made to his house, building on an extra room, and fitting doors made with wood he'd brought back all the way from Stellenbosch.

'Well, that's that,' Jan Joubert said when it was over, raising himself from the bench. 'We'll take our brandy on the stoep, a man can suffocate in this heat.'

The women were only too glad to be rid of them and huddled around clearing dishes, making coffee, each one waiting for the other to speak. Soela went inside to put Bessie to sleep and Drieka opened the subject.

'You saw what happened. That was nothing compared with what he does to her at home. It's getting really bad.'

'How did she get those bruises on her face?' Elsie asked.

'It was about the servant, Katrijn, the one who had the baby. Soela went to see her. She had seen David with Katrijn some weeks before, and accused him of being the father. He hit her in front of the servant and dragged her out by her hair. By the time Willem got there, it was all over, and she was unconscious.'

'I've never hated anyone,' Elsie said. 'It's wrong to hate, the Lord forbids it. But he's raised ugly feelings in me—I can't even bear to look at him. I don't know why I never saw this in him before.'

'You saw it, Ma,' Diena said. 'You didn't want her to go back, remember? You thought he would change. We all hoped for the best for Soela, though we never spoke about it.'

'He's dangerous, Elsie, and getting worse,' Drieka said. 'Something's got to be done. Willem's sick at this whole business. He can't control David, and you know his health isn't good. And he already blames himself.'

'What do you mean?'

'For Roeloff. He feels that David is his punishment.'

'I never did believe that Roeloff killed that stallion.'

'He didn't,' Diena said.

'How do you know?' Elsie asked.

'Sanna said Hennerik saw David and Soela in the barn.'

'I thought it was Roeloff with Soela in the barn.'

'That was earlier. Later, while we were in the kitchen and Roeloff was sleeping, David and Soela went out there. He forced her. When Soela cried, he hit her and said it was to remind her of her sin. He was later seen coming back to the barn by himself. Hennerik was too afraid to say anything.'

'Did you know this, Drieka?'

'I only found out later.'

'Did you tell Willem?'

'What good would that do? Roeloff had already gone.

And things are bad enough. The other day David raised his hand to his own father.'

'It would help Willem, if he knew. That's what's eating at him. If he knew for certain it wasn't Roeloff, he could still do something about making amends. He could send the kommando to look for him, make things right. Willem has to right that wrong. He probably knows in his heart that it wasn't him. Roeloff was always his favourite, Harman told me. That boy reminded him of Lisbeth.' The reference to Willem Kloot's first wife had popped out before she could stop herself.

Drieka coloured a little.

'Then why was he always at him? Roeloff could do no right in his eyes.'

'Who knows? People sometimes do things they don't understand. Why does your brother do what he does?'

'What do you mean?'

'Never mind.'

'I want to know what you mean.'

'I'm sorry, Drieka. That was wrong of me. Forget what I said. All I meant is that everyone has faults. We have no quarrel. Tell Willem what you know, it's not too late.'

'I don't know if he would do anything. You know how he is.'

'Whether he will or not, you have to calm his mind. He's racked with guilt. Now, I must go talk to Soela.'

Elsie found Soela in her childhood room, lying next to Bessie on the bed.

'I've not seen you since October, Soela. You sent no word about how things were going.'

'Things are as you see them, Ma.'

'I can see from those bruises on your face. What did he do, take his fist to you?'

Soela didn't answer.

'There's too much hate. He can't forget the past,' Elsie said.

'I've paid for the past. Over and over. I no longer feel bad about what I did.'

Elsie was not a demonstrative woman. She stood at the foot of the bed and studied her daughter. Soela had changed; her dress had a button missing, and her hair, usually neatly brushed and left loose for special occasions, was a dirty yellow plait tied with an old ribbon. She took the thick braid in her hand, feeling the plaiting with her fingers.

'I'm sorry I sent you back.'

'It's not your fault.'

'It is. You didn't want to go. It was your future I considered, yours and Bessie's, but there is no future. You'll die early if you stay with him. You have to leave for your own sake.'

Soela looked hopeful for the first time.

'What are you saying, Ma?'

'This is your last night with him. You won't go back to Kloot's Nek. Tomorrow he goes home by himself.'

'I don't have to go back? Ever?'

'No.'

'Oh, Ma,' Soela hugged her.

'You and Bessie will be all right here. We're all here to help. There's just one thing.' She put her hands on Soela's shoulders and looked in her eyes. 'Lourens is going to speak to your father about Diena. I don't want you upsetting things.'

'Ma …'

'Your sister will take a husband. Diena has not yet been married. You've already had a chance.'

'Ma, I can't believe you're saying this to me. I've always known about Lourens and Diena. I'm happy for them, they're well suited.'

'Good. I just wanted you to know. Diena has always let you have things she's wanted for herself. But not this time, Soela. Lourens is going to be hers. Now, about tonight. There's no avoiding it; they are staying over. The men will drink themselves to a standstill and fall into bed. You're all right for the time being. In the morning, your father will talk to him.'

'What if Pa doesn't agree?'

'Your Pa will do as I say. Go to bed early and avoid him.'

The night ended as Elsie predicted, with the men drinking until they had passed out on the stoep. She had no idea of when anyone went to bed, but some time after midnight Elsie surfaced uneasily from her sleep. There was no moon, the air was thick and engulfing, and she lay for a few minutes in the stillness, wondering what had woken her up. Then she heard it, a scuffling. She turned to her husband, but Jan wasn't there. Was it him arguing with someone on the stoep? She got up and tiptoed to the door. All was quiet. She returned to bed, and tossed restlessly until finally she drifted off.

At dawn she was jerked out of her sleep by screams coming from the next room.

'... and I'll tell! ...' she heard Soela's voice.

She jumped out of bed and ran into the passage. Willem Kloot, gun in hand, was already at the closed bedroom door and so were her husband and Diena.

'Open up!' Jan Joubert ordered.

'You think I didn't see you? How you encouraged him? And refused me?' There was the sound of a slap, the thump of something heavy slamming into the wall.

Then Soela's voice, loud and shrill.

'Horse killer! You couldn't stand it that he was better than you!'

There was a moment's silence, then a crash of glass. Jan and Willem looked at each other, then put their shoulders to the thick wood of the door. The door gave suddenly, and the men fell over Soela, who was lying on the floor directly behind it, into the room.

'Stay out of this!' David snarled at his father and Joubert.

Willem looked at Soela, unconscious at his feet. David had the end of her plait in his hand.

'Go back,' Willem said.

David jerked the plait, and Soela's head knocked against his boot, blood seeping from her mouth.

'Step back! And let go of her hair!'

David picked up the mirror he'd slammed on Soela's head.

Willem raised his gun. 'David!' The sound of his voice crackled like gunfire over their heads.

'Don't do it, man!' Joubert pulled on his arm.

David had the broken glass poised over his head. He came forward to strike his father.

Willem shot him point blank in the heart.

The shot threw David against the wall, and he landed with a thud, his feet coming to rest in his own blood at Soela's head. There was silence, then screaming and crying as the women became hysterical. Willem Kloot stood over the body with the smoking gun, slack in his hand, shocked at what he'd done.

'I shot him. I shot my son.'

'It's not your fault, man. You had no choice,' Jan Joubert consoled him.

The gun dropped from Willem's hand. He turned and left the house.

When Pietie Retief got the news, he said there was a noose round Kloot's Nek. You couldn't throw kin out like dog bones and expect the Almighty to be satisfied. For all they knew, Roeloff had been eaten by lions, no one had heard from him. Kloot's Nek was cursed. Who would be next? And a father taking the life of his own son? No man could live with that. It wasn't over; death came in threes. He offered the use of his coffin, but David's legs were too long. Joubert, taking charge, knocked out the board at the foot of the coffin so that the cracked boots stuck out over the edge. According to Hennie, the grandson, when the field cornet arrived to take statements, Willem had barricaded himself up in the buitekamer and refused to speak.

'I always said that boy was his father's whip. Mark my words, Hennie,' Pietie Retief nodded sadly, 'there'll be no peace till he makes things right with Roff.'

Chapter Fifteen

Roeloff stood naked at a basin of water at the door to his quarters, scrubbing himself with a rough cloth and a bar of carbolic soap. Twa, rounding the corner, scoffed at the rigorous ministrations.

'Where you going, Kudu, polishing yourself like a leopard?' He'd already forgotten the scolding Roeloff had given him for the lamb he'd slaughtered for his own use.

'There's water. Why don't you give yourself a wash? You might like it.' He knew the hunter's views on washing and said it to tease him.

'What do I want to keep myself like the white man for? Sonqua's lazy, the white man says. He doesn't work, he doesn't sweat. White man's not lazy. He works, he sweats. He *has* to wash himself.'

Roeloff laughed.

'What do you think, Twa?' he pointed towards his clothes.

Twa looked at the new pants hanging on a hook, the white shirt. Roeloff had sold the elephant tusks in Roodezand and bought supplies, including blankets, things for the baby, and tobacco.

'The oubaas's daughter will not know this is you. And leaving your old friend to eat by himself, the inconsiderateness of young people.'

Roeloff let his body dry in the wind while he pulled the comb through his hair. Straight and wet, it reached down to his chest.

'My knife, Twa, over there, please.'

Twa felt the sharpness of the blade and handed the knife to him.

Roeloff bunched the wet hair together behind his head, and cut through the thick mane. He shook it loose, and it bobbed above his shoulders. He stepped into the dark pants, the white shirt, the new boots, then tied his hair back with a leather thong. Satisfied with his appearance, he put on the jacket. He'd never owned one before, and bought it big so he wouldn't have to buy another; the colour was good for both weddings and funerals.

'You look like a chief.'

'You think the oubaas will approve?'

'How can he not approve of one with the imagination to make such a good picture of himself? He'll not only give you his daughter, but all this land. And Twa will have quarters like yours, and two wives. It's cold here in the Cederberg in winter. A man needs two wives so he can slip himself in the middle.'

'Don't worry. Next time we go to Roodezand, we'll look for a woman for you.'

Neeltje stood at the window and watched him approach. For weeks she had waited, every day filled with the thrill of expectation. She didn't know anyone endowed with such beauty, such strength, his hair the colour of ripe mealies, his night-blue eyes that turned grey when troubled. Her feelings had run away with her head, stolen her sleep, sapped her reason. She had a feeling of lightness. She didn't have to eat, she was filled with energy. Roeloff was hers; the smell of him, the feel of him, everything. She hadn't thought any man could invoke such violent longing.

He knocked on the door and stepped into the kitchen.

'I'm here, Neeltje. For opsit.'

'You look ... grand, Roeloff. Those are fine clothes. Did you buy the entire shop in Roodezand?'

'Almost,' he laughed, slipping his hand into his pocket and taking out a pair of silky green ribbons. 'These are for you. I don't know about women's things, but I thought they would look good in your hair.'

'For me?' She was struck by the sweetness of the thought. He had bought her a gift.

'They're from overseas. They have a soft quality.'

'They must have cost as much as a bag of beans.'

He smiled at her practicality.

'A bag of beans is here today, gone tomorrow. These you'll always have. And don't save them. Wear them for me, Neeltje.'

'They're beautiful. Thank you.'

'Your father's here?'

'He ate supper early, he's inside with Harman. He'll come out later for a while before he turns in. We'll sit here in the kitchen, if it's all right. There's no other place.'

'The kitchen is good.'

It was warm and comfortable in the small room, the smell of roast meat reminding him suddenly of home.

'How long does one stay for opsit? It's very comfortable in here, I could sit with you all night.'

'Pa says until the candle burns out. The candle will burn for some time; I lit a new one.'

'You're smelling good, Neeltje.'

She blushed.

'The widow gave me some soap. She made it herself, with apple. Are you ready to eat?'

'And your dress? It's very becoming.'

'It's my mother's. Pa kept it till I was grown. I've never worn it.'

'You're wearing it tonight.'

'Yes.'

'Did you know your mother?'

'She died at my birth. Pa raised me. Pa and a Hottentot servant. And you? Twa said your mother died when you were six.'

'She was bitten by a pofadder.'

'That's horrible. Do you remember your mother?'

'I remember her hair. I always wanted to touch it. After her bath she let me brush it in front of the hearth, or let me watch while she brushed it. And her smell, I remember that, too.'

'I would have liked to have known my mother. What she looked like. I have no memories of her.'

'Mothers are different from fathers. After my father remarried, I had a sister, Vinkie. When I first saw you, I saw something of her in you. I liked you right away.'

'Me, too. A special liking?'

'Like a brother.'

'And Zokho?'

The smile went slowly from his eyes.

'I thought we wouldn't talk about Zokho.'

'We won't after this. She was special?'

'Yes.'

'It's over between you?'

'She lives on in Harman.'

'I know. But, in here,' she pointed to his heart, 'it's over?'

'You ask hard questions, Neeltje. What Zokho did I can never forgive.'

'That's not answering.'

'The pain will be there for a while, but I have you. I have feeling for you. Feeling to make you my wife. You will help me forget.'

'You are honest.'

'I have made mistakes. I'm hoping to make few with you. Now, Neeltje, I'm ready to be impressed by your food. What have you made?'

'Roast lamb and potatoes and, for later, beskuit.'

'You've spent all day in the kitchen.'

'No. I made the beskuit yesterday, the food this afternoon.' She walked to the hearth and turned the potatoes over in the pot, satisfied with their crispness. 'Sit down, I'll dish up.' She had buffed the plates and polished the spoons, but Roeloff was too hungry to notice. He ate everything that was put before him, wiping the plate clean with bread.

'That was very good. I didn't know you could cook like that.'

'You've had my food before, many times.'

'Not like this. This meal was special. The meat was roasted just right, and the potatoes. There was something on it, I think.'

'Marta Reijnhardt gave us some spices when she was here. I put some pepper on it. And mint leaves.'

Wynand came out from behind the partition.

'You've had your supper?'

'Yes. Sit with us, Pa. Harman's asleep?'

'He's just closed his eyes.'

'I see he has a tooth coming out,' Roeloff said. 'I'm grateful he's here. I must thank you. I wouldn't have been able to look after him by myself.'

'We're glad, too. The house has lost its silence. And Pa has a new interest to get him up in the mornings.'

They sat for a few minutes, not speaking.

'I've come for opsit,' Roeloff said suddenly, addressing Wynand Roos.

'I know.'

'And to ask your permission to marry Neeltje. I've nothing to offer except my word that I will love and protect her; she will not want for anything.'

'I'm sure she won't. And she would be happy with you even if she had just the clothes on her back. I've never seen Neeltje so happy.'

'We haven't talked about Harman. His mother's Sonqua, his father an Africaander.'

Wynand looked at the young man who was soon to become his son-in-law. Roeloff had learnt his lessons the hard way. He did not know one more able, or more suitable for his daughter.

'We've had him from his mother's womb, Roff, he's ours. It won't be kind out there for him. He'll have his troubles when he's older, but, he's yours and Neeltje's. Neeltje thinks she's given birth to him the way she fusses. What of his mother?'

'She's returned to her people.'

'She won't come back to claim him?'

'No.'

Wynand took a beskuit from the plate Neeltje had set before them. His expression became serious.

'We're all part of the same family now, Roff. You and Neeltje have my blessing, and you must look on this as your own home. When you're married, we can build near the kopje if you want to live separately, or add on to the house. You don't have to make your home elsewhere.'

'I wasn't planning on leaving you here by yourself. Neeltje might not marry me then.'

'Neeltje would follow you anywhere. And you might move on, for land of your own. This will be yours and Neeltje's one day, and for all the grandchildren that will follow. We want a lot of them running around.'

'Thank you. It's a good place to raise children.' He looked at Neeltje. 'When we're ready and have enough money, we'll go for a few weeks to the Cape. I promised myself I would see it.'

'I don't know if that's such a good idea,' Wynand smiled. 'You might not want to come back. I was down there with Neeltje's mother. It's a beautiful place, and even more built up now, I believe. Lots of people, things to see. There are places where you can go and sit down and take a drink and meet people from the interior, from the community, sailors and merchants and all kinds of travellers to the Cape.' He looked at Roeloff. 'You don't have to wait till you're ready.

We'll have a few free weeks coming up between crops. There's a wagon and oxen. You and Neeltje can go and get acquainted with each other by the sea.'

'That is generous,' Roeloff said. 'But what about all the work here?'

'I'll manage with the Koi-na. Twa can look after the sheep.'

Roeloff turned to Neeltje.

'What do you say, Neeltje?'

'I don't think Pa should be here alone for such a long time.'

'So now you talk as if I'm not here?' Wynand asked.

'What about Harman?'

'We'll take him with us.'

'Or leave him with me,' Wynand got up. 'Twa and I can look after him. Well, you two talk about it. You have lots to talk about. I must turn in—before that candle burns out.'

'I have to leave when it's out?'

'Yes,' Wynand smiled, going behind the partition. 'But Neeltje will know where to find another.'

Roeloff put a thick piece of wood on the fire in the hearth.

'I like your father.'

Neeltje's heart swelled. She had everything: the man she wanted, and her father satisfied.

'I'm glad you and Pa get along.'

He came to sit next to her on the bench.

'When should we set the date, Neeltje? There's no point waiting. How about the beginning of winter?'

'June's four weeks away.'

'It's not enough time for you to get ready?'

'It's plenty. And what's there to get ready? We will just have a few people.'

'You're happy, Neeltje?' he took her hand.

'Yes.'

'Better sit over there, in your father's chair,' he put her hand back in her lap. 'I don't trust myself so near you.'

'Can you read to me, Roff?'

'You have books?' he asked, wondering why he hadn't asked before.

'I have one Stoffel gave me. He got it from an Engelsman who came to discover Africa. The explorer had bad luck at the Cape and lost all his money. He gave the book in exchange for a lamp and blankets. The trade wasn't fair, Stoffel said, but he was impressed by the cover, and it had enough pages to last a winter.' She fetched it and handed it to him.

'He's right, it has a handsome cover. It was good of Stoffel to be so generous. He's been generous to you, Neeltje, giving you dogs and books and everything.'

'He's like that.'

'A man's not like that for nothing. And I didn't know you had lessons.'

'Pa said I should learn just in case. He paid for lessons for one year.'

'Will you read a few pages for me?'

'Some of the words are big. I might not pronounce them right. Why don't *you* read?'

'You first. Over there.'

She went to sit in Wynand's stuffed chair by the hearth. 'From the beginning?'

'Yes,' he leaned back in his chair. 'Don't hurry.'

She opened the book and started to read. It was in Dutch, a story of merchants and spices and Spanish kings, and she read slowly, stumbling over the names. The house was silent except for the music of words, and the odd crackle coming from the hearth as the wood split and burned in the fire. Then his voice, soft and persuasive, entered into it.

'Lift up your dress.'

The request was so unexpected, she thought she'd heard wrong and continued reading.

'Lift up your dress, Neeltje,' he asked again.

This time there was no mistake. She raised the hem of her dress an inch.

He got up and came forward.

'Higher.'

She looked at him. 'No.' She was feeling terribly hot and strange things went on in her body.

He came to kneel at her feet.

'Read, Neeltje, don't stop. Tell me about the emperor.'

'There are no emperors. It's an adventure on the seas.'

'Just read to me. Anything.'

The words tumbled out, dry and incoherent, with no significance. The evening had taken on an unreality and she was swept up in it.

He touched her ankle, the white of her calf.

The book fell from her hands.

'What are you doing?' she slapped his face. 'Go to your quarters, you need rest! You want me to wake Pa?'

'All right, Neeltje,' he said, getting up, his face hot with his efforts. 'Don't wake your father, and don't send me to my room now.'

When Wynand came into the kitchen in the morning, he found Neeltje asleep in the chair, just as he'd left her the previous evening, Roeloff on the bench with his head slumped on his arm.

The wedding took place a few weeks later; a small supper, with a dominee, and a handful of farmers coming for roast lamb and Marta Reijnhardt's botterbeskuit. When the rains stopped in August, Roeloff and Neeltje took Wynand Roos up on his offer and made the trip to the Cape. When they returned a month before Christmas, the wagon stocked with lace and cloth and bedding and glass plates and spices and chairs and tools and enough books to bring enjoyment for several winters, Roeloff was ready to settle into his new life. He had seen what he wanted, and had made good on his promise to look up Oupa Harman's brother. Krisjan Kloot had died, but he located Maria, and Maria's son, Pieter, who had left him the newspaper and book. The mystery was explained. Krisjan Kloot had married the slave girl from Ceylon who had come to work for him after his first wife had died. Their daughter, Maria, a baster with straight hair, light eyes, and brown skin, darkened the strain further by marrying Stefan Cornelius, himself the mixed offspring of a Nederlander and a Hottentot. Maria had two brothers and several nephews and nieces who were fair like the Kloots, but they had moved to Stellenbosch, wanting nothing to do with their dark-skinned relatives. It wasn't uncommon behaviour, Pieter said. There were Africaanders who married Koi-na or slaves, but not all family members accepted this and there was often estrangement as a result. Mixed marriages and half-breed children divided families.

On a wet morning in June the following year, Wynand oiled his gun and saddled his horse for the ride to Jan Dissels Vlei. He had recovered completely, except for an occasional twinge in his legs.

'I lost Neeltje's mother during childbirth, Otto,' he said when he arrived at the German doctor's house. 'I don't want anything going wrong with my child.'

Otto Lieberband spanned in his horses and came with him right away. They were at the Roos house half a day when Neeltje went into labour, in the middle of a storm.

Wynand sat in the kitchen with Harman, listening to the skies rumble and groan, and the rain pelting down on the house. There was nothing he could do except wait, and keep the coffee and hot water going. A scratch at the door made him turn.

'Oubaas?'

'Nothing yet, Twa. You want coffee? Come in out of the rain.'

'Ta!' Harman wriggled off Wynand's lap.

Twa came in and picked him up.

Harman waved his stubby hand in the air, pointing to the door.

Twa's eyes twinkled.

'It's raining, you can't go outside.'

Harman looked at him with big eyes.

'Raining,' Twa said again.

Harman watched his mouth and repeated the word.

Twa laughed from the back of his throat.

'You're Kudu's child all right. Tomorrow Twa will take you to the river and we'll look for tortoise.'

'You're teaching him all this nonsense,' Wynand said. 'The whole day he clucks like a turkey. He can't speak his own language yet.'

'He'll be like his father,' Twa chuckled.

What was the use, Wynand thought. Twa was good-hearted, fond of Harman, and Roeloff encouraged it, speaking to the child only in !Khomani.

A sudden cry from the bedroom made them look up. Roeloff came out of the room for more hot water for the doctor.

'Is everything all right?' Wynand asked.

Roeloff's face was covered in perspiration. He had been running back and forth for hot water and towels, finding the experience a whole lot different from that in a foaling barn. This was his wife, it was her first child. With contractions coming almost every minute, her pain had increased. His own panic rose. He had never heard of a man being in the room with his wife when she gave birth, but Neeltje wanted him there, and there was no one to give Otto Lieberband a hand.

'Oom Otto says it will soon be over.'

Wynand didn't say anything. He was thinking of a night eighteen years ago, only it hadn't been raining, and his wife didn't live to hold her own child. This was different, he told himself. Neeltje was strong. She had her mother's looks, her father's toughness. Everything was going to be all right. They sat close together, he on the bench with Harman on his lap, Twa squatting on the floor near the hearth, drinking endless beakers of coffee. An hour later, a loud scream broke the silence.

Roeloff came out of the bedroom.

'It's a girl!'

'And Neeltje, how is she?'

'Neeltje's fine. She's holding Beatrix and waiting for her Pa to come and see his grandchild.'

The day of his departure, ten days after he'd first arrived, Otto took a farewell drink with Wynand in the voorkamer.

'Thank you for coming and taking care of Neeltje. I won't forget it. I've put two sheep on your wagon.'

'That wasn't necessary, but thank you. So, Wynand, I will go. Your Neeltje's settled with her baby. You're a grandfather. You've found yourself a good son-in-law.'

'I have. You just don't know who the Almighty will send to your door. Neeltje's happy with him. And look what he's done—the sheep have increased, even after that terrible raid, there are a dozen workers, and crops.'

'Don't leave yourself out of it. If it wasn't for you, there wouldn't be anything at all.'

'Maybe so. But he kept this place going during my illness. Last year at the wedding, you drank your brandy in the kitchen. Now, we're sitting in a voorkamer. He built it. That, and an extra room, and that stall in the back for privacy.'

'He's good with his hands, I'll say that for him. And he's mad for Neeltje. All that remains is you, eh? What about the widow, man? She looks like she's lost some of that fat around her neck. She's not bad, and she likes Neeltje and Harman.'

'We don't need two women in the house and I'm too old for a woman's nonsense. A man gets selfish in his later years.'

'Perhaps so, but the fire's not out in the galley. Neeltje might not be here forever.'

Something in his voice made Wynand look up.

'What do you mean?'

'I saw Stoffel. He told me an interesting story.'

'We haven't seen him since the wedding. Where is he?'

'He travels, he hears things. The field cornet was called out to a place a week north from here. A murder in cold blood, self-defence, some say. Talk is that there was trouble over a son cast out over the killing of a stallion. Wrongfully accused, as it turns out. The kommando's out looking for him.'

'Why?'

'The father's ill. He wants him to come home.'

'You waited all this time to tell me?'

'You had other things on your mind; Neeltje, the baby. I wasn't sure.'

'What makes you sure now?'

'I'm not.'

Wynand went to the window and looked out. He didn't speak for a long time.

'It's him. He told me the day he came. "I want you to know I stand accused of a crime I didn't commit." I believed him. I would have believed anything he said, there was just something about him. He didn't have to tell me. He didn't have to tell me many things. There was also that bosjesman girl, Harman's mother. He didn't hide what he felt. It was his eyes and his honesty that drew me to him.'

'What are you going to do?'

'It's his father. I have to tell him.'

Otto came over and patted him on the arm.

'You got used to him, I know. He'll go and he'll come back. If he doesn't—well, my friend, that's how life is. You know the man your daughter married. Neeltje will go with her husband, but her father will never be out of her thoughts.'

Chapter Sixteen

'It's strange how life is, Neeltje. Fifty years ago Willem Kloot was born in a wagon somewhere on these mountains. Today, we're the parents, out here in the dark, and it's the same struggle and danger.'

Neeltje looked out over the fire into the night. There was a moon and she could make out the hilly top of the rant against the skyline. It was a night for two, but Roeloff was in a questioning mood, silent and brooding since learning of his father's illness. He'd told her he didn't know what waited for him at Kloot's Nek, or how long he might be, and she could stay at home with Harman and Beatrix if she wished, or accompany him. He would understand if she didn't want to travel with children through wild territory. There was nothing that she needed to consider. Her father's health had been restored, and he had encouraged her to go. Beatrix nuzzled her face into her mother's bodice and Neeltje put the infant to her breast.

'What do you think, Neeltje?'

'Pa says we come here to learn.'

'Where is the lesson in this? In being disowned and going back home when he's dying, after two years without my family? What am I supposed to learn from that?'

It was amazing to her, men's thinking. They could fix and

provide, but when it came to matters of the heart, things they couldn't physically lay their hands on, of that they knew nothing.

'God's not responsible for the things we bring upon ourselves. What's the good that came from it?'

'What?' Roeloff asked.

'You had a son. You met me.'

He looked at her, surprised.

'You endured pain,' she continued. 'It made you strong. Perhaps it was to prepare you for greater things. Pain sharpens the senses, Pa says. Perhaps you had to leave home to prepare for the task of taking over.'

'Taking over Kloot's Nek?'

'Yes.'

'I hadn't thought of it like that.'

'Men think only of physical things.'

A smile softened his eyes.

'Careful, Neeltje, or I'll take that baby from your breast and show you physical.'

'You have a big opinion of yourself, Roeloff Kloot.'

He laughed, a wonderful sound to her ears.

'You love me, Neeltje? You never tell me.' He moved close, kissing her neck.

Did she love him? Could she breathe without air? She would follow him over all Africa's mountains, just to be near him, to see him with his children.

'Yes.'

'I know it was hard leaving your father. It was hard for me.'

They sat for a few minutes staring into the fire, a comfortable ease between them.

'The first few days will be hard, Roff, you'll feel strange in your old home. You must prepare yourself for the worst.'

'I'm nervous about seeing him after all this time. I've missed him, more than I've wanted to admit to myself. I always put him out of my thoughts, but now that we're so close, I can't wait. I hope nothing's happened. But, are you ready, Neeltje? We will be in Leekenberg tomorrow. Once we cross this rant, we're at Kloot's Nek.'

'I'm ready. I want to see the place where you were born. How will you explain Harman?'

'Harman be who he is. Zokho's blood runs in him.'

Hearing him say the name gave her a strange feeling. The girl's presence would linger forever in the slanted eyes of her son and the blue mark on his back, which was present in some Koi-na and Sonqua children. There was no difference between the children in her affections. Beatrix had come from her own flesh, but Harman had come to her first, naked and abandoned, a part of the man she loved.

'I was only thinking of you, if they asked.'

'If they ask, they'll get answers. Where's Twa? He's been gone a long time.'

'Isn't this where he comes from?'

'The Sonqua have no settled place, they travel up and down. But his people gathered annually at the big river up north. I haven't been there myself. When we left Kloot's Nek he wanted us to go there, but I didn't want to. Just imagine, Neeltje, if I had, we wouldn't have met. A lot of things wouldn't have happened. Even Harman wouldn't be here.'

'So, you're pleased with your own wisdom.'

'Perhaps. Behind those mountains over there, that's where Twa's camp was wiped out. The neighbour, Jan Joubert's farm is right under it.'

Harman poked his head through the flap of the wagon. 'Ta?'

'Twa's not here,' Roeloff said in !Khomani.

Harman retreated.

'He'll climb over all those boxes if he's not tired. We should let him sit with us a while. He feels left out, in the wagon by himself.'

'Bring him out.' Neeltje moved her nipple from the sleeping infant's mouth and covered herself up.

'Harman?'

Harman's face appeared through the crack. He knew by the tone of his father's voice that he was coming out of the wagon to sit with them.

'Pa?'

'You want to come out?'

Before Roeloff could do anything, Harman was up on his stocky legs and had jumped down into his father's arms. He was a big boy for eighteen months, and Roeloff staggered under the impact.

'Easy,' Roeloff said, settling the boy between his legs at the fire. 'Do you want to break your father's back?' His son was a mischievous rascal with the wheat colour hardiness of a Kloot, his slanted eyes giving him a slightly oriental appearance. Restless for adventure, the high point of his day was when Twa fetched him in the mornings to go out into the veld. Twa didn't take the best care of Harman's appearance, often returning him in the evening, dirty and dishevelled, but Harman was happy and content, carrying caterpillars and tortoises.

A short while later he was fast asleep between his father's legs and Roeloff got up into the wagon to put him to bed.

Neeltje got up with the baby.

'I'm turning in. We have to be up early in the morning. What do you think's happened to Twa?'

'I don't know. Otto's ointment isn't helping that leg. I'll sit here and wait for him.'

'Don't come to bed too late.'

But Roeloff didn't get to bed at all. All night he sat with his back to the wheel of the wagon waiting for Twa, dozing off intermittently. Drawing nearer to the Hantam he had felt the change in Twa. His wrinkled face, usually pleated in a smile, was pinched and shrunken, and there was little laughter in the black eyes.

At dawn Roeloff felt his presence and saw the figure come limping over the veld. Something in his manner told him all was not well.

'You are up, Kudu.'

'I waited for you.'

Twa offered no explanation. There were coals on the fire, and he stirred them with his foot and sat down.

'You look like you've seen a ghost.'

'The ghosts of my family. That's where it happened, over there. When the horses came and the guns smoked and my wife and unborn child and all the rest of my people were killed.'

It came out in a torrent: his life with the Ein-qua, their days beside the big river up north. Twa had told many stories in his time, but never before had he talked this much about his family. Roeloff looked at the little hunter. He seemed suddenly very old. A wife? A child not yet born? He'd never thought of Twa like that, in the role of a married man, never heard him talk with such passion. There was nothing mad or devilish about him now.

'We came from up there to look for ostrich and springbok. Some of our people were here, behind the rante. If you go there now, you'll see the smoke of their fires on the cave walls. I had taken a wife, my child was coming. I had a sister, young like you were when your father threw you out. We lived by the mercy of the gods, and only took from the white man when there was nothing to eat. We didn't kill people.' He lowered his eyes to the dying coals. 'We were sleeping at our fires when the riders came and shot us where we lay with our heads to the ground.'

Roeloff said nothing.

'They got me in the leg. They thought they'd killed me. I played dead. With my eyes closed, I listened. There were only three of them, but they reminded me of hyenas at a kill.' He paused, and looked up from the fire. 'You're one of them, Kudu. I've wiped your behind, you've filled my belly. Why did they do it?'

Roeloff couldn't bear the pain in his eyes.

'Fear, Twa. Of the unknown. Sonqua taking their animals. Not enough land.'

'This land stretches to the end of the earth. It's big enough for all.'

'Big enough for the Sonqua. The Sonqua have no animals. A farmer without grazing land will perish.'

'His animals take precedence over people?'

'They take precedence over everything, even his family. Without it, he has nothing, his family dies.'

Twa took out his tobacco and continued talking.

'When they left, I counted the bodies. My sister, Shy Little Tortoise, was gone. They'd taken her. We'd heard from others that when the white man killed the Sonqua, he took their children to work on the farms.'

Roeloff lowered his gaze so Twa wouldn't see the shame in his eyes. That was exactly what his father and Jan Joubert had done to Zokho.

'So, when I came to your grandfather's farm, I felt I owed him something for saving my life, but knew I wouldn't rest till I found Shy Little Tortoise. When I disappeared from time to time, I was looking for her. The years went by, and I looked and looked, but never found Shy Little Tortoise.' He paused for a moment to stuff his pipe. 'Then, one day, you will remember the day, Zokho came to Kloot's Nek and I thought the gods were playing cruel tricks on me.'

'What do you mean?'

'She had the same slanted eyes and colouring as my sister.'

Roeloff felt his heart pick up a beat.

'I thought you all had the same colouring and eyes.'

'Not all white people look the same, Kudu, so how can we? We are different colours of the sun. The morning sun which is light, the afternoon sun which is deep. And our eyes, depending on whether we're from up there or over there where the sun gets up in the morning, would determine the thickness of the skin over them.'

'You're saying something serious, Twa.'

Twa looked at him. 'I asked Zokho about her mother. Her mother was not from the tribe she was living with. She had run away from the people who had captured her years ago, and met up with them. She became the wife of one of the hunters.'

'Are you saying that she …'

'Zokho's mother was Shy Little Tortoise.'

Roeloff sat very still.

'Do you know what that means? It means that you're Zokho's uncle. My son, Harman …' He left the sentence unfinished. If Twa was telling the truth, then his father and Jan Joubert had killed Harman's grandmother the day they raided the camp and captured Zokho. 'Why didn't you tell me before?'

'I never even told Zokho. She doesn't know her mother and my sister were one.' He took a deep drag on his pipe. 'We must keep this secret, Kudu. I only told you because I thought if you knew, you would understand things about yourself and your son.'

Roeloff gave a small laugh.

'I understand many things, Twa. The world's not as pure as we think.'

'You will tell him about his mother and his crippled old grandfather?'

'Harman will know his history when he's grown.'

They sat in silence for a long time, watching the first light come over the rant.

'My time is nearing, Eyes of the Sky. I've brought you home, you are safe. When the big sleep comes, you must bring me here, to the rante. The second cave, near the eye.'

Roeloff felt a pain in his heart. Twa had told him once that a Sonqua could tell from the ache in his bones when he was coming to the end of his journey. Had Twa come to Kloot's Nek to die? He couldn't bear the thought.

'You're not going anywhere. Who'll teach Harman to use the bow and arrow?'

Twa's face puckered into a mischievous smile.

'Twa's wild blood's in him, he'll teach himself. He will not be like your other children, Kudu, and you'll have many. Be careful with him.'

'He'll grow up like his father.'

'His father?' Twa chuckled. 'Who's his father? His father's white, but his heart's the heart of the little hunter.'

When Neeltje saw the house and trees in the distance, her heart picked up a beat. The road leading up to it was long, edged with kareebome and jagged rock formations, the friction as the wagon rolled slowly over the dry clay whipping up pockets of orange powder. She could imagine her children playing on the grass below the rant on their left. On their right was a large stone kraal, dusty and dry, in disrepair, and further along, stables and buitekamers leading up to the thatched- roof house on the rise. In front of the house, and at the side, there were four wagons.

'All these wagons and horses. It doesn't look good. Twa?'

Roeloff called to the hunter in the back of the wagon. 'We're here. We're at Kloot's Nek. Come and sit here with us in the front.'

Pietie Retief was on the stoep with Joubert and a few others when Hennie pointed to the dust.

'The kommando?'

'It's a wagon. It looks like, it looks like …'

'Who does it look like, man?' Retief dug his elbow into his grandson.

'I can't see.'

'It looks like Roeloff,' Joubert said. 'All that hair.'

'Roeloff? I can't believe it. Did you say Roeloff?'

'Inheritance will bring back the devil.'

The old man looked at him askance.

'Nonsense! His father sent the kommando. They found him. I'm surprised he's come, though. After the way he was kicked out, I wouldn't have blamed him if he stayed away. Always said there was good in that boy.' He stretched his legs and walked to the end of the stoep. 'And it would stand everyone in good stead to remember it's his land we're standing on now.'

Joubert took out his pipe and filled it.

'What do you mean? There's Drieka.'

'He's the son.'

'A wife takes precedence.'

'Not a second wife. Not over children. Kloot's Nek is Roeloff's and Vinkie's.'

'Well, Willem's still with us. We shouldn't be talking about that.'

Retief said nothing. He knew Jan Joubert. Joubert was

already orchestrating the running of the two farms, and on the lookout for a place for Diena and Lourens.

Word of Roeloff's arrival got to the women inside and they came out. It was Sanna, breaking the rules, who ran from the stoep to meet him.

'Roff!'

The wagon came to a halt and Roeloff got down. He had travelled in his working clothes, but had put on his jacket shortly before they arrived. He cut a grand figure in his boots and long hair, and everyone was staring at him.

'You've come back!' Sanna embraced him. 'Look at you, you've become rich?' She looked at the girl in the wagon. 'Who's that?'

'My wife, Neeltje, and Beatrix and Harman.'

'You are married?'

'Yes. And those are my children. There are many people here, Sanna—what's going on? The kraal's empty. Where are all the sheep?'

'He took it to his place. And the horses.'

'Joubert?'

'Yes.'

'And all these people?'

Sanna looked at him. Her eyes told the whole story.

'Oh, no …'

'He's very sick, Roff. Oubaas Retief and his grandson brought the … they brought the …'

'The coffin?'

'He's not like he was when you last saw him. The disease has eaten his flesh.'

'Is that Vinkie over there next to Drieka? She's grown tall.'

'That's her. She's taking it very hard.'

'What happened to David?'

Sanna nodded sadly.

'Your father shot him.'

'What?'

'The morning after Christmas. David woke up with the devil in him and hit Soela in her parents' home, took the mirror to her head. Your father stopped him from killing her. When it was discovered that she—well, you'll soon hear. That child standing next to Diena, Bessie, it's Soela's. Diena's married now. That's kleinbaas Lourens, her husband, next to oubaas Retief.'

'What happened to Soela?'

'She sits all day looking out the window. Doesn't speak. Diena looks after her. It's sad what's happened here, Roff. Your father changed after you left, and after David, he went downhill. I'm glad you're back.'

From where she sat on the wagon, Neeltje looked at the large Koi-na woman talking to Roeloff. Sanna had the same sallow complexion as the workers on her father's farm, and wore a red cloth wound round her head. Neeltje took an instant liking to her, and handed Beatrix down to her.

'Welcome back, Roeloff. It's good to see you.'

Roeloff turned and greeted Jan Joubert, who had come up behind him. Joubert had changed only in weight; his smile was buried under a bushy beard, only a hint of it reaching his eyes.

'Good to be back. This is Neeltje, my wife. Her father

be Wynand Roos. And my son, Harman, and daughter, Beatrix. Hello, Oom Piet, Hennie.'

Pietie Retief grabbed hold of him.

'Welcome, welcome. You've come back for good?'

He understood the question.

'I don't know.'

'Glad you're back, man. This place was dead without you and the bosjesman.'

Roeloff smiled. You could always count on Pietie Retief to call the devil by his name.

Then Joubert spoke again. 'You know your father's sick?'

'Yes.'

'Drieka has had her hands full since the illness. Diena and Lourens moved in to give her a hand.'

'That was good of them.'

Then the women arrived and everyone talked at once, ushering them up on the stoep. Elsie hadn't changed much, except that her lips seemed thinner, but Diena was a surprise, with her hair cut short to ear level, and several months pregnant. Drieka had thickened around the waist, and she had blue circles under her eyes. Vinkie, who had shot up like a sunflower, was smiling shyly at him. Her shyness lasted only a few seconds, then she rushed into his arms.

'Roff!'

'How are you, Tinktinkie?'

'I've missed you, so much,' she hugged him. 'Oh, Roff,' and she started to cry.

They held each other for a few moments, then he released her and introduced his wife to everyone.

The kitchen was as he'd left it: the heavy table, the

benches, the cupboard against the wall holding dishes and condiments, plates of beskuit, the guns and powder horn on the wall in their usual place, the fire in the hearth burning winter and summer, glistening black and silver with kettles and pots, emitting wonderful aromas. But it wasn't the smell of mutton roasting or bread baking outside that registered first, it was the stench of living flesh rotting. It brought him instantly to the putrid death smell at Oupa Herman's funeral.

'The kommando didn't let us know they found you. We could have prepared,' Drieka said.

'They didn't find me. The news got to me in the Cederberg through the doctor who came to deliver Beatrix.'

'We're glad you're back,' Pietie Retief said again. 'It's a sad thing to come home like this. Brace yourself, son, before you go in.'

Roeloff nodded. Now that he was in the kitchen with his wife and children, he didn't know where he should put down his things. Diena noticed his discomfort.

'You can have your old room, Roff. Lourens and I are happy to give it up now that you're here.'

'I don't want to disrupt things. We can stay in the voorkamer.'

'Your father's in there. And don't worry, Lourens and I want to get back, you can have your room. Come, Neeltje, you look tired. Let me show you where things are.'

Neeltje left with Diena and Vinkie, who seemed taken with Harman and the baby. Roeloff looked round at the others, then braced himself and went into the voorkamer.

There was an awkward silence when he left. Cups were

stirred, benches shifted, but no one spoke. The prodigal son had returned. Along with his wagon and horses and wife and children, he'd come upon them like the wind, fast and unexpected, and no one wanted to be first to give his opinion.

'His wife's the image of Vinkie,' Joubert said. 'Have you noticed? He picked well. I haven't heard of her family.'

'Who do you think the boy looks like?' Drieka asked. 'His eyes. There's something strange about them. Like I've seen them before.'

'There's nothing strange,' Retief said. 'He looks like Roeloff.'

'Well, Neeltje's not his mother, that I'll say.'

Everyone looked at Drieka. That was dangerous talk.

Elsie waved her Bible in front of her face.

'Don't go stirring things up, Drieka. Oom Retief's right. He looks like his father. Leave it there.'

The others looked at Elsie and nodded wisely.

'He says he's not sure if he's coming back,' Jan Joubert said.

Drieka stirred her coffee. 'He'll stay. He won't let go of this land.'

Pietie Retief coughed politely. 'It's his, isn't it?—shouldn't he hold on to it?'

Joubert and Drieka looked at each other. There were too many ears around. He would speak to Oom Retief alone later. He didn't want any wrong impressions to be formed, knowing the old man's habit of repeating things.

In the voorkamer Roeloff stood anxiously at the door. The curtain was drawn to give coolness, and the foul air was marked with the sickly sweet smell of white flowers. The bed had been placed near the window, and he drew in his breath when he saw the wasted figure of his father. The strong face was hollowed and grey, the thick hair the only indication that Willem Kloot wasn't very old.

He studied the face in repose, gaunt with approaching death. He'd seen it before, the sharpening of the features when a man lay inches from his fate. No prayer could bring his father back from that. He was on the lip of whatever it was that waited for him on the other side.

His father opened his eyes. There was a long silence, then recognition.

'Roeloff …'

Roeloff fought to control his emotions. 'I'm here, Pa.' He lifted the skeletal hand in his. It was cold to the touch.

'You … came …' the words struggled out.

'Don't talk, Pa. You're straining yourself.'

Willem's face was pinched, his eyes dark sockets in his head.

'I'm sorry …'

'Don't be sorry. It's I who am sorry. I'm sorry for all the things I did that upset you.'

Willem's eyes filled with tears.

'I was … wrong.'

Roeloff cried freely. He felt the pressure of the hand as his father tried to communicate with the last of his strength.

'Vinkie … the farm …'

Roeloff bent down, straining his ears to hear.

'Take care … of them.'

Roeloff waited for him to continue, but Willem Kloot didn't speak again.

'Pa!'

There was a small gasp, then his father's eyes rolled back in his head. Roeloff watched him drift slowly away, the hand coming to rest on the sheet. He didn't go out to the others. He was angry, angry at the unfairness, angry at God. How could he come back now, after so many years, only to have his father taken away? Hadn't he lost him before? He sat by the bed, sobbing into his hands, his grief welling up like a hot spring—for the lost years, for the grandfather who'd loved him, for his brother's betrayal, for the child sitting by himself when they carried his mother away. He'd never acknowledged that child. Never took time to deal with his pain. He'd carried the pain inside him all these years, silent and sleeping. The grief ripped from his chest in a groan.

The others found him lying almost on top of the corpse, and Pietie Retief came over to console him.

'Be content, Roff. It's hard, but he waited for you. You made your peace.'

Roeloff cried into his shoulder.

'He was always so strong, Oom Retief. How could he go just like that? I didn't have much of my father.'

'That's how life is, son. We come for a few minutes of pleasure.'

'I loved him. Even then.'

'And he loved you. That was what ate at him. He wasn't the same after you left. He knew he'd made a mistake, that it wasn't you who'd killed that horse. That horse caused a lot of trouble. One shouldn't say this about brothers—and may God rest his soul—but you were the one he loved most, your mother's child. He never got over Lisbeth.'

Sanna came in carrying the tin tub for the women to wash down the body, and he noted with a certain detachment that Jan Joubert was directing things. He was too numb to think. Neeltje was right, he should have prepared himself, but as always he didn't like to think of the worst and other people always saw further than he did.

He left the house through the kitchen and walked down the path to the dam. There was a certain comfort in seeing the familiar faces of Hennerik, Kupido, Kleintje, and some of the other Koi-na. No one knew whether to come forward to commiserate with him, or to keep at a respectable distance. A few minutes later he arrived at the spot where he'd once pulled his sister from the muddy water, and sat down. It all seemed a lifetime ago. His father, the stallion, his brother. It was still hard to think of David, but the grief had lessened, there was remorse where before there had only been pain.

'Roff?'

He turned.

'Ma said to come get you. People are asking for you.'

'Sit down, Tinktinkie.'

Her face brightened a little.

'No one calls me Tinktinkie anymore.'

'Are you too grown up for that?'

'No. Will you go away again, Roff?'

'No.'

'You will stay on Kloot's Nek?'

'Yes.'

She started crying suddenly and pressed her face into his shoulder.

He held her close, letting her cry out her grief. He could hear again the voices of Drieka and Sanna and Diena as they came running across the grass, their shouts as he pulled Vinkie from the water. He had raised his voice to his stepmother that day. It was all silent now, the pieces of driftwood sticking out of the milky brown water, the stillness of the trees. In a few hours his father would be put in the ground. Consigned to darkness and silence. He would never hear Willem's voice again.

He got up and she put her hand into his.

'I knew you would come back.'

'How did you know?'

'Pa told me.'

They walked slowly back to the house.

The kitchen was filled with faces he knew, and some he saw for the first time. Six new families had trekked to the Hantam. People spoke in whispers, and embraced him with their sympathies, filing in and out of the voorkamer paying their respects. Neeltje was feeding Harman at the table, and he went with Vinkie to sit next to her, where he listened to Jan Joubert at the other end telling Retief of the sheep he'd recently lost. Roeloff waited for him to finish speaking.

'I was thinking that perhaps the funeral should be in the morning instead of the day after next.'

Joubert looked at him, surprised.

'We're waiting for more people, Roff. And the field cornet has to verify the cause of death. It's customary to wait three days.'

'I could send a message to the field cornet and let him know. My father's been lying here—well, we can't have the corpse ripening in the heat. If it wasn't dark, I'd do it now.'

The room fell silent. The new master had spoken. And what he proposed was unthinkable.

'Now?'

'I don't want to upset things, but the smell …'

'It's not too late, man,' Pietie Retief said. 'Hennerik and Kupido can bring the lamps. The hole's dug.'

'It's not proper,' Joubert said.

'Aagh what, a man doesn't need all this praying and displaying if he's lived his life right. I'm with you, Roff, if you want to do it. Hennie can help.'

Everyone looked at Pietie Retief. There was no brandy on the table, he was talking on a clean stomach. It was unheard of, burying at night, no night vigil, all the mourners not yet arrived.

'It's wrong, Roeloff. You're not serious, are you?' Joubert asked.

Roeloff turned to Drieka.

'I'd do it, if my stepmother agreed.' It was the first time he'd called her that. It didn't go unnoticed.

Drieka blew her nose into her hankie.

'Well, it's not the way, but perhaps Roeloff is right.' She blew her nose again. 'Perhaps it makes sense in this heat.'

There was a murmur of disapproval.

'That's it, then,' Roeloff said. 'We'll do it. Oom? Hennie?'

Joubert looked from his sister to Roeloff. Roeloff had gambled. Drieka had taken up her position: the power structure had been established.

For the rest of the mourners, it was wood for a hellfire. They would talk about it for months.

An hour later, Roeloff, Hennie and Joubert carried the coffin in the dark to the grave prepared next to Oupa Harman's in the family cemetery. Under the light of lamps and the moon, the mourners' faces etched with disbelief, Roeloff said a few words for the safe passage of his father's soul, then helped to lower the coffin with rieme. The distant cry of a jackal lent an eeriness to the proceedings.

Neeltje, staying behind with the children, stood with Harman at the back door. She could see the dots of lamplight in the distance, and hear voices. She picked up her son.

'Your father's come home, Harman,' she held him close to her heart. 'This is where you and Beatrix will grow up.'

The next morning Roeloff was up early, careful not to disturb the mourners who'd arrived late and camped out in the voorkamer. Sanna was already in the kitchen.

'Morning, Sanna. I smell coffee.'

Her face brightened when she saw him.

'I knew you would be up early. There's coffee and bread. It's all ready.'

He sat down on the bench and she put a mug of coffee in front of him on the table, and two thick slices of hot bread on which a fat smear of pale yellow butter was melting.

'The people are sad about your father. But also happy that you're back. We're even glad to see that bosjesman.'

Roeloff smiled.

'Twa doesn't like it when you call him that. He's Sonqua. You looked after Vinkie well, Sanna.'

'Her mother did. Well, Sanna a little bit also. She never

forgot you. Talked about you all the time. She never was that close to her other brother. And when he … well, no use talking about it.'

Mention of his brother brought mixed feelings.

'How was my father after it happened?'

Sanna's eyes narrowed with the memory. She poured herself coffee and sat down next to him.

'It was a sad time on Kloot's Nek. Your father punished himself. Didn't talk to anyone, not his wife, not Vinkie, not the people who came here to ask questions. He had nothing to do with the funeral. Grootbaas Joubert did everything.'

'Grootbaas Joubert seems to have been in charge of a lot of things.'

'He brought kleinnooi Diena and kleinbaas Lourens here during your father's illness. There was talk that they would run Kloot's Nek.'

'And Soela? Does she come here? I didn't see her at the funeral.'

'They don't bring her. But Bessie, she comes with kleinnooi Diena. The kleinnooi's fond of her, everyone is, especially the grandfather.' Sanna turned to him with sad eyes. 'But things are not right there, Roff. The child hardly speaks, no one's ever heard her laugh. They say she's seen too much.'

'What?'

'Her mother and father. They fought over her, Roff, all the time. He said bad things.'

'My brother?'

'Yes. He never accepted that child. There was talk.'

'What kind of talk?'

Drieka came into the kitchen and Sanna stopped.

Roeloff got up.

'I'll go out and take a look at the kraal. That was good bread, Sanna.'

He fetched Twa from his hut and went to inspect the kraal for evidence to show how long ago the sheep had been there, and how many there had been. They found the kraal derelict, the stones missing in several spots, the gateposts gone.

'What do you think, Twa? How long ago were they here?'

Twa was happy to be back. Many of the old Koi-na were still on the farm, their differences a thing of the past. He'd been away with the kleinbaas. Sonqua or not, he was privileged. But, however much he smoked and told stories, he never told them about Zokho. Zokho was Kudu's business. They would not hear from his lips that Harman was mixed. He kneeled down on his good leg and examined the dried-out clumps of manure. There was still a bit of a commotion going on in his head from the previous night's drinking with the Koi-na, but he felt better just being back.

'A long time. Look at this,' he picked up a piece of manure, rubbing the grains between his fingers. 'Dust.'

'How many?'

Twa laughed, and immediately held his head.

'You're asking hard questions, Kudu. I'm Twa, not a sorcerer.' He studied the indentations, limping from one end to the other, bending down, shaking his head.

'It's hard to tell,' he finally said. 'But six moons ago, at least five hundred.'

Roeloff laughed. When he had first met Twa, the hunter

had had a strange method of counting, starting from one to ten, then going back to one, and doubling the result. He'd since taught Twa the right way, but occasionally he slipped back into his old method and his calculation was hopelessly out. Five hundred could easily be as low as fifty or a hundred.

'Five hundred! When we left here, there were four. He couldn't have increased it by a hundred.'

Twa shook his head at his stupidity.

'That's why I said five hundred. The tracks are right up against the fence. They stood crowded.' He paused for the effect of his next pronouncement. 'Hennerik said he also bought about fifty of that thick-woolled sheep.'

'Merino? How did he get them up here? They're hard to come by, those sheep.'

He returned to the house and found Joubert in the yard saying goodbye to Diena and Lourens who were returning home with Bessie. He looked at the child. He'd not had a good look at her before. She was almost three years old, a quiet little girl with blue eyes big as saucers, and long hair washed in gold.

'Hello, Bessie. You're going home today?' He was struck by her eyes, by their intensity.

She looked at him curiously, but didn't say anything.

'She's not one for talking much, Roff,' Diena said. 'She'll have to get used to you.'

Roeloff reached up and touched her hair. It was soft and silken. He felt a cold wind blow through his heart. Had he come back to Kloot's Nek for a reckoning of his sins? Was this what Sanna was trying to tell him?

'See you soon, Diena. Maybe this afternoon. You, too, Lourens.'

The wagon rolled off and he turned to Joubert.

'I was hoping to catch you out here by yourself. I believe you have our sheep at your farm.'

'Your father couldn't manage. It was easier looking after them there.'

'I'm grateful. I want to ride out this morning with Hennerik and Twa to fetch them back. And the horses. They're there too, I believe.'

'It looks like you've decided to stay.'

'Yes. And I'm anxious to get started on the work that needs doing. I understand we also had merino. In all, we should have about five hundred sheep.'

Joubert laughed.

'Whoever told you that had too much to drink. There are far less. Jackals and disease took most of them. But, seeing as we're on the subject of what belongs where, perhaps we should talk about Drieka. I have her interests to think of. I'm also her executor. If you hadn't come back ... well, you know what I'm leading up to; Kloot's Nek would be hers.'

Roeloff smiled. They were finally at the place where there was no pretence.

'Pa had a regard for you, and you helped him, Oom Jan. I'm grateful, not indebted. You're your sister's executor, not his. Tante Drieka will have her share. Tante Drieka and Vinkie and no other.'

Jan Joubert kept his composure.

'And what would that be?'

'A place here as long as she wants. If she wants to remarry, well, that be something else. Kloot's Nek will not change hands.'

Jan Joubert put his hands in his jacket pockets, rocking slightly on his heels.

'You've got a lot of wind for one just returned. A man needs his friends in the Karoo.'

'I agree—if he has any.'

Roeloff arrived at Joubert's farm ahead of him that afternoon.

Diena greeted him and invited him into the house. 'Do you want to see Soela while you wait for Pa?'

'Yes,' he said, a little unsure of himself. He was anxious to see her, but also a little apprehensive.

Diena took him into the voorkamer to wait. It was years since he'd been there, and he looked around with interest. Jan Joubert had improved his life. There were mats and tables, and an oak-trimmed mirror above a handsome cabinet with delicate carving on the drawers. On its polished surface stood six glasses like soldiers next to a matching bowl, an ostrich egg decorated with animals painted in brown, and a jar of dried flowers. The riempie chairs at the window were a better quality than the ones at Kloot's Nek. He wondered at the handiwork of the painter of the ostrich egg, and the one who'd put the room together.

His eye was caught by a box under the table. He looked at it, the splintered wood and the lid. ... *a wooden box with a green lid ... the dockets of the first settlers*. It had to be the box his grandfather had talked about. What was it doing at the Joubert house? Had his father given it to Joubert for safekeeping, or had the farmer taken it?

He strained his ears to try to determine Diena's whereabouts in the house. He was in two minds whether to take her into his confidence and ask about the box. People changed after marriage. He heard movement at the back of the house, and fell quickly to his knees. What he was doing was wrong, and it was bad manners to pry in other people's things, but he had to know. Taking a small knife from his pocket, he picked at the lock on the box. It was rusty, but opened with a dull click. It was obvious it hadn't been opened; a thick mat of dust sat on top of the little bundle underneath. He moved the spiderwebbed dirt carefully aside, and lifted out the dusty treasure. It was a handful of papers, thin and brittle with age, wrapped first in duiker hide, then in coarse, green cloth, bound with string. The handwriting was faint with age, the paper so yellowed he could hardly make out the words. Snaking on top, denting the page and blotting out some of the handwriting underneath, was a small leather necklace with markings on it. He picked it up, measuring its length with his hand. A baby's. He glanced quickly at the top entry on the first page.

D ... Y OF ANNA KLOOT
December 1651—Cold and wet aboard the Drommedaris. Wind blowing strongly ... ship so cranky we can carry no sail ... topsails taken in—heavy swells—ship almost flung on its side—grave fears of capsizing.

The next few entries were blanked out, either by dampness or age, he could make out the words only here and there.

... unbearably hot ... up on deck, trying not to think of the fatherland, the preciousness of water. When Sven asked for me ... the appointment of junior surgeon ... chance to go with the able Commander great opportunity ... father approved of marriage, not of the journey to an unknown land ... completely dependent on the vagaries of the wind ... water supply no more than 28 leaguers. April 5, 1652—heaven-high tops of Cabo da boa Esperance sighted ... very high mountains, one of which is as flat as a table.

... 25th ... number of men down with bloody diarrhoea and fevers from the cold and discomfort. Not yet told Sven the news ... other women have children, but we are more curious about the women of the Goringhaikonas and Goringhaiquas with their long, narrow breasts which hang down half an ell long like leather bags, and these they throw to the back to give suck to the child hanging there ... sallow complexion and slanted eyes from squinting all day into the sun, and when they speak they make clucking sounds ... clothing the undressed hide of goat or sheep which they drape over their shoulders like a cloak. In winter they turn the hair inwards to keep warm, in the hot weather, outwards—over their privities, a scrap of fur. When we kill sheep or cattle, they take the guts between their fingers and press out some of the dung, and lay this on a fire until slightly shrivelled, and gobble it down. Everything eaten in great haste with blood dripping from their mouths. What they cannot eat they wind round their arms and legs to keep warm and as ornament. This rattles in tune with their voices when they dance ... religion addressed to the moon. They believe there's a great captain above and a great captain below. The captain above is sometimes good when he gives good weather, and sometimes evil when he gives storms and cold. The captain below is always good

since he gives them cattle for their food and sustenance. They find it strange that we Christians work, and say that we gain nothing from our toil, and at the end are thrown underground so that all we have done is in vain ...

He wanted to go on reading, but was too conscious of his unlawful search of the box. He flattened the papers, fingered the faded leather necklace between his fingers, and put it back, wrapping everything up carefully. He would have liked to put something in the box to replace the bundle he'd taken, but there was nothing he could think of and there was too little time, as he heard footsteps coming towards the voorkamer. He moved the webbed dust back in place, clicked the lock shut, and slid the duiker-skin parcel gently down the front of his shirt. He hoped that what he had taken belonged to the Kloots and not to someone else. When Diena appeared at the door, the box was in its place under the table, and he was back in his chair.

'She's ready.'

He followed her into the kitchen. His first impression of Soela was from the side, a still figure sitting in a chair, looking out the window. Diena must have just changed her dress for she looked hurriedly prepared, her hair still bristling from the way the brush had gone through it, one sleeve not fully pulled down over her arm. But, even without looking into her face, the silence pained him.

'Soela, look who's here. It's Roff.'

Roeloff came to stand in front of her. Her illness had made her look younger, almost angelic, and she looked at him without moving her eyes.

'Hello, Soela.'

She looked at him for a moment, then returned her gaze to the window. There was no life or laughter in her. A feeling of despair rose in him. This wasn't the flirtatious girl he'd known and offended. As he watched, a tear rolled from her eye and sat between her nose and cheek.

'Don't take it hard, Roff. She's not aware.'

'Can I be with her alone for a moment?'

'Yes.'

Roeloff knelt down in front of Soela.

'I don't know if you understand me, Soela, but you recognised me. It's Roeloff. I'm sorry for what I've done. I was young and stupid.'

Soela sat unmoving as before, staring at something only she could see on the distant horizon.

He took her hand and squeezed it.

'Bessie needs you. Get better for her.'

Her lashes flickered, and presently, the tear rolled down her face and dropped into her lap.

He left her and returned to the stoep to wait for Joubert.

Diena came out with coffee.

'Did you speak to Soela?'

'I did.'

'You look well, Roff. Your time away did you good. I didn't have time to talk to you much at the house. I'm sorry about your father.'

He looked at her. The short hair, the colour in her cheeks—Diena had blossomed. She no longer had that pinched, reserved look and was much more forthcoming.

'Thank you. You've done well, too, Diena. A husband, a baby coming. Lourens seems a nice man, pleasant. Are you happy?'

'Yes. I was fortunate to meet someone like him.'

Bessie came to the front door and watched them.

'Don't stand there like a little lost lamb, Bessie. Do you want some of this coffee?' Diena asked.

Bessie turned and went back into the house.

'Who does she look like, do you think?' Roeloff asked suddenly.

Diena looked up from the coffee she was pouring.

'Soela, of course. Everything about them's the same.'

Roeloff took a sip on his coffee, and put the mug down.

'Her eyes are not the eyes of her mother and father.'

Diena looked at him, hard. The ease with which she'd spoken earlier was replaced by a hint of concern.

'You're scaring me, Roff,' she laughed nervously. 'Of course they're not the eyes of her mother and father. They could be like her grandfather's, Oom Willem, or her great-grandfather, Oupa Harman. There are blue eyes on your side of the family.'

'I didn't mean their colour.'

'What did you mean?'

Roeloff looked at her.

'You know what I mean. You know whose child she is.'

Diena's lashes flickered. She didn't say anything.

'I am told there's a Slams in Roodezand. He doesn't treat broken bones or snakebites, but has another speciality. He might know how to cure Bessie's sadness.' He paused a suitable time. 'It might also help if Bessie played with other children, Harman and Beatrix. It will be good for them to grow up knowing each other.'

The evenness in her breathing returned.

'They must know each other, yes.'

'She must come often to Kloot's Nek.'

'She will.'

'I could send for her every five or six days.'

Diena paused with the mug at her lips.

'I'm sure it'll be all right.'

'I don't mean to disrupt the two families. That's not what I want.'

Diena looked at him. He looked back at her. There was nothing more he had to say. She understood; he would leave things as they were. Diena would be the go-between for him to see his child.

Joubert and his wife arrived as they finished their coffee. Roeloff accompanied the farmer to the kraal where all the Kloot sheep had been collected.

'I count three hundred and sixty without the merino,' Roeloff said after a considerable time. 'We're short by about a hundred.'

'Your father had about thirty merino. The rest is mine.'

Roeloff turned to Hennerik.

'Hennerik?'

'Grootbaas had fifty merino. He didn't cut holes in their ears as he was the only one with them in these parts.'

Roeloff turned back to the farmer.

'I find it strange that my father would not have marked them, he must have been very ill. But, there you've heard

Hennerik; he didn't. I believe the merino are all ours. You would have marked them if you had any.'

Joubert kicked his boot against a post, more to give himself time to think than to rid it of dirt.

'You're taking the word of a Hottentot over mine?'

'Yes.'

Joubert narrowed his eyes.

'Take his word then, if you wish. You won't put your hand to them. Take your thirty and leave.'

'Take them, Kupido, and the other sheep,' Roeloff said. 'Hennerik, you and Twa get the horses.' He turned back to Joubert. 'It's always better to see the enemy in its original clothing. The merinos are a small price to pay.'

Chapter Seventeen

Neeltje stood at the door of the voorkamer and watched him at the table, silhouetted against the circle of light. He'd been there all afternoon, bent over some papers, oblivious to the hours slipping away. She studied him from the back; his hair tied in a thong, his head tilted forward. Already the burden of charge sat in his shoulders. She didn't know the nature of his concerns, but it had locked him away in this room.

Three days at Kloot's Nek and she already knew the lay of the land. The new master wasn't loved by all. Drieka acted one way in his presence, differently behind his back. Roeloff was responsible for her brother's dispossession. She wasn't going to forget it.

Neeltje came quietly into the room.

'It's time to come to bed, Roff. Tomorrow it will all look different again.'

He turned.

'Sit with me for a while, Neeltje.'

She came in and sat next to him on the bench.

'These papers must be very important to keep you in here like this.'

'They're the handwritten words of Anna Kloot, a hundred and sixty years ago.' His eyes filled with tears. 'You should read it. She tells how they came from the Fatherland in three ships and lived with the wind and the rain in their flimsy tents on the wild shores of Africa, and their encounters with the people with the brown skin and clucking sounds who roamed the land with their cattle and sheep. This necklace,' he picked it up and handed it to her, 'was Adriaan Kloot's, the first Kloot born in the Cape, given to him by a Koi-na woman. Hear how she describes his birth:

'Adriaan Kloot born on the 10th with the wind and rain competing with his screams in the tent. One of the Koi-na women, Vygie, sat with me throughout the night. She's called Vygie after a desert flower, and said to have been fathered by one of the yellow-skinned men of the interior. She's different from the other women, being smaller in physique, also yellower in complexion due to her Sonqua blood, although none of us have seen these mountain men of the interior of whom they speak. She sang to me in a thin and childlike voice, dabbing my forehead with herb juice so that for whole stretches I would be unaware of the awful wrenchings in my belly. When the big pains came at the end, her hands were gentle. She wanted to rub the baby with cow dung to protect him, but Sven wouldn't hear of it. These women know things. They're not sick like us, their babies live. When Sven was in bed with a fever and the chief surgeon's medicine didn't help, I folded one of her powders into his food. Vygie also gave a leather necklace for Adriaan to wear. This will protect him from evil spirits.'

Neeltje felt the tiny markings on the faded leather with the tips of her fingers.

'She kept it together with her notes. It's wonderful, Roeloff, that you have these memories.'

'I know.'

Neeltje looked at the necklace lovingly.

'One of our children should have it.'

'Which one?'

'Harman.'

'I agree.'

She gave the necklace back to him and took one of the pages delicately into her hand. The script was difficult to read, but she understood what it said.

'She writes well, Anna Kloot, the way she describes things. It's no wonder there's a gift for writing in the family.'

'There's more than writing.'

'What do you mean?'

'Vygie had a daughter, little Eva, the image of her mother. She and Adriaan played together as children. When they were older, they were caught in the grain field showing each other their private parts. Anna Kloot's husband, Sven, gave both of them a good hiding. A few years later when little Eva became the wife of a chief, Adriaan went missing. A party went out and searched for him. They found him after several days with a party of Koi-na, his face smeared with grease, heading for the interior. It turns out he was upset about the marriage. He was possessed by these people and their ways. No manner of punishment could tame him.'

Neeltje smiled.

'That's not the worst. After leaving her parents and coming to this country as a new bride and enduring the harshnesses of a strange land, Anna Kloot suffered betrayal.

She discovered her husband with Vygie. There was a child.' He paused for a moment. 'Things repeat themselves, Neeltje. Nothing's changed. Not the Kloots, not the struggle for land.'

'What happened to the child?'

'He went with his mother into the interior. There's no further mention of him. Sven went back to the Fatherland on an outgoing ship. Anna Kloot remained with her sons, Adriaan and Frederik. She married a farmer who had lost his wife. After everything she had suffered, she stayed. She says here, *There is no wind like the wind that blows here, anywhere else, but also not mountains and oceans and God's beauty all in one place.*

He got up and put his arms round her waist.

'We will stay on Kloot's Nek, Neeltje.'

'I know.'

'When you are ready, I will tell you what happened between Soela and me.'

Neeltje reached up and ruffled the softness of his hair.

'That's over, Roff. We'll have enough to do raising children and sheep to bother with scratching about in the past.'

He drew her close and kissed her.

'I am lucky to have you, Neeltje.'

'You've made your own luck, Roeloff Kloot. Did you think you had nothing to do with it?'

Behind a kopje far, far away, three hunters approached a waterhole and sniffed lightly at the air. As they leaned forward to drink, they moved back suddenly and knelt with their hands to their mouths. A torso, hollowed out, lay halfway under a bush a few feet away—a carcass of scarlet ribbons, the eyes sightless under a cascade of beads. They wondered at the identity of the woman. It was the work of lions, they knew, from the punctures in the neck and the kaross torn to shreds in the struggle. It was easy to see what had happened. She'd come to drink and not smelt them. Her spirit was tainted, she'd lost her skill.

One of them reached for the digging stick lying unmarked in the sand, then withdrew his hand. It was bad luck to linger, and bad luck to take her possessions; they couldn't even drink the water. They looked at each other with sad eyes. Their journey had been for nothing. But they were used to the cruelties of the gods. Desire for water was carved into their souls.

Taking a last look at the remains, squinting their eyes into the sun, they marched resolutely in the direction from which they had seen lightning fork the land.

Glossary

baster	half-breed
bijwoner	someone who works on a farm and usually lives on the premises
biltong	strips of dried meat; used for long journeys
blesbok	antelope characterised by white blaze on the head
bliksem	expletive; abusive mode of address or reference to someone, roughly equivalent of 'bastard' or 'swine'. Can also be used as a verb. Normally, however, it means 'lightning'. Thunder and lightning = donder en bliksems (see 'dondering')
bosjesman	Bushman; today called San
botterbeskuit	dried-out, bread-like type of cake that could be kept for a long time; used for long journeys
buitekamer	outside room
caffre	derogatory term used by the Dutch for blacks; 'kaffir'
dagga	hemp, marijuana
dassie	small, harelike mammal
dominee	preacher, minister
dondering	see 'bliksem' (from 'donder')

doopmaal	meal served to celebrate a christening. 'Doop' = christen, baptize; 'maal' = meal
doringboom	thorn tree
druppels	drops
duiker	small pieces of antelope
grootbaas	term used by servants or workers to address the master
hok	hut or shed
Hottentot	name given to the Koi-na by the Dutch; today called Khoi or Khoikhoi
jakkalsjagter	someone who hunts jackal
jong	derogatory term used by the Dutch for male person of mixed race
kapje	head-covering worn by women; bonnet
kareeboom	indigenous tree species (plural: kareebome)
kaross	leather cloak worn over the shoulder by Sonqua
kleinbaas	form of address used by servants for the master's son
kleinnooi	form of address used by servants for the master's daughter
kloof	ravine
knecht	foreman on farm; usually white and usually residing on the premises
Koi-na	brown-skinned people of the early Cape; today called Khoi or Khoikhoi
kolganse	Egyptian geese
kommando	group of farmers or burghers on horseback; usually used in a military context
kopje	hill or hillock

kraanvoëls	cranes (birds)
mijn	Dutch word for 'mine' or 'my'
nachtmaal	holy communion
oom	uncle
opsit	to signify courtship, where the potential groom visits and stays up with his betrothed after the rest of the family has gone to bed
oubaas	form of address used by servants for the grandfather or oldest male
oupa	grandfather
rant (plural: rante)	ridge of mountains or hills
rieme	thongs of softened rawhide used instead of rope for numerous purposes
riempiestoel	chair with a seat and back thonged with fine, narrow rieme (see above)
schiet hom vrek	shoot him dead
skaapbos	bush usually eaten by sheep
skerm	Bushman shelter built with twigs and branches, in the shape of a beehive
Slams	derogatory term for 'Muslim'
smous	trader
Sonqua	Bushman, today called San
teewater	tea water
trekboer	farmer who moves from one place to another to find grazing for his cattle; also refers to the Voortrekkers (Boer pioneers who moved from the Cape Colony to the Transvaal in 1834 and 1837)

trekgees	the urge to move; 'trek spirit'
vaderlandse schaapen	fat-tailed sheep of the early Cape; 'sheep from the fatherland'
vastrap	traditional and spirited folk dance
veldskoene	shoes or boots fashioned out of animal hide by the early farmers
voorkamer	front room of the house designated for visitors
voorloper	the leader of a team of oxen; usually a young boy of mixed race
vrijburgher	freeman or free burgher
vygie	succulent plant found in arid land
witblits	potent apricot or peach brandy brewed by the early farmers

About the Author

Rayda Jacobs is an award-winning author and filmmaker. She was born in Diep River, Cape Town in 1947 before moving to Toronto, Canada in 1968.

She published her first collection of short stories, *The Middle Children*, in 1994. Jacobs went on to receive the Herman Charles Bosman Prize for English fiction for her debut novel, *Eyes of the Sky* (1996) and the Sunday Times Fiction Prize for her 2003 novel, *Confessions of a Gambler*. She later co-adapted the latter into a feature film and has produced and directed numerous documentaries for television.

She is currently the author of ten novels and multiple short story collections.